P9-CCO-395

A Cruel
Deception

This item is no longer property
of Pima County Public Library
Sale of this item benefited the Library

ALSO BY CHARLES TODD

THE IAN RUTLEDGE MYSTERIES

A Test of Wills	*The Red Door*
Wings of Fire	*A Lonely Death*
Search the Dark	*The Confession*
Legacy of the Dead	*Proof of Guilt*
Watchers of Time	*Hunting Shadows*
A Fearsome Doubt	*A Fine Summer's Day*
A Cold Treachery	*No Shred of Evidence*
A Long Shadow	*Racing the Devil*
A False Mirror	*The Gatekeeper*
A Pale Horse	*The Black Ascot*
A Matter of Justice	*A Divided Loyalty*

THE BESS CRAWFORD MYSTERIES

A Duty to the Dead	*An Unwilling Accomplice*
An Impartial Witness	*A Pattern of Lies*
A Bitter Truth	*The Shattered Tree*
An Unmarked Grave	*A Casualty of War*
A Question of Honor	*A Forgotten Place*

OTHER FICTION

The Murder Stone	*The Walnut Tree*

A Cruel Deception

A Bess Crawford Mystery

Charles Todd

An Imprint of HarperCollinsPublishers

This is a work of fiction. Names, characters, places, and incidents are products of the author's imagination or are used fictitiously and are not to be construed as real. Any resemblance to actual events, locales, organizations, or persons, living or dead, is entirely coincidental.

A CRUEL DECEPTION. Copyright © 2019 by Charles Todd. All rights reserved. Printed in the United States of America. No part of this book may be used or reproduced in any manner whatsoever without written permission except in the case of brief quotations embodied in critical articles and reviews. For information, address HarperCollins Publishers, 195 Broadway, New York, NY 10007.

HarperCollins books may be purchased for educational, business, or sales promotional use. For information, please e-mail the Special Markets Department at SPsales@harpercollins.com.

FIRST HARPERLUXE EDITION

ISBN: 978-0-06-294429-0

HarperLuxe™ is a trademark of HarperCollins Publishers.

Library of Congress Cataloging-in-Publication Data is available upon request.

19 20 21 22 23   LSC   10 9 8 7 6 5 4 3 2 1

FOR:

Mommy Kitty, so tiny, so pretty, so strong in spirit,
who survived so much before finding a home and
the love she so deserved. Love she gave back
for seventeen *wonderful* years and left her paw print
on our hearts forever. God bless her!

Mark McLucas, whose heart failed him too soon,
and yet it was his kind heart that endeared him
to those who cared about him. He was an artist,
a lover of all things Harley, a lover of dogs
including his wonderful Jenny, who was with him
to the very end. A father who loved his young children
and fast cars and movies. Who left no mark
on this world, and yet who left it
a kinder and better place for having been in it.
May he find peace at last . . .

Jackson, so beautifully marked, a bashful giant,
a veritable lapful, who offered love and loyalty
and a wonderful spirit to the very end.
Who found his forever home,
alas without his brother, Jesse,
and had his own special place
in two big people's lives.

A Cruel Deception

Chapter 1

England, Late March, 1919

I was changing the surgical dressing on a patient in Ward 3 when Matron sent for me.

For some weeks now I'd been posted to a clinic in Wiltshire, for surgical cases like this abdomen. A piece of shrapnel missed in earlier surgeries had worked its way into the colon and caused a massive infection. Sergeant Higgins had been recovering well when this happened, but Dr. Johnson had done a marvelous piece of surgery to locate a source of the infection. It had almost been too late. Another few hours and the infection would have spread to the abdominal lining.

I finished what I was doing, smiled at the drowsy Sergeant, and handed my patient over to Sister Newman. "That should do for now," I said, and went to wash my hands before going down to Matron's tiny ground-floor office.

She was writing a letter when I knocked, and I stood quietly by the door until she'd finished it.

When she did look up, she frowned, and I felt suddenly like a schoolgirl who'd been caught in some mischief. As far as I knew, I'd done nothing wrong, but her frown had the power to make a saint feel guilty. It was one of her best weapons against carelessness and stupid mistakes.

"You've had a remarkable career until now, Sister Crawford," she began. "Have you given any thought to the future?"

Oh, dear—!

"There's still much to be done for the wounded," I replied. How very unoriginal! But it was all I could think to say.

She nodded, looking down now at what must be my file. "London headquarters has asked for someone capable, discreet, and able to act independently. I've considered my staff, and you strike me as the most suitable candidate."

Worse than I thought! I was being considered for a training post in London. My spirits plummeted. Last week Sister Caldwell had been persuaded to return to the hospital where she had done her own training, to teach probationers. I wasn't sure she was happy about that, but she had taken it philosophically, telling the rest of us in the ward that it was an honor to be asked. But I didn't want to teach. I wanted to continue to work with the wounded who still needed skilled care. Like Sergeant Higgins.

She was waiting for a response.

"Yes, Matron?"

"Would you consider traveling up to London to speak directly with the person making this request?"

"If you think it best." What else could I answer? Although I wouldn't mind a few days' leave in my old flat at Mrs. Hennessey's, the question was, how was I going to convince London—politely—that I'd prefer to return to a clinic?

"I do," she said, and nodded as if satisfied with her decision. Looking down again at the letter and the other papers on her blotter, she added, "Say nothing of this, if you please, to anyone else. But be prepared to leave at six tomorrow morning. Take your full kit with you, as it is unlikely that you'll be returning to us. You are relieved of your present duties and can hand your patients over to one of the other Sisters. If anyone asks, you've been granted a brief leave."

"Yes, Matron." I had heard speculation that the Queen Alexandra's was considering what to do about the hundreds of new nursing Sisters trained in the early months of the war. They couldn't possibly find positions for all of us, even though quite a few, like my former flat mate Diana, had resigned at the end of February, in order to be married.

I really hadn't thought about my own future. I'd been too busy with the wounded who hadn't gone home at war's end. Men like Sergeant Higgins or Private Tomkins, who were still in clinics like this one. They deserved the gratitude of their country.

I realized that Matron was still giving me instructions. "There will be a car waiting for you tomorrow morning. And may I add, the very best of luck to you, Sister."

"Thank you, Matron. I shall be sorry to leave this clinic."

"We are sorry to lose you. Good-bye, Sister."

I was dismissed.

Outside the door, I took a deep breath and tried to think what I'd done that had made Matron so eager to be rid of me.

But there was no time to dwell on that. Six o'clock would come soon enough.

By the time I'd stepped out of the motorcar that had been my transport from the railway station, and walked up the steps to the Queen Alexandra's headquarters in London, I had marshaled every argument I could think of to stay on the active-duty roster. They seemed lamentably thin, given how very many we were. The staff could choose from the finest.

Putting on the best face I could, and remembering my great-great-great-grandmother who watched my great-great-great-grandfather hurry off to stop Napoleon at Waterloo, I opened the door.

This could very well be *my* Waterloo.

I was surprised to find myself expected and ushered directly into the office of the Chief of Nursing. I had met her once before, when we had finished our training and she had come to congratulate us and wish us Godspeed to France.

This wasn't the same person. One of her assistants?

She was an older woman, with a stern expression and gray streaks in her brown hair. And nearly as formidable. I could feel a sense of doom falling over me.

But she smiled as I entered and said, "Sister Crawford reporting, Matron."

"I'm very pleased to meet you, Sister. I knew your father out in India. In fact, that's one of the reasons I was happy to see your name at the top of my list."

"If it's for a teaching position—" I began, but she cut me short.

"Were you not told why you volunteered?"

Volunteered?

"No, Matron. Just that I was to report here today."

She smiled but it was with a great sadness, I thought, not humor. "You must be thinking this is some cloak-and-dagger assignment."

Looking away for a moment, she paused, and I braced myself for dismissal from the Service.

"No, I'm afraid the truth is rather simple and rather embarrassing. My son is in Paris for the peace talks, and I'm worried about him. He was wounded last October, and he hasn't really been well since. He's assured me for weeks that he was recovered and was busy attending discussions at the Peace Conference—he's attached to the staff of one of our delegates. And then a friend who has just returned from Paris informed me that over the past few weeks, he's not been in attendance at any of the meetings. I could ask through channels—but if he's in some sort of trouble, it would finish his career. He's staying in the Army, you see. Your father's old regiment."

"You fear that he's had a relapse?" During the war that was one of our concerns—a man who tried to persuade us he was able to return to active duty, when he was not. But this would surely explain why she needed a nursing Sister.

She faced me again. "Not in the usual sense. I have reason to believe it isn't his wound that's troubling him." And I saw that it wasn't an easy admission for her to make.

"If he's well—if he's fully recovered—it might be more helpful to send a friend rather than a Sister." And then I wished I could take back my words. All at once, it occurred to me that it might be something else we always worried about. A drug dependency from all the medications we'd have to give a severely wounded man.

Some change in my expression must have told her I'd guessed. And yet she couldn't bring herself to say the words.

"I would like you to find him, assess his condition, and report to me. If there is a medical issue, I can see that he's given the proper care in the proper place." She hesitated. "If the war were still on, I wouldn't spare you for such a personal task. Your skills would be needed elsewhere. But we are not short of nurses, now, and I am told you are—discreet. As well, you are familiar with the Army."

I could interpret that to mean that she was desperate to know what was wrong and had nowhere else to turn. She could depend on a Sister to keep her observations to herself and report them to a superior. To her, not the Army.

"Would it not be possible for you to take leave yourself?"

She took a deep breath. "My appearance would draw—attention. Speculation. I'm not sure that's the wisest course at present. And my son would resent my interference." A wry smile flicked across her face and was gone. "He's rather like his father, you see, and he feels he's long since out of leading strings and a Nanny. But this might not be something he can deal with on his own."

She was right, a drug dependency too often wasn't.

I could hardly refuse her. I could tell how worried she was—even to send for me took far more courage than she wanted me to see.

"I expect you will need little more than a few days of—leave—to make a brief visit to Paris and return." She looked away. "Of course, if you need more time . . ."

Images from my last visit to Paris suddenly came welling up from my memory. Wartime then, with everyone trying to make do with bread that tasted of sawdust, meat that was gray, and coffee that barely deserved the name. Soldiers everywhere, and the German guns still far too close for comfort. Women in handsome gowns, laughing and pretending all was well. Had the city recovered? Apparently I'd soon find out for myself.

"Let's hope it won't require more than that." I summoned a smile, although I was already wondering what sort of news I would bring her. There could be any number of reasons why her son was in trouble, and not all of them good. What's more, I wasn't certain he'd welcome having his mother send someone to spy on him. That would be how *he* saw it. After all, he had been through the war, he'd consider himself his own man now. Had she thought about these possibilities?

I was casting about for a polite way to ask when she interrupted me.

"Then you'll go?" she said, striving to hide the eagerness I could see in her eyes.

I knew now how Sister Caldwell must have felt, after she'd been talked into teaching: cornered. Resigned to what Matron proposed. But if I could finish this affair successfully, it might go a long way to earning me more clinical duty instead. That wasn't selfishness. It was my belief that I could offer more skills working with the wounded than I could ever do as a teacher.

"Yes, Matron. I'll be happy to do what I can."

There was relief now, replacing the eagerness, as she tried to hold back tears.

"This will not go on your record—it's leave, after all. But I shall see that you are rewarded, Sister Crawford, for your kindness."

Still, I felt a surge of guilt, as if she'd read my thoughts.

She was handing me several sheets from a file open in front of her.

"These are the papers you will need to travel, and here's my son's address as well. Look them over and then I'll put your name in the blanks."

I did as she asked. Travel documents, letters showing that I was on official business, even a letter of credit allowing me to draw whatever funds I might need from an account on a French bank. An envelope containing English pounds and French francs. Tickets for the crossing and for trains. An introduction to a French doctor in Paris. Even a photograph of her son, so that I could recognize him. It was that last that worried me. I began to wonder if she suspected more than I'd realized.

"I'm sure I won't require half of these, but I appreciate your concern for me."

"You may tell anyone who asks that you're conducting a survey for me. Conditions in the remaining clinics, and so on. And that I've given you a few days of leave in Paris to visit an old friend of ours who has survived the war. That shouldn't arouse any suspicions at this stage. I would be remiss if I didn't send messages to my son about friends of his who are home now." She shook her head. "So sadly few. Well. It will have to do." She passed another letter to me.

I returned the documents to her, and she filled in my name in all the proper places.

When we had finished our business and I was preparing to leave, she thanked me again. And as I opened the door, she added, "Sister Crawford?"

"Yes, Matron?"

"May I say, you are your father's daughter."

It was a compliment of the highest order.

"Thank you, Matron. I am proud to be his daughter."

And then I was in the passage again, wondering just what I'd got myself into.

I went to Mrs. Hennessey's house, and she was delighted to see me.

At the start of the war, she'd converted her large and spacious home into flats for nurses like me undergoing the rigorous Queen Alexandra's training program, and we had kept them for a pied-à-terre whenever we were on leave in London and didn't have enough time to travel on to our homes. I'd kept mine at war's end, since I was still in the service. Diana had married, but Mary and Lady Elspeth had kept their rooms as well. It still was frowned on for a woman to stay in an hotel alone, but even that was changing with the times. We'd left too many men in the muddy fields of Flanders and France.

Mrs. Hennessey and I caught up on news over her precious hoard of tea, and she asked if I had leave and intended to go to Somerset. I told her that I was going to Paris on official business but expected to be back in a few days.

We pressed all my uniforms, packed them in a valise rather than my kit, and then I had dinner with my mother in one of our favorite restaurants.

I'd sent my parents a telegram to let them know I'd be in London, ostensibly for a brief bit of leave, and so I was rather surprised when the familiar motorcar pulled up in front of Mrs. Hennessey's door and only my mother stepped out.

She smiled. "We might as well be back in the war, darling. The Colonel Sahib is busy with something or other that he can't talk about, and Simon has disappeared into the heather in Scotland. At least that's what I gathered from his note."

My father had been called back from his early retirement to help with the war effort, and most of the time we had no idea where he was or even if he was safe.

Simon Brandon, my father's former Regimental Sergeant-Major, had been recalled as well, and he'd often been involved in training recruits. There had been secret work too. What that was I was never sure, but I'd guessed from various comments afterward that he had been behind enemy lines more than once. I do know he'd appeared and disappeared, sometimes without a word, even in France. And he seemed to relish the action, but he'd also been wounded a time or two, once quite seriously. That had worried my father, who often treated Simon like the son he'd never had. My mother was quite fond of him as well, and he would do anything for her.

Simon had lied about his age and joined the Army shortly before my father's regiment was posted to India, and I'd always thought he must have lost his own parents very early, to have so readily adopted us as his family. I'd never heard him mention them or any other relatives. My earliest memory of him was walking into my father's study one afternoon in India, as Simon, tall, rebellious, and resentful, was being dressed down by my father. Five minutes later, as penance for some infraction, he was ordered to escort the Major's little daughter to another child's birthday party. And I'd wanted my father to take me there. We rode away as enemies—and came back tentative friends.

"Oh, dear. I expect it's the two of us for dinner, then." I followed her back to the motorcar, and got in next to her. She was quite an experienced driver, and as she smoothly pulled out into the evening traffic, I added, "What's happening in Scotland?"

My mother cast me a look that I interpreted as putting a good face on doubt. "I'm not quite sure. I asked Richard about that, but he didn't seem to know, either. Simon has been broody lately. We haven't seen much of him, even though he's been in the cottage these past few weeks."

"That's not like him," I commented, thinking about it. His cottage was just beyond the wood at the bottom of our garden. Close enough that he'd often come up to dine with my parents.

"Iris told me the other morning that he must have a lassie up in Scotland."

Iris was our maid, and she'd been with the family forever, keeping up the house in Somerset when my father was posted abroad, taking my mother and me with him.

"A lassie?" I repeated blankly. Somehow it had never occurred to me that Simon might have a life outside our family. "He was in the north often enough during the war, but I never quite imagined—" I shook my head. "Well, well."

My mother said nothing, appearing to concentrate on threading her way to the Strand. I could sense the tension in her, though. She wasn't about to admit that she was worried.

As we found a place to leave the motorcar close to the restaurant, she said lightly, "You know Iris. She'd marry the dog to the cat, just to attend the wedding."

I did. Outwardly the most practical of women, she secretly adored novels of romance and danger from Jane Austen to *Jane Eyre*, and still mourned her young man who was killed in the Boer War. Even though my father had said privately that Ronnie was completely unsuitable for her, his handsome photograph in uniform and his heroic death had endowed him with all the virtues a woman might hope for in a husband. And no one had had the heart to tell her otherwise. She had said to me once that she hoped I would find the love she'd known, however briefly. I had been touched.

We had a remarkably good dinner, my mother and I, talking about everything from what was happening in Paris to what was poking up in the gardens at home, showing the first signs of spring. A few of the daffodils already had buds waiting for a warm day to open.

And the ghost in the room, so to speak, was Simon away in Scotland, although neither of us mentioned him again.

She took me back to Mrs. Hennessey's, told me to write when I could, and left. I stood at the door, in spite of the chill wind, waving her out of sight. Back to Somerset and all the familiar things of my childhood.

It brought home something I'd been avoiding thinking about. What was I to do in the months and years ahead? Continue in nursing, with gall bladders and kidney stones replacing the work I'd done at the Front, or find something else that I could love as much as I had my duties with the Queen Alexandra's. Mrs. Hennessey had said that I would find my next step in due course.

"Don't rush the future, my dear. It's best to let the war settle in your memory before you look ahead."

There had been some truth to that. I'd wanted to help bring the severely wounded back to England, I couldn't leave the Service with that undone. I'd discovered since then that for too many of them there would never be much of a future. Medical care had saved their lives, but it couldn't make them whole again.

Trying to push aside gloomy thoughts that matched the gloomy day, I went inside and prepared to leave for France.

The next morning I took the train to Dover. There I found a ferry waiting for half a dozen high-ranking officers coming down from London by motorcar, and was told there would be space for me as well. A light rain was beginning to fall, and I went to my quarters to put my valise inside. But it was stuffy in there, with that typical smell of salt and damp that was familiar from my many crossings during the war. And so I went to the bridge, taking shelter in a corner, out of the way. I was about to shut the door when I saw two staff motorcars draw up to the quay, and seven officers got out, shook hands, and three got back into the first vehicle. The others set out for the ship.

I didn't need field glasses to recognize the tallest of the four.

It was the Colonel Sahib, my father.

So much for all Matron's careful instructions! This was to be a quiet journey, drawing as little attention as possible. And my father would surely want to know why I was not in Wiltshire, where he'd last seen me, and instead on my way to France. Would he believe that I was going to inspect the last of our clinics? He would probably know precisely how many there were, where they were located, and how soon they expected to be closed.

I hadn't been able to lie to my father since I was

three. I'd have to think of a way of telling him the truth, just not all of it—and hope for the best.

He looked up at that moment, as if he'd sensed my presence, and when I waved, he saw me, smiled, but kept on walking.

Happy as I was to see him, I groaned inwardly and started down to what we euphemistically referred to as the salon, although it bore no resemblance to the elegant salons of the P&O. It had been converted to a canteen for troops crossing to France and seating for the walking wounded returning to England. The chairs had been mended several times, and the tabletops were scarred with initials and various insignia carved into the wood.

I heard voices approaching, and then the door from the outer deck opened and my father stepped in. He smiled at me but to my surprise didn't speak. Instead he continued his conversation with his companions.

I could feel the ship beginning to move as we cast off and set out for Calais. One of the crew came to where I was sitting and asked if I would care for a cup of tea. I accepted his offer.

I had almost finished my tea when the meeting ended and my father accompanied his companions as far as the salon door. When they had gone, he turned and came over to my table.

"Fancy meeting you here," he said with a grin, and pulled out the chair across from mine. "Does your mother know you're on your way to France?"

I returned his grin. "We had dinner together in London last night. I seem to remember I failed to mention it."

"Posted to a base hospital, are you?"

I knew and he knew that most of them were being closed as patients were stabilized and beds were found in England for them.

"Actually, I'm carrying out a survey for the Queen Alexandra's." Near enough to the truth to salve my conscience. "Mother seemed to think you might *already* be in Paris."

His good humor disappeared. Glancing over his shoulder to be sure we couldn't be overheard, he said quietly, "The American president's fourteen-point plan is causing trouble. The Canadians want to be represented, not just as part of the British Empire. So does Australia, but she'd like to have New Guinea as part of her territory. Both lost thousands of men, they feel they earned the right. Everyone seems to be here, wanting something. The biggest problem is the French position. She is set on punishing Germany. Heavy reparations. After all, Germany has crossed her borders before, in the lifetime of many who remember. But given the state of the German economy, this could cripple the country for years to come."

"Surely the point," I commented.

"Yes. A poverty-stricken Germany won't rearm for a generation. But will they be angry enough to want to try again? I'm not comfortable with that thought. And there are other problems. The Arabs expect to be given part of the Turkish empire for their role in liberating it. German possessions in Africa are being divided up, and this new concept of Wilson's, that a people should determine their own destiny, has set the cat amongst the pigeons, even for us—" He broke off as a member of the crew came in and filled a cup with tea, then took it with him. "At any rate, it's clear that any number of parties are muddying the waters, and we'll be lucky if we have a treaty by summer," my father went on somberly, as soon as the door had closed behind the man. He sighed. "We've been in talks in London. I'm on my way back with new instructions. By the way, our old friend Captain Barkley is in Paris. You might want to look him up."

Captain Barkley and I had a checkered history. My father had sent him to keep an eye on me when there was the possibility that I was in danger. He was an American who had joined the Canadian Army well before his own country had entered the war. I quite liked him, although his irritating insistence that I was in need of protection often put us at loggerheads. My parents had brought me up to be independent and resourceful. And while his concern was charming in an old-fashioned way, it was difficult to make him see that I could take care of myself.

"Yes, I'll look forward to seeing him again," I said, determined to avoid him at any cost.

My father looked sharply at me, then changed the subject.

Simon's name never came up.

I didn't see the Colonel Sahib again except at a distance as he and the other officers stepped into a waiting staff motorcar. But a burly man in a smock appeared as I left the ship, touched his cap, and gestured to my valise. Deciding that my father had sent him to assist me up hill from the docks, I nodded, and let him take my kit as well.

I started up the sloping road to the town proper. Many of the houses at the top were still in ruinous conditions. Billets, bars, brief shelter for the worst of the wounded, ambulances waiting to offload and return to the Front, new officers looking for transport to their regiments, and refugees hoping for everything from a chance to earn a few sous to searching for relatives—Calais had been little short of chaos. Now it was almost quiet by comparison, although the Army was repatriating soldiers as quickly as possible.

Still, the street was busy with people going about their business, and in the distance I could hear men marching. Looking over my shoulder I could see that another ship was coming in. It appeared to be a transport.

Just then someone shouted, "Sister?"

I turned to see a medical officer coming out of a now-derelict house that had once been used to store medical supplies as they were unloaded, until they could be sorted and sent on.

His uniform was streaked with what appeared to be soot, and there was a dark smudge on one cheek. I stopped. "Sir?"

"Over here. I need your help."

I called to the porter, who was still trudging ahead of me, and he reluctantly halted as I turned back toward the house.

Frowning now, the officer stared at me. "I'd expected an orderly. Well, never mind, you'll have to do."

I asked the porter to wait, but by that time the officer was already clambering through a doorway that appeared to be a black pit. As I followed him, I realized that this must lead down into the cellar of the house.

Behind me the porter was calling to me, and I told him again to wait, that I would attend to him in a moment.

Just then a tall, lanky man came up the road behind me and said, "Don't worry, ma'am, I'll keep an eye on him. You go ahead."

I recognized the colorful uniform. He was one of the pilots of the Lafayette Escadrille, the American flyers who had come to France early in the war, eager to do their part long before their country had entered the fighting in 1917. Instead of the traditional kepi, he wore a high-crown broad-brim hat. I didn't know him.

The medical officer had reappeared in the doorway, impatiently calling to me. I had no choice. I hastily thanked the man, and hurried toward the opening. A set of stairs disappeared down into the darkness, and as I started down, he held up a torch to guide me. Then he was walking back into the shadows, and I followed, nearly tripping over an overturned stool or an empty box, I couldn't be sure which.

The doctor was saying, his voice echoing, "I'd been told there were deserters living in some of these places. I almost missed these two, couldn't see them at all even with my torch. But they're in bad shape."

His light flicked over two men slumped on what appeared to be mattresses that had seen better days. One looked to me to have a fever. His face was flushed, even in this dim bit of light.

The doctor set his torch on another overturned box, and knelt beside the sick man.

"He's wounded. Well, it's half-healed. Or got infected, living in such conditions. Here, help me cut away his shirt." He handed me a pair of scissors, and I began to work on the shirt as the officer searched in the satchel he must have brought with him. Together we got the shirt away from the wound, and he drew the torch closer as we examined it. It was along his ribs on the right side, raw, angry, and oozing fluids. The skin around it was scraped as well.

"Infected," the doctor said, rocking back on his heels. "We'll have to get him to hospital. Then hand him over to the Foot Police."

"Here!" the other man in the shadows exclaimed. "We're not deserters, we've got our papers."

"Then what are you doing here?" the doctor snapped.

"There's naught to go home to, is there? His wife died in the influenza, and mine's left me. We've been doing whatever work we could find, then he took a fall trying to help a Frenchman repair a shutter, and the fool wouldn't pay us then. There was no money for a doctor, and the landlord of the house where we'd been staying accused us of fighting, and kicked us out. I brought him here, but that cut got worse two nights ago. I tried to steal a bottle of wine, to clean it with, but the police chased me, and it wasn't until last night I could circle around and come back." He began to fumble in a bundle lying beside him, and finally found papers, waving them at the doctor.

The man with the wound groaned, and tried to sit up. We got him back on the mattress, and the doctor said, "Small wonder he's infected. Are those rat droppings? And God knows what's on the mattress." He began putting a clean dressing on the wound, and then as he held the man upright, I wound the tape around his chest to keep the dressings in place. He badly needed a bath.

Satisfied, the doctor turned to the other man. "What's wrong with you?"

"Nothing," he answered sullenly.

"You've been favoring that arm. Let me see."

It took some persuading, but in the end, the man removed his shirt, glowering at us all the while.

There was a large boil on the man's shoulder, and the doctor set about lancing it and putting a dressing over it.

Then he turned to me. "Go back and tell them we'll need a stretcher and orderlies to get that one back. Our other friend here can walk."

"I'm afraid I just landed from England. I'm on a mission for Matron. I'm not attached to a clinic here."

Surprised, he said, "Then why did you come to help me?"

"You didn't give me much choice, sir."

"Damn it, then what became of the orderly I sent for?"

"I don't know."

He was on the brink of swearing again. "All right. Can you manage these two while I'm gone? There's a clearing hospital, temporary, just down the road, where we treat whatever is brought to us. I won't be long." He stared at me, frowning. "What's your name, Sister?"

"Crawford, sir."

"Greene. Archie Greene."

I didn't relish standing here in the dark with our two patients. "Leave me the torch, sir?"

"Oh—yes, of course." And then he was gone.

I was just starting to question the second patient, when a shadow loomed in the brightness of the doorway, and the flyer who had promised to guard my luggage called, "Ma'am? Are you all right?"

He had a slow way of speaking, almost a drawl.

"Yes, I'm fine. We have two patients here, and the doctor has gone for a stretcher. It shouldn't be very much longer."

"I don't care for the fact that he left you in this cellar," he said. "I'll be right here, in the doorway, if you need me. I can see your porter from here as well. He's not of a mind to go without you. Not now."

"What did you do to him?" I asked, alarmed.

"Nothing," he said in an aggrieved voice. "Just a little friendly reminder that we'd helped him when his country needed help most."

I heard a quiet chuckle from our second patient, the one with the boil. I didn't find it quite as amusing as he did.

Turning to him I said, "Where are you from?"

He said, wariness in every word, "Begging your pardon, Sister, but do you really need to know?"

"No," I replied, but I rather thought his accent was from Shropshire. "How long have you known your friend, here?"

"We were in the same company most of the war. He said he wasn't going home, and I wasn't in much of a hurry myself. So we didn't. We'd tried to find work in Rouen, but there's the language, you see. Neither of us can speak it very well. Just mam-zelle and mon-sewer, and parlay-voo. There was a woman in the bar who said she'd teach us, but she wanted more money than we could pay. Still, we were getting by well enough, until Teddy here got hurt. It was a nasty fall."

And yet he'd stayed by his friend.

He was adding anxiously, "If he's taken to hospital, will they put us in prison for not going on the transport with the rest? We didn't desert. We just didn't go home."

"If you have your papers, you should be all right." But I wasn't sure the Army would see it that way.

Just then I heard footsteps, men talking, and then Dr. Greene was back, this time with two orderlies and a stretcher.

There was more argument about going to hospital, but in the end it was clear to Teddy's defender—we had learned *his* name was Hank—that if they didn't go, Teddy could be in far more serious trouble with that wound.

The orderlies got Teddy onto the stretcher as I held the torch for them, and then we made our way through the clutter to the stairs. They managed the stairs with the skill of men used to trench walls, and the little party, led by the doctor, started off. He'd thanked me, and I'd been grateful that he hadn't asked me questions too. I hadn't wanted to explain about reviewing the clinics, for fear he'd demand that I start with his own.

In the light of day, looking down at my boots, the hem of my skirts, and my cuffs, I could see that they were the worse for wear after kneeling on what must have been a filthy cellar floor. I sighed.

The flyer who had kept my porter from deserting me said, "You might wish to go to hospital, where you can freshen up."

But it was the last place I wanted to go. "Is there a respectable hotel or lodging house where I could take a room for a few hours?"

"Yes, ma'am. If you'll allow me to guide you, I'll take you there."

The difference in the town was astonishing. I could remember lines of wounded waiting on the road to the docks, ambulances moving back and forth, new recruits marching off troop vessels and climbing to the top of the cliffs in perfect order, some faces filled with excitement, others with dread. Refugees huddled in the railway station where officers and other ranks stood around awaiting transport as they went on leave. Now some semblance of normal life was stirring, although there were uniforms everywhere. Only the wounded were missing.

We found the house not far from the Gare, and the woman who owned it took one look at my skirts and hands and said, "Oh, did you fall? Are you hurt?"

I assured her I wasn't and took a room for the afternoon, paying off my porter and thanking the young officer for leading me here.

He told me it was his pleasure to help out, and walked on.

In the event, I stayed the night, for Madame allowed me to clean and hang up my uniform, then offered to press it for me after breakfast the next morning.

She even provided my dinner—for a price—and joined me at the table to ask endless questions about nursing and England. I finally got to bed shortly after eleven, and after breakfast, I took the train to Paris. A day late, but I didn't think it would matter.

As I was about to put my valise overhead in my carriage, the American flyer put his head around the door and said, "Let me put that up for you, ma'am."

I thanked him, then said as courteously as I could, "The proper form of address is 'Sister.'"

He grinned. "Yes, ma'am, I do know that. But you don't look much like my sister, and so I find it hard to remember." And with that cheeky rejoinder, he disappeared down the corridor. I didn't see him later as we pulled into Paris and I got down at the Gare du Nord. But then it was possible he'd left the train at Rouen. Nice as he was, I didn't wish another Captain Barkley following me around offering to help at every turn. At least not until I'd found Matron's son and learned exactly what I would have to deal with.

Lieutenant Minton, like many of the people at the conference, had taken a flat in Paris rather than live in an hotel. As I reached the outskirts of the city, my companions in the compartment began to collect their belongings, and the older man across from me offered to lift down my valise when we arrived. He was being kind, I thanked him, and let him help me.

There were taxis waiting outside the Gare du Nord, and I gave the driver the direction of the flat.

Paris had changed—and yet was very much the same. The shells of destroyed houses, the depressed air of the average citizen, uniforms everywhere, that was familiar. But the uniforms were more varied— some I couldn't immediately identify—while men in the dark suits of the Foreign Offices hurried toward meetings, and the streets were crowded with all manner of traffic.

The address I'd been given was in a quarter of nineteenth-century houses, and as I looked up at the grillwork at the windows and the mansard roof, I thought Lawrence Minton was living rather well for a minor attaché at the Peace Conference.

I asked my taxi to wait for me, and went up the steps to knock at the black door.

An older woman wearing a dark dress that looked very much like mourning answered, and I asked for Lieutenant Minton.

I was told that he was not at home.

"His mother has sent me to call on him," I explained. "May I wait for him to return?"

She considered my uniform and must have concluded that I wouldn't be put off with excuses. Or else that I looked too respectable to be anything other than a nursing Sister carrying out a task for the Minton family.

"I am afraid Lieutenant Minton has not been in Paris for some time. The flat is paid for through September, and I have kept it for him. But he has not been in residence."

This was unexpected. I had to think fast.

"His mother, Madame Minton, is not aware of this," I replied. "She will not be pleased that I couldn't find her son. Is he not attending the Peace Conference?"

The woman made a face, a typical French reaction to being put on the spot. "I cannot answer that—I have not been taken into his confidence."

"Where is he then? Has he returned to England?"

She hesitated. "How can I be sure that you are here at the request of Madame his mother?"

Oh, dear. This had an ominous sound.

I found the letter of introduction given me by Matron. "Perhaps this will serve? I promise you, I have come to help the Lieutenant if I can. Not to create more problems for him."

She read the letter, laboring over translating from the English phraseology. I watched her expression, hoping she would accept the letter as legitimate.

Looking up from the sheet of paper in her hand, she said, "I am not certain of this information. But you might look in the village of St. Ives. Number twelve Rue des Fleurs. I understand that is where a young woman lives. She had cared for Lieutenant Minton when he was taken ill some weeks ago. Then she arrived one day and took him away with her. I have not seen nor heard from him since."

I repeated the address, to be sure of it. Then I asked if I might see his rooms, thinking I might find something there that would help me understand why he'd left Paris—and why he hadn't informed his mother. He had *volunteered* to attend the talks, according to Matron. It was good for his career.

Madame refused, adding that she did not have permission from him to allow anyone in the rooms. "And my other lodgers will not be happy about this."

"There are other flats here?" I asked, looking up at the floors above my head.

"Yes. Since the war began," she said. Philosophically she added, "One quickly learns to make do."

I thanked her and went back to my waiting taxi.

After conferring with the driver, I learned that my best option was to take the train to St. Ives, some fourteen miles north of Paris. I thanked him, and in due course, I was deposited at the proper station, where I found that there was a train leaving in the next quarter of an hour. I bought a return ticket in the event this was a wild goose chase, then sat down in the busy waiting room to await its arrival.

I alighted in the village of St. Ives in watery sunshine. The railway station was tiny, and there was no sign of the stationmaster when I looked around. Nor was there a taxi waiting for any local passengers. I resolutely picked up my valise and my kit, and looked toward the church tower, which was surely in the center of the village. Avoiding the rain puddles in the ruts in the road, I made my way toward it.

Though the village had been spared the worst of the war, it was shabby, and I saw two houses that looked as if a shell had missed its target and fallen on them instead. Pigeons flew up from the ruins as I passed.

The house I was looking for at 12 Rue des Fleurs turned out to be a short side street beyond the small church. It too was rather shabby. North of Paris, where the Germans had charged down the Marne Valley in the first days of the war, the damage had been horrific. They had been stopped well short of St. Ives, but many of the residents here and in nearby villages had prudently fled. Only in the last few months had some of them returned—as I walked, I could see small signs, like a newly painted door or smoke from the chimneys, even though the rest of the house still hadn't been kept up.

A few trees were striving to produce blossoms, but the typically French window boxes were still straggly and winter brown. It had been unusually chilly of late, but I thought perhaps no one had had the heart to plant geraniums in the spring for a good four years.

I went up the two steps by the door and lifted the knocker, letting it fall.

No one answered the summons, and I knocked again.

Finally the door opened barely a crack, and a young woman's face appeared in the narrow space. She was quite pretty, with dark hair and eyes, and a pert nose. And younger than I was, by two or three years. I hadn't quite expected that, from the description Madame had given me in Paris.

I was beginning to wonder if *she* had given me the

wrong address. On purpose, or because she too had been given it?

"*Oui?*" The young woman stared at my uniform, then at my face.

"Good afternoon," I said briskly in English. "My name is Sister Crawford. I've come to call on Lawrence Minton." Shaking her head, she began to shut the door in my face, and I added quickly, "No, please, I'm here at the request of his mother."

She hadn't expected that. Stammering in French, she seemed to be telling me that he was ill and not receiving visitors, speaking too quickly for me to follow her.

This was, apparently, the correct address.

"I'm very sorry to hear it," I answered in French. "But I am a nurse, you see. May I come in?"

She wasn't prepared for that either.

"No—I tell you he is not well."

"Yes, yes. That's why I am here."

That seemed to worry her even more. But before she could answer me, I heard a male voice from inside the house. "Who is it, Marina?" He spoke in French, but he was definitely English.

"*Votre mère*—" she began, and I heard him swear roundly.

"*Mon dieu*—" He must have thought it was indeed his mother at the door, because I heard a flurry of movement now, as if he was hastily making himself presentable.

I put the flat of my hand on the door, and before Marina could stop me, I pushed it wide, and she gave way before me.

The entrance hall was as shabby as the exterior. There was a small table with a lamp on it, and nothing else besides the stairway to the upper floors. To my right was an open door, and with Marina at my heels begging me to stop, I marched straight in there.

I didn't need the proof of my eyes. My nose had already told me what Lawrence Minton was ill from.

The miasma was a blend of stale sweat, unbathed body, and the sickening sweet odor of opium. Minton was standing in the middle of the room, staring at me, jaw dropping as he realized I wasn't Matron.

I could see at once that he was his mother's son—he had her blue eyes fringed by dark lashes and brown hair with streaks of lighter shades, like caramel. The resemblance ended there, for while the shape of their faces was similar, his was thin and haggard.

He was still staring blearily at me, frowning now.

"Who are you?" he demanded in French.

"Good afternoon, Lieutenant Minton," I said cheerfully in English, setting my valise on the floor. "Your mother has been worried about you. I've come to see why you haven't responded to her messages."

This wasn't the way I'd expected to begin my task, but I really didn't have a choice. And so I had adopted a Matron's direct, no-nonsense approach. It usually worked, even on the most recalcitrant patient.

He looked up at me, confused. "You aren't my mother," he said after a moment.

"I am her emissary," I told him bluntly. "She has given me instructions to find you and report to her."

"I don't need a nursemaid," he retorted, batting at the air with one thin hand, as if bothered by a fly. "Tell her I'm fine."

"No, you aren't," I said firmly. Turning to the young woman, I asked, "This is a large house. Is there a room I could use while I am here?"

"You will stay?" she asked, taken aback. "You have seen him, you can now report to his mother."

"He isn't ill," I told her unequivocally. "Lieutenant Minton is an addict. I have instructions from Mrs. Minton to report to her, but my first duty is to take care of him."

"It's hopeless," she said, dropping her voice to a whisper. "I have tried, but he refuses to let me do anything."

"He won't refuse me," I told her, knowing even as I said the words that I was very likely going to find the Lieutenant as difficult as she had. But it was important to give the impression that I intended to be successful, and that was that. I also knew the Lieutenant was listening to the exchange. "Can you show me to this room? I should like to freshen up, if you please."

Marina cast an anxious glance at Minton, but he had shut his eyes, ignoring me.

"I'm sorry, I don't know your name," I said, in an effort to distract her.

"Marina Angeline duBois Lascelles," she told me, still watching Minton.

"Thank you, Mademoiselle. Now, my room, if you please?"

With no help forthcoming from Minton, she looked at me, uncertain, and then she said, "This way," and turned toward the staircase.

With a nod to the Lieutenant, I picked up my valise and my kit and followed her. He made no effort to stop me or to carry my things for me.

As we climbed the stairs, I asked, "Why is the Lieutenant here, and not in his flat in Paris?"

"I was afraid," she said reluctantly. "But his—his illness was beginning to cause talk. I thought it best—I didn't know what else to do."

"He isn't ill," I told her, repeating what I'd said down-stairs. "He's addicted to opium. How did that happen?"

She stopped in front of a closed door. "All was well with him. His wound had healed, he was here to attend the talks, he was the man I remembered, the man who had done so much for my family. And then something happened. He began having nightmares and asked for laudanum to help him sleep. But he told the doctor, as I learned much later, that it was the wound, he had reinjured it playing tennis. And so it was given him. Now he needs it more often than when he sleeps. As you see."

Opening the door, she stepped aside.

The room was large, had two pairs of windows over-looking the street, but it was stale, airless, and smelled a little of damp.

Apologizing, Marina crossed the room to open a window. "I have had to let the maids go. There is no money, you see. And the cook as well. We do what we can. I am so sorry. If you feel you'd rather leave . . ." Her voice trailed away.

"This will do very well," I said briskly, as if I were used to such problems, all the while wondering what Matron would make of her son's circumstances. In London we had both wondered about the possibility of drugs. But surely she had had no idea that he was at this stage in his addiction. It was one thing to suspect—quite another to know.

Setting down my valise and my kit, I said, "Is that where the money has gone? To buy his laudanum?"

"No honest doctor will prescribe it in such doses. But there are other ways. He is not attending the conference meetings, and therefore he has not been drawing his pay. The Army believes he has gone to England, you understand, to have his wound attended to. To be sure there is no trouble over this, he had to leave Paris, and I was afraid to leave him to himself. I brought him here, to the house of my parents."

"Are they here as well?" I asked, surprised.

"They haven't returned. Life is a little better in the south."

When I didn't answer immediately, wondering what her family would think of Marina bringing the Lieutenant here, wondering too just what their relationship might be, Marina asked anxiously, "Can you help him? Without telling his mother what has happened? I can do nothing with him."

"I don't know. I'll do my best."

She shook her head. "The English are always so calm. I wish I could be calm, as well."

I turned to look at her. "Forgive me for being intrusive," I said after a moment. "Are you engaged to the Lieutenant? Do your parents approve of his staying here with you?" I needed to know, if I too intended to stay here.

She held my gaze, but I could tell that she was actually trying to hide her embarrassment. "It is my family's house, yes, that is true," she replied with an effort. "And they are still in Lyons at present. I am living in Paris now, and they have entrusted me with the responsibility for this house. To prepare it for their eventual return. They don't know that I am living here at the moment. Or that the Lieutenant is also here. I don't care to lie to them, but my conscience is clear. Lawrence is a friend of my family's, but I am not his—his mistress, if that's what you are asking. But I think they would understand what has happened, that I am trying to repay his many kindnesses to my parents during the war."

"I'm sorry. I misunderstood." I smiled. She meant what she was saying, and I believed her. Still, I wondered if she hadn't yet recognized something more than a family debt. I suddenly felt years older in experience. One grows up quickly in aid stations near the Front or in hospitals where men died even as one struggled to keep them alive.

Still, it was probably for the best that I said nothing more about propriety, or made her feel uncomfortable about a situation neither of us could change for now.

"I must bring you fresh water." She took the pitcher from the washstand and hurried out of the room.

Well, I'd discovered why the Lieutenant wasn't in Paris and hadn't been attending the meetings he was supposed to be there for. Matron had been right to worry about the rumor she'd heard. But I didn't think she knew about Marina. If she'd suspected her son had turned to laudanum, she'd have told herself it was because of the old wound. But was it?

While I believed Marina when she said she wasn't involved with the Lieutenant, still, there would be talk if she wasn't careful. A young woman living alone in the same house as an English officer? Especially in a small village like St. Ives, there would be speculation, rumors. How quickly would they reach the ears of Marina's parents? The repercussions could destroy her reputation and her future.

It occurred to me, as I waited for Marina to return with my pitcher of water, that Matron had judged her emissary well. Not only would I do what I could to protect the good name of the Queen Alexandra's Imperial Military Nursing Service, but I'd also protect my father's former regiment. Not because I'd grown up with its traditions and reputation, but because my father would expect me to see that it wasn't dishonored. Now I had another responsibility—somehow to save the man downstairs from himself. And given my reception here, where I had had to force my way inside, it wasn't going to be an overnight miracle.

I hadn't met the Lieutenant before this, when he must have been a very different man. But I knew what laudanum could do to the strongest men, and I also knew that to help him, I'd have to put away any feelings of pity or sympathy.

I stood there for some time, considering what to do. I couldn't walk away. Send for Matron? Let *her* take on the task ahead? But she had sent *me*, in her place. At the very least I must try to do something about his addiction, before I reported to her. If only to take the measure of what it would require to help him. I owed her that.

And meanwhile, my presence might offer some protection for Marina's good name. I could see, even in such a brief encounter, that she had neither the experience nor the strength to work with the Lieutenant. She felt an obligation, a strong sense of duty, but I gathered that her determination hadn't been enough to stop him from using the drug.

I took off my coat and put it in the armoire, feeling the chill in the room as I did.

Calling on my training, I began to assess the situation.

Marina had indicated that the change had been sudden, not gradual.

What *had* happened to Lieutenant Minton? He didn't strike me as shell-shocked, and Marina had just told me that he'd got over his wound without any problems. He'd been attached to the English delegation to the peace conference, which meant that he was not taking drugs then, or showing signs of any emotional distress. I think Marina would have known if there had been a romance that went wrong.

Removing my hat and putting on my cap from my valise, I went to the window and looked down at the street below. The houses across the way were, from the look of them, still unoccupied.

If there was no money for coal or food or common necessities, that must be my first responsibility. Thank heavens Matron had given me access to funds. I was going to need them. But how was I to explain my use of them, without telling her what I'd walked into here?

Chapter 2

The water in the pitcher that Marina brought up to me was lovely and warm, and I washed my face and hands, then tidied up my hair and set my cap on again.

There was nothing for it now but to go back down to the front room and confront Lieutenant Minton.

But he wasn't there.

I went in search of Marina and found her in the large kitchen.

"Where has Lieutenant Minton gone?"

She sighed. "He locks himself in his room when he doesn't want to talk. I have grown accustomed to it."

Looking around me at the empty kitchen, I asked, "Why doesn't he contribute to the expenses of housekeeping? If he isn't drawing his regimental pay, surely he must have money of his own."

"I think he may be in debt."

"Gambling?" He wouldn't be the first officer to have taken up gambling, only to find themselves in over their heads.

"I don't know. He won't talk to me about his troubles, you see. But I don't believe it's cards." Her eyes filled with tears, and she brushed them away angrily. "There's something wrong, Sister Crawford. I don't know what it is. But I think he's desperate. Despairing. I worry that he will do something foolish. That's the other reason I brought him here, where I could watch over him. And I thought it would make a difference, somehow, being away from Paris."

"Is he being blackmailed because of his addiction?" I asked, for surely that would explain a little of his actions.

"I don't believe so. I think—whatever it is, it has to do with the war. And yet how could it be that? The war is over. Has been over for months."

I took some francs from my pocket. "His mother has provided me with money, in the event I needed it to help her son. The first thing we must purchase is food. And some coal, if you can find it. Can you cook?"

She smiled a little. "In the war, I learned to do many things that I'd never expected to do. Yes. I can cook."

"Then find something for our dinner. Something you believe the Lieutenant might like."

"He has a very small appetite. And there isn't much in the shops yet. A few eggs. A little cheese. And even these things are expensive." She sighed. "It will be better when we can grow crops again. Still, it will be months before a harvest."

"We must eat. Go on and see what you can find." I hesitated. "Do you live mostly in Paris? Or here?"

"I was a teacher in a school in Paris. My father was an artillery officer. He was captured early in the war, although for two years we thought he was missing, perhaps even dead. But he'd sent my mother to Lyon, the house of her sister, out of harm's way. The Lieutenant helped us find out what had happened to my father, and when a few very ill prisoners were released, he made certain Papa was amongst them. It was a good thing. He had been wounded, and it hadn't been cared for, that wound. He may still lose his leg."

"Why are you here, and not at your post in the school?"

"I lied," she said, not looking at me. "I told them I was needed to care for my father. But it was really Lawrence—the Lieutenant—who needed me. They believe I am in Lyon, and so the Head Mistress is holding my position for my return." Turning to face me, she added more than a little defiantly, "There was no one else to care for him, you see."

"He's fortunate to have you," I said, and smiled, trying to soothe her ruffled feathers. I hadn't meant to upset her, but I had to have some feeling for the situation I had walked into.

"Meanwhile," I went on cheerfully, "while you're away doing the marketing, tell me which room belongs to the Lieutenant?"

"It's no use, he won't come out."

"That's probably true. On the other hand, I ought to try, don't you think?"

"The room of my parents. Upstairs, to your right. Third door."

Thanking her, I went back up the stairs, found the third door, and knocked. From the front hall came the sound of the outer door opening and closing. I was just as happy not to have Marina as a witness to anything that was about to happen.

When there was no response, I said, "It's Sister Crawford, Lieutenant. I'd like to speak to you, if I may."

But Marina was right. He had no intention of coming to the door. After a moment, I left. It wouldn't serve either of us if he thought he could make me beg.

We ate our dinner—just the two of us—although Marina tried to take a tray to Lieutenant Minton. It was still there when I went up to bed, sitting outside his door. She had found some eggs and cheese and a few potatoes and made an omelet. There had been a cabbage as well, and we steamed that.

I knocked at his door and said in Matron's no-nonsense voice, "Lieutenant? You're being childish, wasting good food."

Once more there was no answer. I hesitated, and then reached out to see if the door was locked.

To my surprise, I found it wasn't. I opened it and stepped into the room.

There was no lamp burning, nor had the curtains been drawn. I could just see him stretched out across the bed, dressed in shirt and trousers, and when I went closer for a better look, I found he was sleeping like a man drugged. I'd given enough sedatives to the wounded to recognize the signs. And even though I touched his shoulder and spoke his name, he didn't respond.

The room was icy cold. I drew up the coverlet to cover his shoulders and arms, then pulled the window curtain to.

It wasn't necessary to tiptoe out of the room. Lieutenant Minton wouldn't have heard me leave. I doubted that he'd have heard a stampeding herd of elephants.

I could understand now why Marina hadn't felt as certain as I had that something could be done for this man. Picking up his tray, I took it back to the kitchen.

Well, I thought, finally going to my own room, whether he liked it or not, tomorrow we would talk. I had to know more about his state of mind.

Over breakfast the next morning—the last of the omelet warmed over, and the remains of the cabbage—I chatted with Marina again. It was chilly this morning, and I'd have given much for a porridge.

First, I asked her to arrange for enough coal for fires in my room and hers, one room downstairs, and to keep the cooker going. And then I asked her if she knew why Minton was at the Peace Conference.

She shrugged. "He wishes to stay in the Army, or at least he did wish to. He speaks quite good French as well as German. He can translate while someone is still speaking. It's a gift, to do that. And some of the delegates have no language skills at all. Besides, he is—was—the sort of man people like. Good company, is that what you say in English? With everyone at the conference seeming to have no patience with the views of anyone else, he was sometimes able to get things done without any fuss. That is also a gift."

"How long have you known Lawrence?"

She picked up our dishes and carried them to the pan in the sink. "Since early in 1916. He came to Paris on a short leave, and that afternoon he called on my brother, who was recovering from his wounds. They had known each other for some time. I was taking care of Pierre, as well as teaching, and so I met Lawrence then. In the end, he spent his entire leave with us, cheering up Pierre. That's when I asked if he could find news of our father. We had heard nothing for months, and the Army could give us no news. And then in April 1917, Pierre was killed. Lawrence wrote to us to offer his condolences, and he came to call as soon as he could. We corresponded after that. When he was sent to Paris, he looked me up."

"I didn't know you had a brother. I'm so sorry."

"He was a flyer. The Germans shot him down. Their commandant wrote to my father, telling him that Pierre was dead before the fire. It was a relief, knowing. One of Pierre's squadron had reported that his aircraft had burned on impact, and I tried to keep that from my mother. But the Germans had pulled him out of the cockpit in time. It was kind of the commandant to give us that peace." She shivered. "I'd thought— I'd dreamed of him in that burning aircraft, calling for help as the flames crept closer. Sadly, Pierre never knew my father had been found and was alive."

I had treated more than a few flyers with severe burns. Others had died before they could be rescued. It was a horrible fate.

She changed the subject quickly, but I'd seen the tears she was trying so bravely to hide.

Lawrence came down shortly after we'd done the washing up, pale, unshaven, and trying to conceal how badly his hands were shaking. He had no appetite, and five minutes later, he shut himself up in the sitting room that had belonged to Marina's mother.

"He's nearly out of laudanum. I don't know what he'll do if he can't find more," Marina said quietly, watching him go. "He can't go to the regiment's medical staff. And one by one the French doctors he saw in Paris refused to give him more. He claimed that there was a piece of shrapnel still there, pressing on his spine. But it's a lie."

I had knocked on the sitting room door shortly afterward, but Lawrence had ignored me, and this time the door was locked from the inside. Frustrated with him, I asked Marina if she had any skeleton keys that would unlock the door from the outside, but she didn't know of any.

I went with Marina to buy a little coal, helping her carry the sacks home again, and we were filling the scuttles when there was a knock at the house door.

My hands were black with coal dust. Marina, glancing at me in surprise, quickly wiped hers on her apron and hurried to the door. I slipped up the back stairs and was just out of sight at the top of the staircase when a male voice spoke to her in halting French. She responded rather coldly, then I heard two sets of footsteps walking back toward the sitting room.

I couldn't see the visitor at all, but I thought he must be English.

She was tapping at the sitting room door, informing Lawrence Minton that he had a visitor.

I could hear the key turning in the lock, the door opening, then closing. After a moment Marina went on to the front room, shutting that door behind her with what sounded suspiciously like a slam.

I was already on my way back to the kitchen, hastily washing my hands, picking up one of the full scuttles, and carrying it toward the parlor.

She was sitting there, staring at nothing, when I stepped in and closed the door behind me. Setting the scuttle on the hearth, I said, "I gather the Lieutenant wanted to see his caller?"

Marina grimaced. "It's Lieutenant Bedford. I don't care for him. I don't think he's good for Lawrence."

"Did they serve together? Or is the Lieutenant on the staff of one of the delegates to the conference?"

"I don't believe they served together, but he is attending the conference and they have flats in the same house. I am not even sure that they are friends—but Lawrence encourages his visits. He's another reason I brought Lawrence here. But Lawrence wrote to him, telling him where he was. I was quite angry about that."

"Why do you receive him then? It's your house, you could refuse to let him in." But even as I suggested it, I knew she couldn't do that. Not if Lawrence Minton wanted to see the other man.

"He doesn't take no for an answer. I tried several times, but he simply waits outside until Lawrence sees him, and after he leaves, Lawrence is angry with me." She lifted her chin. "But this is my home, I have the right to turn visitors away."

Lieutenant Bedford stayed for half an hour, and then left. I made it a point to be by a window upstairs, to have a good look at him.

Rather rakish, I thought, watching him walk down the street. There was a jauntiness in his stride that spoke of satisfaction, and I learned later on that day that he had found some laudanum and brought the bottle to Lawrence.

There was no doubt about that—Lawrence was in a happy mood, and then slept for several hours.

While he was still in his happy mood, I confronted him, asking what had brought his friend to the house.

"That's none of your affair. Nor is it Marina's. I've told her that."

"Of course it's her affair," I reminded him. "This is her house, not yours. And what would your regiment think, seeing you now? And *here*, rather than in Paris? If your commanding officer discovers what you're doing instead of attending the talks, you could very well find yourself cashiered."

"I've changed my mind, even if no one believes me. Let me make it clear to you as well. I don't intend to stay in the Army," he retorted. "I'm sick of the Army, and of Paris."

"You're also abusing Marina's hospitality. Did you know? There was barely enough money to buy dinner last night. She's no longer teaching. There's no income for her to live on."

That surprised him. "She has money. She's told me so."

"How long ago was that, pray? Whatever she may have had, it's gone now."

"She can return to teaching, if she wishes it. I'm all right here on my own."

"And who will buy your food and cook your meals, if she's not here?"

"I'm not interested in food. I'll manage."

"That's what many people addicted to laudanum tell me. And after a while, they simply die. Is that what you want?" It was severe, but it had to be said.

He looked at me then, and I saw such anguish in his eyes, I caught my breath.

"The world would be a far better place without me in it," he said harshly, and turned on his heel, walking out of the room. I could hear him taking the stairs two at a time, and then the sound of his bedroom door slamming.

I stood there, his words still ringing in my head.

This was more serious than I'd expected.

There were many reasons for addiction. I'd seen them during the war, when men with severe wounds became dependent on something to take away pain that wouldn't ease or even end. Clearly Lawrence Minton was a different case. Something was driving him, and he was seeking not relief from pain, but oblivion. And yet there was nothing in the information Matron had given me to indicate shell shock. If not that, then what?

Or did she not know? That was always possible.

He appeared to be shutting down his mind so that he didn't have to think or feel.

And if that was true, his situation was far more serious. He wasn't looking for escape, the good feeling that opiates offer in the beginning. When the laudanum didn't give him what he sought, the alternative might well be death.

If there was any chance of saving him, I'd have to find out what had happened to him and why. Any way that I could.

That evening over a meager dinner, I asked Marina what she knew about Lieutenant Minton aside from what he'd done for her father and her family.

Considering the question, she said, "When we first met him, he spoke so warmly of his mother. His father had died when he was only fourteen, but he'd loved him very much. I expect that was why he helped my father, so that we wouldn't lose *him* too soon. He told us about his parents' home in the Cotswolds. They went to live in London after the war began, and his mother joined the Queen Alexandra's. He told me about a setter, liver and white, he had had as a child, the school he went to, his friends. Such a happy childhood. It explained the man he'd become, thoughtful, kind. I liked that man very much."

"Yet you have stayed with him, in spite of the changes in him."

Marina shrugged. "But of course. One does not abandon a friend."

"Did he speak of the war at all?"

"No. But it is hard for many soldiers to talk about the trenches. I saw nothing wrong with that."

"When did you begin to see this change in him? Do you remember?"

Frowning, she thought about the question. "The war was over, and at Christmas he went to England for a short leave. He went home—not just to London, but to the house where he was a child. And he spent a fortnight there. He came back to France, and I saw him in late January. He was excited about being posted to the conference; he even stayed a few days with us in Lyon. Somewhere he'd found a little coffee—real coffee—and he gave it to my mother tied up with the most enormous bow. At the end of February or perhaps the first week of March, he called and took me out to dine and then to the cinema. It was a lovely evening, and at the end of it, he asked if I'd help him to find a nice gift for his mother's birthday. That was a Monday. I told him yes, I'd be happy to help. It was only a week away, that birthday, and he was to collect me at eleven the next morning. But he didn't come that day, or the next. I didn't know why, I was worried, and by Tuesday of the following week, I found one of his friends at the conference and asked where he was. I'd thought he might have been sent back to England to clarify instructions.

Something to do with the conference. But no one had seen Lawrence for days."

"What did you do?"

"I was afraid to make too much of a fuss. I smiled and pretended all was well. But on the Sunday I went to the house where he'd taken rooms, hoping the woman who owns the house might be at Mass. But she was there, and she wouldn't let me come in. It wasn't proper, she told me, and I'd have to leave. I explained that my mother had sent me—it was a lie, but I thought she might help me if she saw I wasn't there to visit him myself. That's when she informed me he was ill, he hadn't left his room for days, but he refused to hear of a doctor being summoned. I found his friend again, and I asked him to go to the flat and find out how ill Lawrence was. His friend was shocked—Lawrence looked terrible, he told me, as if he hadn't slept or eaten or taken care of himself at all. Thin, a beard from not shaving, his clothes unwashed. I was very worried by that time."

"Why didn't this friend try to help him? Why was it left to you?"

"He wanted to report what he'd seen to one of the officers. I knew that would not be the best thing for Lawrence. Or his future in the regiment. I told him a lie, I said that my father would come from Lyon,

that Lawrence would listen to him. And I watched
the house for two days, until I saw Madame go out.
I went in then, found Lawrence, and hired a taxi to
take him to St. Ives. The driver wanted no part of
him—Lawrence was in a terrible state, I had to pay
extra just to the Gare. You can imagine what it was
like on the train. I had to tell more lies—he was my
brother, I was taking him to my parents in St. Ives,
he was still recovering from a head wound—whatever
I could think of at the time. Nevertheless, I got him
here, and I found two maids and a cook who were glad
of the work. But then I couldn't pay them any longer."
There were tears in her eyes. "Still, I made him bathe
and shave, I cut his hair and kept his clothes clean. I
told him I would write to his mother if he didn't take
care of himself. I think he would have left then, but
he had nowhere to go."

Madame must have come home—seen her taking
Lawrence away, and was glad to hand the problem to
someone else. Yet she had kept his room.

"He never told you what had happened? Or tried to
account for this change in him?"

"Before, we had talked easily. Laughed, even. Now,
he won't speak, he won't eat, much less tell me anything. If I press, he walks away and locks his door. So I
stopped asking. It was better that way."

I could see how tired and worn she was. Lawrence Minton had changed, but he had changed her as well. And refused to see that he'd done this. He took whatever she gave him, food and warmth, a roof over his head, but he offered her nothing in return.

"Let me try," I said, in an effort to lift her spirits. "I've had some experience with men who were ill. It may take a while. You must be patient."

That only alarmed her more. "Is it *illness*? Something—something dreadful?"

I smiled, although I didn't feel much like it. "I think he's worried about something. Something that might have happened the night you dined together. Between seeing you safely home and the next morning. I can't imagine what it might have been. But I intend to find out." And once I did, I could summon his mother—

"He won't tell you. If he won't tell me, how will *you* manage to break through his silence?"

"I won't ask him. That's the difference."

The next day I walked down to the station, and took the morning train to Paris.

My first stop was the flat that the Lieutenant had taken when he was first seconded to the peace conference.

The woman who had opened the door to me the first time was there again, and before I could greet her with the usual *Bonjour,* she said, "Did you not find the Lieutenant?"

I realized that she had been worried as well.

"I have found him," I told her. "But now I'm looking for a friend of his, to ask his help in caring for the Lieutenant. Perhaps you know where I might find him? I believe his name is Bedford. I also believe he's an officer, but I'm sorry, I don't remember his rank."

I had expected her to turn me away, but she said, "Yes, he also has a flat here in my house. But he is not receiving visitors."

"I'm not a visitor," I said rather bluntly. "And it's urgent that I speak with him. If you will please tell him that Sister Crawford is here?"

"Does he know you, Sister?" she responded. And I thought there was more than a hint of suspicion in her voice.

"He does not," I said firmly. "But I am representing Lieutenant Minton's mother, who is unable to come to Paris just now. If he is truly a friend of the Lieutenant, then he will wish to hear what I have to say."

"I shall ask, of course," she said. "But I do not expect he will wish to be disturbed."

She shut the door, leaving me there to wait in the cold. The minutes ticked by. I watched a street sweeper, a nanny pushing a small child in a pram, saw two men exchange greetings on the corner of the street, and was beginning to think she had deliberately shut me out, when she opened the door again.

"Lieutenant Bedford was late at the talks last evening. He asks that you come another time."

She was about to close the door again, but I'd brought my umbrella, and I wedged it into the opening as she intended to swing it shut.

"That will not do, Madame. I have told you this is an urgent matter. If you are unwilling to persuade Lieutenant Bedford to come down, I'll be happy to do that for you. But I intend to see him, you understand." We'd been speaking French.

A voice behind me said in English, "Hallo. What seems to be the problem, Madame Periard? Sister?"

I turned to see a British officer standing behind me. Summoning a smile that would have made my flatmate Diana proud of me, I said pleasantly, "Good morning, Major. I'm here on behalf of Lieutenant Minton's mother, and I've come to see Lieutenant Bedford, who is, I'm told, a friend. But he refuses to see me. I—um— believe Lieutenant Minton is traveling, and it's urgent that I get a message to him."

The last thing I wished to do was give this officer any reason to think that Lawrence Minton was troubled or even in trouble. The Major wore the insignia of the Lieutenant's regiment—and my father's.

He nodded, and said, "In that case, perhaps I can help you. I can't invite you in, but there's a café just around the corner. The coffee is terrible, and the tea is much worse, but at least we'll be out of this cold wind."

I was getting nowhere with Madame. But at this juncture, if I couldn't find a way to help Lieutenant Minton, I didn't foresee much hope for his career anyway.

"Could you instead persuade the Lieutenant to see me?"

The Major shook his head. "I don't think you'll get much satisfaction from Bedford even if I dragged him to the door."

I took a deep breath. "Then I will accept your kind invitation."

Relieved to be rid of me, Madame thrust my umbrella out of the way and shut the door in my face.

I salvaged my dignity with an effort and let the Major lead me to the café he'd mentioned.

"We haven't been introduced, Sister. My name is Webb. Harry Webb."

"Sister Crawford," I said, hoping that wouldn't remind him of a past Colonel of his regiment. But apparently it didn't, and he nodded. "A pleasure to meet you, Sister, although I must apologize for the circumstances." He cleared his throat. "I'm sorry. I really don't believe you'd have had any luck trying to talk to Bedford. He can be very—difficult."

"Unfortunately he appears to be the only person who can tell me anything at all about Lieutenant Minton."

He looked down at me. "You mentioned that you were here on behalf of his mother?"

Oh, dear. I'd used Matron as an acceptable reason for calling on Lieutenant Bedford, but I could hardly tell the Major why I'd come.

I said, "She asked me to look in on Lawrence while I was in Paris."

"Ah. A duty call," the Major said as we turned the corner and felt the full force of the wind in our faces. I put up a gloved hand to keep my cap in place.

"It's just there," Major Webb assured me, pointing. And I saw the sign above the door halfway down the street.

Le Cochon Bleu. The Blue Pig.

"That's an odd name for a café," I said, glad to change the subject.

"The story is, the owner inherited a blue pig from his father, and sold it for enough money to travel to Paris. He went to work in this café, and when he'd earned enough to purchase it from the original owner, he renamed it for that pig."

"Was it truly blue?"

"God knows. Probably gray or black. But blue is more interesting, don't you think?"

We had reached the door, and he held it open for me.

The café wasn't much different from a dozen others I'd seen in Paris, except for the oil painting of a blue pig over the bar, gloriously blue. And judging by its size, more hog than pig as well.

We took a table away from the door, out of the draft as it opened and closed. The breakfast patrons had gone, but it was still quite busy here. Of the twenty or so tables, eleven of them were occupied by Frenchmen, some of them with women, others alone. They stared as the English officer and the nursing Sister came in and sat down.

The Major ignored them, signaled to the waiter, and asked me if I'd prefer the coffee or the tea.

I chose the coffee. The tea must have been added for the British here for the peace conference, but I didn't hold out much hope that it tasted anything like real India tea.

Keeping his voice low, the Major said, "I'm sorry. I must tell you, if you're looking for Lieutenant Minton, that he's not been in his flat for some time."

"So I discovered when I called earlier. The only other name I knew to ask for was Lieutenant Bedford's."

He raised his eyebrows at that. "I'm surprised that Minton mentioned Bedford to his mother."

Oh, dear.

"It was Madame who told me he was a friend."

"I've asked her if she knows where Minton is at present. But she swears she has no idea."

Was she protecting Minton? I had a feeling she might be, and not just because he'd taken lodgings there until September. After all, she'd told me where to look for him. But I'd been a different matter, representing his mother. She couldn't simply put me off. Matron could raise questions about whether or not her house was suitable for officers' billets.

"His mother is going to worry," I said, rather than lie to him about what I'd been told about Lawrence's whereabouts. "This is the only address she could give me."

Our coffee came, black mud smelling of chicory.

"Best not to drink it," Major Webb said, smiling.

I looked at him. Fair hair, blue eyes, a straight nose and firm jaw. Not precisely handsome, but attractive in the way that a man who knows himself often is.

The smile faded as he went on. "Madame is a widow. Her only child, Armand, was killed at Verdun. Decorated for gallantry under fire, posthumously. Her husband died of the shock."

"I didn't know."

"I believe he was a rising artist. He had a studio on the Left Bank, but he made a living painting sets for the theater. I have a feeling she's glad of our presence. Certainly our money makes a difference, but she tends to mother us." He grinned wryly. "It's a lovely house, or else I'd move on."

It occurred to me that her losses might be why she was sympathetic toward Lawrence Minton. *His* mother was worried about her son too. If all else failed, if Madame refused to confide in me, perhaps Matron could speak to her and find out if she knew why Lawrence had changed so abruptly.

I was still considering that when the Major frowned, clearly making up his mind about something.

"I ought not tell you this. It will worry his mother even more. But there's something amiss with Minton."

"Do you know what it might be?"

"I could understand if he drank too much. Or if there were—um—women. This is Paris, after all. But I don't think it's either. For one thing, Madame guards the door as if she were Cerberus at the gates of Hades.

And there isn't an excessive number of bottles in the dustbin, no odor of alcohol as one passes his door. I haven't seen him staggering in at all hours. I do know his rooms are rather unkempt. I caught a glimpse inside when Madame was bringing clean sheets around. I hadn't expected it of him."

I took a chance and said, "Perhaps he's been unhappy in love."

"There *was* a girl, French, I think. Quite attractive, and clearly from a good family. I'm not sure what her interest in Minton was. According to Madame, her family knows him."

Madame was sounding more and more like the French equivalent of Mrs. Hennessey! Keeping the secrets of the men in her house, just as Mrs. Hennessey protected her young ladies.

And Major Webb was very observant, reminding me a little of Simon Brandon.

"I had expected her to invite me into her parlor," I said with a sigh of frustration, "and bring Lieutenant Bedford there, to speak to me. She could have been present, I only wanted to ask about Lieutenant Minton."

"I have a feeling that she didn't want you to meet Bedford. She's rather old-fashioned about propriety. When my sister was here, visiting, she gave me a list of restaurants where it would be unwise to take her."

Yes, very like Mrs. Hennessey!

"The Lieutenant couldn't be that terrible." But I remembered the rakish air about Lieutenant Bedford as I watched him walk away from the house after he'd called on Lawrence.

"Terrible, no. I understand he was quite popular with his men during the war. But he's rather rough around the edges. A battlefield commission."

Which meant he'd come up through the ranks, and many officers looked down on such commissions. As for popularity with his men, that depended on how he used it. Respect was not always the same thing as popularity. "Another source tells me Bedford was reckless to the point of foolhardiness. I can't comment on the truth of that either. But it gives you some feeling for the man."

"Then why were he and Minton friends?"

"*Were* they friends?" he asked, curious.

"I assumed they must be. If Madame suggested it."

"I don't know," he replied doubtfully. "They had so little in common."

And yet Lieutenant Bedford had come all the way to St. Ives to call. And bring more laudanum? Was that truly *friendship*?

"What kind of officer was Minton?"

"Quite good, cared for his men, was mentioned in dispatches several times. But for bravery, not foolhardiness. Twice went out under heavy fire and brought in his wounded."

I considered him. "You've been looking into his records."

"Yes, I was just worried enough to be curious." He smiled again, as if to make light of it. "I'm not usually the sort to go around coddling younger officers, but there's the regiment to think about."

Very like my father. The Colonel Sahib had seen through Simon's rebellion against authority and found something he liked. And he'd been right. He taught Simon strategy and tactics and most importantly, patience, discovering along the way that his protégé had a gift for languages and diplomacy. Then watched him rise through the ranks. The only time Simon had defied my father was when he'd suggested that Simon go to Sandhurst to train as an officer.

I stirred the coffee with my spoon, surprised that it hadn't melted, and considered the man across from me.

Major Webb was friendly, helpful even. But I'd been brought up with a regiment, and despite his explanation, I couldn't help but wonder why a Major was so interested in the affairs of a lowly Lieutenant like Bedford. Yes, they shared a lodgings. And of course they were in the same regiment. Still. From what I'd observed so far, Lieutenant Bedford didn't have Simon's abilities. And before he'd changed, Lieutenant Minton apparently was the better man.

I found I was glad I'd been circumspect.

"It does you credit, that you're concerned about a fellow officer," I said, looking up at him with a smile. "I'm not quite sure what I ought to do now. Matron will expect me to write and tell her how her son looks and what messages he sends back to her. How his lodgings are, if they're in a good part of town. The sort of thing a mother wants to know."

There, that ought to give Major Webb an opening to tell me not to worry, that he'd keep an eye out for Lieutenant Minton, and see that all was well. After all, what mother wouldn't be pleased to have a higher-ranking officer taking an interest in her son, especially when he was expecting to make a career of the Army?

But I'd underestimated the man sitting across from me.

He pushed his cup aside, and said, "You have your duties here in Paris, and I have mine. And we can't neglect them. Still, I don't see why, between us, we can't find Minton. I'm willing to try, if you are."

"I wouldn't even know where to begin," I said, giving him the chance to lead me in whatever direction he had in mind. "I know Paris a little. But hardly well enough to search the city for one man."

"Perhaps Madame will confide in you. If you keep trying."

That surprised me. "Do you think," I asked, trying to sound earnest, "she knows more than she's told either of us?" Then I added, "She hasn't given me that impression. Why do you believe she hasn't already told me all she knows?"

"It's just a feeling I had." He turned to look out the window. "I can't tell you why. Possibly Minton reminds her of her son, before the war. There's a photograph of him in her sitting room. Rather handsome, in a Bohemian sort of way."

Drawing a breath, the Major added, "Well. What do you say? Shall we try to find Minton? I can't think he's in any difficulty, I expect he's just young and easily distracted. But the Army won't take his absence lightly."

I agreed with him about the Army. I said, "I'll do what I can. I must travel with my duties. But Paris is my base for the moment."

"Where are you staying?"

Oh, dear.

I gave him the address of the house where Matron had arranged for me to stay. It was the home of a French doctor and his wife, and she had known them before the war. "I'd hoped to make my duty call on the Lieutenant first thing, and put it behind me. I've hardly had the chance to settle in." I'd traveled to St. Ives instead. Now I'd have to be sure to call on them, before the Major did.

He nodded. "That isn't too far from here. I'll find you a taxi."

"That's very kind of you."

He went to the bar to pay for our coffees, and then walked with me back to the corner, where he hailed a passing taxi.

Settling me inside and giving the driver my direction, he said, "I'll leave word for you if I learn anything. And you know where to find me."

"Yes, of course." I thanked him again, and the taxi pulled away.

When I looked back through the tiny rear window, the Major was still standing there, looking after me. As if to make certain I went where I was supposed to be going.

Chapter 3

All the way to the house where I was supposed to be staying, I wondered why the Major had been so open with me—a perfect stranger—about Lawrence Minton. It was not very British for one thing, and an officer would surely be more guarded about his men.

Unless of course he was telling me what he thought might elicit what I knew?

After all, I hadn't been very forthcoming, either, but then I was on an errand for Matron, and I was certainly not about to tell him *her* business . . .

The taxi's driver glanced over his shoulder. "We are here, Sister."

I paid him and got out.

A very respectable neighborhood, a street of fairly

large white houses with those distinctive mansard roofs. Matron's friend in Paris must be a specialist, then.

A maid let me in, taking me to a small morning room where Dr. Moreau and his wife were sitting, going through a box of letters. They rose to greet me. He was a man of medium height, graying, with the black-rimmed spectacles that I'd seen so often in France. His wife was slim and very attractive, her hair still dark and fashionably cut. Her smile was warm.

They were very happy to see me, and Madame asked the maid to bring us tea.

Apparently, Matron had told them when to expect me. Oh, dear.

"But you didn't arrive, and we were worried. *Alors,* you are here now," Dr. Moreau said. Turning to the maid, he added, "Sister Crawford's luggage can be taken up to her room."

"I'm so sorry," I said quickly. "I stopped to see a friend on my way to Paris, and I'm staying with her for a few days. I wanted to call in and let you know that I was in France."

They politely inquired about my journey to Paris, asking if I found the city much changed since the war, making me feel at ease here.

Dr. Moreau asked if I intended to remain in the Queen Alexandra's. Evidently Matron had told him a little about my training and my experience in the field, and he was curious about some of the English doctors I'd served with. I discovered he'd known several of them personally, and I also learned that he himself had served in the war. He had been at Verdun, as bloody a battle as our Somme.

Tea came, and after Madame Moreau had served us and the maid had withdrawn, they mentioned Lawrence for the first time.

"Helena is worried about her son," Madame Moreau said. "Have you any news of him? I can write to her for you."

"He's not in his lodgings," I answered, "at the moment. But I shouldn't worry her at this stage. He could be visiting friends. I gather the peace discussions are not moving at a speedy pace." I hesitated, then said, "There's an officer who tells me he'd like to help me locate Lawrence. But I'm not comfortable taking him into my confidence."

"Is there a problem?" the doctor asked, his gaze sharpening.

"He's a Major in Lieutenant Minton's regiment," I explained. "He may feel that he ought to report him, if he overstays his leave."

"*Mon Dieu,* that's very wise of you," Dr. Moreau assured me. "We saw Lawrence when he first came to

Paris, and he was very enthusiastic about remaining in the Army."

"Major Webb may call here—he asked where I was staying, and I felt it best to suggest a friend had introduced me and you'd kindly invited me to stay here. It's part of the truth, of course, but I was afraid he might make too much of the fact that you knew the Lieutenant's mother, and I'd been sent to Paris to look in on him."

"Of course," he agreed.

We'd finished our tea, and Madame offered to show me to my room. "You'll stay for lunch," she insisted.

"That's very kind of you," I replied, and followed her into the passage and up the stairs.

As we climbed, she said, "At least the war is over, and we can look forward to better times." Pausing on the landing, she pointed to a portrait of a very handsome young French officer. He had Madame's eyes, and I knew at once he must be their son.

"André," she commented. "He was our happiness."

"I'm so sorry."

Smiling sadly, she went on up the steps, adding, "He was Army mad. Just like Lawrence. I feel so for Helena, worried about Lawrence. He suddenly stopped coming here, you know. It must be nearly six weeks since we've seen him. And finally, two weeks ago, I wrote to ask if he'd been posted back to London. When Helena told me he was still in Paris, I made discreet inquiries amongst our friends at the Conference and discovered also that he hadn't been attending for some time." We had reached the first floor, and she turned left. In a quieter voice that wouldn't carry, she said, "I knew *something* must be wrong. But Helena asked me to do nothing—she wished to deal with the matter privately. Michel was quite upset—he's very fond of Lawrence. He feared he might be ill, perhaps too ill to send for him. And so he made the rounds of French hospitals, searching for him. But to no end."

"What did you think might be wrong?" I asked as we stopped at a closed door.

"Well, of course—a young man, single, in Paris. I thought he might have—contracted something un-speakable." She reached out and opened the door. "One of Michel's colleagues reported someone coming to him for opiates, but he suspected the man used a false name, and he turned him away. But there is a market for such things, if one knows where to look . . ." Her voice trailed off.

I couldn't tell her what I'd witnessed in St. Ives. She would wish to contact Matron immediately, and I wasn't sure that was the best solution. Until we knew why Lawrence had suddenly cut off all ties with Marina and the Moreaus, I didn't think Matron herself could help him.

With only a nod, indicating agreement, I stepped into my room.

It overlooked the back gardens, and was very pleasant, done up in shades of yellow that ranged from the pale walls to darker shades covering the bed and at the windows. The carpet was a pattern of greens. So much prettier and more comfortable than where I was presently living. A fire was ready laid in the hearth, and I could see that Dr. Moreau and his wife were expecting me to come and stay sooner rather than later.

Turning to her, I said, "Madame, would you mind terribly if I stayed where I am for the moment? I think I might be able to—to learn more if I am on my own. I can't explain why, not just yet. It's someone else's privacy I'm dealing with. And I'd rather not put this person at risk."

"At risk?" she repeated, more than a little alarmed.

"In the sense that this person is afraid of losing the Lieutenant's friendship by confiding in me. I don't know much of the story yet. I hope to learn more. But I rather think the Lieutenant is in some difficulty and just now he's not willing to seek help from anyone." I'd said more than I'd intended, but it was the only way to explain myself.

"Gambling? A woman?" she asked, worried.

"I don't believe so. A war memory?"

Nodding, she went to the window to look out. "My husband has had some experience dealing with that. If you need help from him, I promise you he's discreet. I have tried to shield him from worry about Lawrence. After we lost André, Michel turned to Lawrence. Writing him letters as he used to write to André. Wanting to see him whenever Lawrence was at all close to Paris. It helped, a little, to ease the pain of our loss, you see."

I could understand that. All the more reason not to bring up the laudanum. Not yet at least. As a doctor's wife, she would know how dangerous that was. And it would worry her even more.

Turning from the window, she asked, "Have you seen him, then? Do you at least know where he is?"

"Please don't ask me. I'll tell you everything as soon as I can."

I thought she was going to argue with me, but she shook her head, drew a deep breath, and said, "I will hold you to that, Sister Crawford."

"My name is Elizabeth. My family and friends prefer to call me Bess."

"Bess," she said. "It's rather informal. Would you prefer Elizabeth?"

"Bess will do nicely," I said, summoning a smile.

"As soon as you can, will you tell me what you know? I shan't tell my husband until I must, but it would help to understand . . ." Her voice trailed off.

"If you promised not to write to Matron. I don't think he will want her to—to worry prematurely. And she has responsibilities in London. Wait until we see that coming to Paris is the right decision."

I couldn't help but think, *if only I could manage to bring Lawrence here, where he could have proper medical care.* But how on earth was I to do that? At this stage? And removing him forcibly from that house in St. Ives would very likely make matters worse. He wouldn't trust anyone, then.

Madame smiled fondly although rather sadly. "I remember Lawrence as a child. Such a lively little boy, full of curiosity and energy. He learned French very quickly, and my daughter adored him. She was three years older, you see, and treated him like one of her dolls, to be petted and looked after."

I wondered if I had been given her daughter's room. It was so pretty and bright, very feminine. But where was she?

Almost as if she'd heard the thought, she added, "She married a man from Toulon. A naval officer. I was so grateful—she was well out of Paris and our fears that the Germans would be upon us at any moment.

She has a daughter of her own now, and we shall finally be able to travel to visit her."

She left me to rest, although I had a feeling it was to give herself time to recover. Instead I stood for some time at the window, looking down into the back garden. A white wrought-iron love seat just below my window was inviting, sheltered from the wind, and later would have the best view of summer's blooms. Farther along, a man was working, clearing away winter's debris, dressing the beds, and turning over the kitchen garden so that it would be ready for planting when the weather improved. I couldn't see him clearly—he wore a usual workingman's smock and a broad-brimmed hat that shaded his face. But I thought he must be an ex-soldier, the way he carried himself. A few minutes later he wheeled a barrow filled with the tools of his trade—I could see hoe, pitchfork and shovel, secateurs and string—to the shed at the bottom of the garden, stowing them away.

It reminded me of home, and Bertie coming into the kitchen for his tea, telling Cook that our tulips were poking their noses up, and which trees were budding well.

Suddenly homesick, I turned away and went down to the elegant dining room.

After we'd dined, Dr. Moreau pulled on his heavy coat, reached for his hat, and accompanied me to find a taxi. There was an avenue, he said, three streets away.

As we walked, he asked about me, polite inquiries about my parents and how they had felt about my nursing, but I could tell that his mind was really on Lieutenant Minton. He said finally, "Whatever you learn about Lawrence, you must tell me. I don't want my wife to be worried. She hasn't really recovered from the loss of our son. Meanwhile, if there is anything I can do, as a doctor, as a friend, please come to me. Anything you need."

I thanked him, and then remembered something. "You corresponded with Lawrence during the war, I think?"

"Yes." He shook his head. "We comforted each other, in a way. He'd lost his father, I'd lost my son. It helped me, those letters. I'd like to think they helped him as well."

"So many men were changed by the war," I began carefully. "Was there anything in particular that affected Lawrence?"

He paused, and I stopped beside him. "Early on, I think there was something. It was before I got to know him so well. It was at Mons—after Mons—I might be wrong, of course, but he never talked about those first days of the fighting. It was intense. Things happened. The British Expeditionary Force was battle tested, but they were outnumbered. As we were along the Marne, in the beginning. We could see no hope, it appeared we couldn't stop the Germans. We knew the taste of defeat."

A taxi was approaching, cutting off the conversation. Dr. Moreau raised his hand to signal it, and as it pulled up beside us, he took my hand. "Anything," he said firmly. "Anything you need. Promise?"

"I will remember," I said, not wishing to give him a promise I might not be able to keep.

I got in, the door closed behind me.

And for the second time that day, a man had stayed where he was until my taxi turned the corner, out of his sight.

I caught myself drifting into sleep on the train, much to the amusement of the man across from me. He wore the black suit of a shop clerk, a silver watch chain in the pocket of his waistcoat, his hair slicked down with Macassar oil. I could smell it from my seat opposite.

I was back in St. Ives in time for supper, such as it was, and I gave a moment's thought to the dinner I'd have enjoyed in the home of the Moreau family. Still, I had had my taxi wait while I bought a large canvas holdall and filled it with whatever I could find in the shops before continuing to the Gare. Cabbage, the outer leaves looking rather winter-weary, a few carrots, some eggs, onions, a half round of cheese, and miracle of miracles, a tin of milk and a little tea I saw on a high shelf. In another shop I found a pot of honey, dark with age but, I hoped, still good.

My fellow passenger kindly helped me lift my purchases down and took them off the train for me, but there was no one to carry them up the slight rise to the house.

With the money I'd left her, Marina had found a scrawny chicken, and we made a pot of stew, filling the house with its aroma. She had also found more coal for the cooker and the fires.

When I asked if she'd seen Lawrence at all that day, she shook her head. "He's avoiding us." Sighing, she said, "I should go back to Paris. He doesn't want me here, and no doubt I'm making matters worse. But if I go, what then? What will become of him?"

And then she admitted, not looking up from the onion she was chopping, "I thought perhaps you'd not come back. I wouldn't have blamed you."

"My valise is here," I said lightly.

"Yes, but you could have sent for it."

"That would have been rather cowardly, don't you think?"

That brought a fleeting smile. "I am glad not to have to face this alone."

But Lawrence Minton was not as pleased.

I encountered him in the front room, after Marina and I had finished in the kitchen. The Lieutenant hadn't joined us for dinner, and I hadn't seen him since my return. I'd gone into the room to close the curtains and found him sitting in one of the chairs, apparently asleep. He was pale, disheveled. A lamp was burning on a table by the door.

I stopped short when I saw him there, and I was about to slip out of the room when he came awake with a start. When he realized who it was, he got to his feet, angry with me. "I thought you'd had the good sense to go."

"You are a guest in this house, just as I am," I replied, purposely making my voice cold. "You can't order me to leave." Reaching up for the curtains, I added, "Do you really expect me to report what I've found here to your mother?"

"There's nothing she can do about it."

"That's rather callous of you. I'd be ashamed of myself, in your shoes."

His face flushed. "But you aren't in my shoes, are you?"

"No, thankfully, I'm not. All the same, I'll help you, if you will let me."

"I just want to forget." There was sudden anguish in his voice, as his face twisted in almost physical pain.

"And when this level of forgetting isn't enough to stop the memories, then what?" I softened my tone.

"Who said there were memories?" He was instantly menacing, moving toward me. I realized that I'd touched something I didn't really understand.

Backing up, I said, trying to keep my voice calm, steady, and sensible. "It stands to reason, doesn't it? Why else would you want to dull your mind, except to escape from something?"

"You don't know what you're talking about, Sister Crawford."

Just then Marina came into the room. She looked from one to the other of us, and said, "Lawrence—" as she saw his flushed face.

"I won't be spied on," he said harshly, turning to her. "My mother sent her to spy."

"I can't ask her to leave at this hour," Marina said, pleading with him. "There's no train tonight. Nowhere for her to go."

"I don't care where she goes or what happens to her. I won't have her here."

Marina was about to respond when he added, "Either she leaves or I shall."

She turned to me, looking for support.

I snapped in the voice I used with recalcitrant patients in the wards. "Stop being childish, Lieutenant. Neither one of us is leaving tonight. I was just going up to my room. Good night."

Marina threw me a grateful glance, then said, "You've missed your dinner, Lawrence. Come and eat something. You'll feel better afterward."

He put his hands to his head, his eyes closed, his body doubling over, as if he was in pain. "Don't you understand? Food won't help me. Nothing will. Nothing short of oblivion."

That frightened her—she took that to mean he intended to kill himself.

"Lawrence?" She went to him, putting a hand on his arm. "You don't mean that. It's wrong—the church says—"

I'd reached the doorway, and I stopped there.

He pulled away from her. "Just leave me alone," he said, straightening up. "You don't understand, you can't possibly *understand*." Shoving her out of the way, he walked to the door, brushing me aside as well, before taking the stairs two at a time. He disappeared into the darkness, and after a moment I heard a door slam.

Marina had heard it as well, and she looked at me, tears in her eyes and despair in her face. "What am I to do?" she asked me. "I don't know how to help him."

"There's only one way—find out what's haunting him, and then try to break its spell."

But even as I said that, I could see that she didn't believe me.

I don't think any of us got any real sleep that night. I tossed and turned, trying to find a comfortable spot in my bed. The room was cold—we needed to be sparing with our store of coal—and in the middle of the night there was nothing to be done about it. The hot water bottle that I'd brought up to bed with me and an extra blanket from the cupboard helped a little.

Marina looked tired and worried when she came down to the kitchen the next morning. Lawrence Minton didn't appear at all.

I said, trying to be cheerful, "You found a chicken yesterday. That was wonderful. If we can buy a little more coal, we might have enough to keep our bedrooms warm at night. What do you think?"

"I have no money. And I can't let you go on paying. It isn't right." She picked up the bowl in which we'd put the eggs, looked at it for a moment, and put it down again.

"Marina, it isn't my money. Lawrence's mother has given me carte blanche to use whatever I need from her account. I think she had a feeling that all would not be well with her son. She isn't wealthy, but she's comfortably situated, and she would want me to help. At least until we can decide what to do about Lawrence. I can't in good conscience write to her and tell her what's happening here, when I don't know why."

She looked around the kitchen. "How long can *she* afford to keep up two households? I feel so uncomfortable, you see."

As I began to slice the bread to toast, I changed the subject. "Were you as wretched as I was last night? The wind must have come up, and when I looked out my window this morning, I was sure there had been frost. After breakfast, we might collect blankets from the other bedrooms. I know I could use more. And why don't we fill more hot water bottles?" I pointed to the dresser against the wall where the extra hot water bottles were stored on the top. Smiling, I added, "It appears there are enough that we could have two each."

But it would take a fire in the hearth to rid the bedrooms of the pervasive damp that seemed to permeate everything, even the clothes in my armoire.

Looking up at the dresser, she said, "I should have thought of that myself. It's just—to be honest, I am a teacher—I thought, this is a house with servants, I can manage. I wasn't prepared for—for this." She gestured around her, sadness in her face. "How will it end? I ask you."

For a moment I wondered again if she was in love with Lawrence Minton. On the whole, I decided, she wasn't. He had saved her father's life, and in gratitude, she was trying to help him. But she was right, she wasn't prepared for no money, no servants, and a man who was too selfish to see what he'd brought her to.

"I miss my own life," she said forlornly, her voice very quiet. "My students, preparing lessons. Going to the cinema with friends. Visiting my parents on school holidays. I'd so hoped that after the war, life would be a little better. But it hasn't been, has it? When the fighting stopped, we realized that nothing would ever be the same again."

We heard the sound of someone knocking at the house door, and Marina quickly turned away, hurrying up the stairs to answer it.

I took the eggs she hadn't prepared and began to break them in another bowl before whipping them with a fork.

She was back in less than a minute. "A poor soldier, looking for work. I couldn't even give him a sou or offer him a crust of bread." She watched me prepare the eggs. "It's so sad. What are they to do?"

"If you want to leave, I will stay here and do what I can. If all else fails, I'll send for Matron. His mother."

She shook her head vigorously. "That is the worst possible thing for him. To lose his future in the Army? It will be disastrous."

"Don't you think that every day he fails to appear at the Peace Conference is going to cause comment and eventually put that in jeopardy?"

Her face sad, she sat down in one of the chairs at the servants' table and stared at me. "But if they had found him incoherent from—"

The sound of footsteps coming down the passage, slow and erratic, reached us. Marina rose quickly and took my place at the cooker, pushing me aside.

As the half-opened door swung back against the wall with a loud *thump*, Lawrence clung to the frame in the opening, looking very ill.

"I think—" he began, his face gray. "Poison." And before either of us could move, he slipped to the floor in a heap.

I reached him first, turning him over as he vomited so that he wouldn't choke, undoing his collar so that he could breathe more freely, then reaching for his pulse.

It was rapid. But that could be the vomiting. I'd been given a brief overview of poisons in my training, and I tried to remember details. One didn't expect to find them on the battlefield, and so I'd had little actual experience with them.

There were some where vomiting was dangerous, and others where it was the only treatment, getting it out of the system before it could circulate throughout the body.

Dry heaves racked his body now, and he lay on the cold floor, shivering violently.

Marina was white as her apron, her hands at her throat, as if to ease his suffering.

"Blankets—towels—quickly," I told her firmly, cutting through the shock.

She fled, and I held Lawrence's body, trying to ease his suffering. He didn't fight me, his skin pale and clammy, eyes unfocused. "Oh, God," he managed to say, then began to vomit again.

I was rapidly going through what I knew. He wasn't having spasms, arching his back in pain. And a corrosive poison could get into the lungs, if vomiting was severe. If it was arsenic, he hadn't shown any of the usual symptoms of paleness, lethargy, dry hair from a slow poisoning. The various food poisonings were less likely, because we'd eaten the same meals, Marina and I, and we were all right.

She was back, dragging a large feather duvet behind her, arms full of towels. "It's awful," she was saying. "He's been sick in his room, down the stairs—"

I took the duvet and wrapped him in it, handed her a towel and instructed her to wet it for me, to clean his face, and put another over the puddles beside him.

Lawrence was still trembling, his eyes closed, his hands cold. Curling up like a small, sick child, he moaned once or twice as new waves of nausea hit him. Marina had poured warm water from the kettle over the towel, and I washed his face and hands with that.

"Are you in pain, anywhere?" I asked as I worked. *Appendix, a twisted intestine, gall bladder . . .*

"N-n-no," he managed to say. "J-just—this."

Unable to watch his suffering, Marina had found a pail and a mop and was starting out of the kitchen to begin cleaning up after him. I said, mouthing the words rather than speaking them, *The bottle.*

She stared, uncomprehending, and then she seemed to grasp what I was trying to say. Nodding, she hurried on.

I took two clean towels and made them into a pillow, and put that under his head. He lay there, exhausted, eyes closed, breathing still rapid but easing, and when I tried his pulse again, it was slowing a little.

Was the worst over? Or was this only a brief respite before the violent waves began again? I couldn't be sure. My legs were beginning to go numb, kneeling there on the cold floor beside him, but I didn't want to disturb him by moving, risking setting him off once more.

It was nearly half an hour before Marina was back, her apron off, a pillowslip full of soiled towels in one hand, the pail and mop in the other. She was struggling to manage it all, but when I didn't get up to help her, she cast a quick glance at Lawrence.

"Is—is he—?" she asked, horror in her face.

He did look quite bad, but I shook my head, giving her a smile. She disappeared into the backyard, left her burdens, and came back to wash her hands.

Coming over to me, she said, "I'll burn the lot. But not just now." Reaching into her pocket, she brought out the blue bottle with a cap on it. I covered it quickly with my own hand, and put it out of sight.

Lawrence lay where he was for another hour. By that time I couldn't feel my toes at all. Marina had found a cushion that helped, a little, but I was quite cold as well as numb.

Finally he opened his eyes. He frowned when he saw

me, started to move away, then stopped as swiftly as he'd started, trying to take deep breaths. After a time he mumbled, "What was it?"

"I don't know."

"Will—will I live?"

"I think you might," I said, not sure how much I could promise him.

"His bed is clean and made up," Marina said.

"I don't know that he can cope with the stairs. A bed in the parlor? And a fire on the hearth?" I wasn't certain we could carry him that far, and he didn't seem to have the strength to walk far on his own.

Marina was about to say something about the coal on hand, then thought better of it. "I'll see what I can do," she said.

When she'd gone, Lawrence said to me, his voice still only a halting thread, "You—you should have—have let me die."

"I thought for a while that you might," I told him. "It seems you are stronger than you think."

He closed his eyes. "I couldn't get my breath. Waves of nausea—"

"You came for help. I'm glad you did. I didn't relish the idea of writing to your mother tonight."

He might claim that he wanted to die, but when it

came down to it, he had the same will to live that drove all of us to keep fighting. I found that interesting.

It was another two hours before we could help him to his feet and half carry, half drag him to the parlor, where the fire was a pale shadow of itself, but on the hearth rug, the blankets and quilts would be warm enough.

He didn't lie down so much as fall down. It occurred to me that as little as he'd eaten, he'd had no strength to fight off whatever it was that had made him so ill.

I left Marina to watch over him when I slipped back into the kitchen and took out the blue bottle of laudanum.

Removing the cap, I smelled it, and it was the usual sweet odor I recognized. But there was something else as well. I took the tiniest bit on my finger and tasted it.

There was laudanum, that was certain. But it had been thinned with something else. It took me several minutes to decide what else had been in the bottle.

I'd been thinking poisons—but there wasn't any poison.

What had been added, with only enough laudanum to cover the taste, was a strong emetic. Used to induce vomiting in poisonings, it irritated the stomach and forced it to expel anything that was there.

I stood there in the middle of the kitchen. Who had done this?

My first thought was Marina, to stop him from using laudanum, to make him so ill, he would turn away from it.

But where would she have found such a thing as an emetic? Or known how strong to make it?

The emetic itself could be a poison in high enough doses.

I remembered her reaction at seeing him so ill. That hadn't been guilt. She had been genuinely frightened. And why would she bring me the bottle if she had tampered with it? She could have said it had been broken in the first throes of Lawrence's nausea, or that she couldn't find it.

Who, then? Lieutenant Bedford, who had brought the vial here?

I was interrupted by footsteps coming toward the kitchen, and I hastily recapped the bottle and put it back in my pocket. I wasn't certain just how much I should tell her.

Marina came in, bursting with questions. "I think he's asleep. You are a Sister—what did that to him? *Was* it poison? I can't imagine who would do such a thing. He has only eaten what we ate—should we throw away what is in the larder? To be safe?"

I said, trying to calm her, "It wasn't the food. We haven't been ill, after all."

"Then the bottle—was it in the bottle? I don't know how many others he has. If that's the only one."

"I think it must have been," I said slowly. "But he shouldn't use any more of the mixture in the bottle. And we should be sure we have all that is left of what Lieutenant Bedford brought him." I was already considering taking it to Dr. Moreau, to be absolutely certain of what it contained.

She shivered. "I've never seen anyone so ill." Looking around her, she said, "I'll clean up here. But we need to eat, you and I. I feel faint from missing breakfast." She did look as if she was on the verge of collapse— fatigue, the fright, the lack of food, had taken their toll on her as well.

"I'll clear away in here and prepare breakfast. Stay with him. Keep him calm. He needs to rest more than anything right now."

She was hesitant, remembering that I was the guest in the house. But I said, "I tend to annoy him. Best if you are there when he wakes up. I have a little tea that I found in Paris. We'll make a cup for him later in the afternoon. He'll need liquids now, lots of them."

Marina made a face. "I think we need a little wine, you and I. There's some in the cellar. Shall I fetch it?"

"Later, perhaps. For now, don't mention the bottle. One of us should search his room, all the same, and collect anything we might find."

She stood there in the middle of the kitchen, looking quite lost. "I only wanted to help him," she said then. "I seem to have made a muddle of it."

"Don't give up now," I told her. "Perhaps the fright he's just had will turn around his insistence on ruining his life."

But even as I said it to make her feel a little better, I knew how unlikely that hope was.

Chapter 4

We had a very late breakfast. Neither of us had much of an appetite. I sat with Lawrence for an hour or more, letting Marina rest, and then she spelled me. I was nearly certain he wasn't asleep, although his eyes were closed. More than likely he was ignoring me. I wasn't in the mood to talk, either, and so it suited me to sit there by the window and keep a watchful eye on his breathing.

The nausea had passed, but it was afternoon before I made a cup of weak tea, a little honey in it, but no milk, and asked Marina to help him sip it.

While she was occupied with that, I went up to my room, sat down in the chair by the cold hearth, and shut my eyes. I still wasn't sure just why someone had put an emetic in the laudanum. To make him ill? To turn him away from the very habit-forming sedative? Good intentions—or evil? I had no way of knowing. The question was, Should I tell Lawrence Minton what I suspected?

I became aware of a tapping at my window, turned to look, and there on the sill outside was a pigeon, mostly a russet color but with a white tail. He—she?—pecked at the glass with a steady movement of the head, and eventually I rose to go to the window and have a closer look.

He didn't fly away as I approached, and I got quite close to the glass before he stopped his pecking. It was then I saw that he had an injured wing, and as I slowly changed my position for a closer look, I noticed something else. On his leg was the metal capsule used by the British Army to send messages by homing pigeons. This was a military bird. Accustomed to people. Accustomed to being handled.

I opened the window a very little, and he tried to come into the room. I had to put out my hand to prevent him from flying straight in. He was hungry, I thought, and I went quietly down to the kitchen, remembering that Marina hadn't finished her toast. It was there in the dustbin, and I fished it out, took it up with me and crumbled it on the window ledge where the pigeon could find it easily. He ate with such relish, I realized he must have been very hungry.

The room was already quite chilly, and I shut the window again as quickly as I could, while he huddled in one corner of the ledge. I pitied him but didn't know what else I could do for him. Rubbing my hands together, I watched him for a moment, then went back to my chair. Drawing a quilt around my shoulders, I slipped into an uneasy sleep.

When it was time to prepare dinner, I discovered that Marina had gone out, using the rest of the francs I'd given her earlier to buy more food. She was in the kitchen, and the first thing I noticed was how red her eyes were.

"How is our patient?"

"I think he's sleeping. I can't be sure." She turned her back on me for a moment, then said, "Who could have poisoned him?"

"I don't know. Has he said anything? Do you think he knows?"

"It was that man—Monsieur Bedford—who brought the laudanum. But why should he wish Lawrence any harm?"

"Perhaps he didn't know what was in the bottle. Or bottles." I hesitated, then asked, "Did you search the Lieutenant's room?"

"Yes." She was busy cleaning carrots and chopping them up. "There were two other bottles. I have hidden them in the linen closet. For now."

"Shall I go and sit with him?"

"Yes. Please."

I walked away, went up to the parlor, and stoked the fire a little where it had burned unevenly. I was aware of Lieutenant Minton's gaze on me as I worked, but when I turned to sit down in the chair by the window, his eyes were closed.

After a while, I said, "Could you drink a little more tea?"

He didn't answer.

On the far side of the street, a woman was hurrying by, her umbrella up as a light rain began to fall. It had been gray most of the afternoon, clouds heavy with rain that had held off until close to dusk. I hadn't bothered with the lamps, and the room was lit only by the flickering flames in the hearth.

When Lawrence Minton spoke, breaking the silence, I was caught off guard.

"What was the poison?" His words were weak, but clear.

Should I tell him the truth? I hadn't mentioned my suspicions to Marina, and I wasn't certain that I should tell the Lieutenant.

"Do you think it was poison?" I asked.

"What else could have made me so ill?"

When I didn't reply straightaway, he added, "You're a Sister. You must know. Tell me."

"The greater part of my training was dealing with wounds," I replied. "We didn't expect to find poisonings on the battlefield."

He grunted. I couldn't quite make out what he was saying, but I thought he was swearing to himself. After a time, he spoke again. "It was in the laudanum, wasn't it?"

"I'm afraid it must have been. Neither Marina nor I have been ill."

"Oh, dear God." Then, raising himself on one elbow, he glared at me. "It was your doing, then."

"It was not!" I told him emphatically. "In the first place, where would I have come by a poison? In the second, why would I wish to harm you?"

"You went to Paris."

"I did. To see the family with whom I was expected to stay, while in the city. I owed it to them to explain why I was not coming to them after all. How do you think I might have brought poison into my conversation with them? *Could I beg a little arsenic for some rats infesting the house where I've chosen to live at the moment?* Perhaps you ought to ask the friend who brought you the bottle."

He lay back down, covering his eyes with one arm. "Go away. I don't need you *hovering*."

I stood up. "That's a very good sign that you're beginning to recover."

I was at the door, reaching for the knob, when he said, "On your word. You didn't put anything into my laudanum?"

"I give you my word." I opened the door. "But someone did. If it wasn't me, and it wasn't Marina, you might wish to consider whether or not you have an enemy who wants you dead."

He didn't answer. I closed the door to keep what little heat there was in the room, and shivering at the cold in the rest of the house, made my way down to the kitchen.

By nine o'clock, a cold rain had set in, and when I went up to bed, two hot water bottles wrapped in my apron, I found two more blankets as well. Marina had gone to look in on the Lieutenant and see to his fire. I'd left her to it.

The pigeon was huddled in his corner, looking thoroughly wretched, as I began to draw the drapes. I debated what to do, then went down to the kitchen. In the back hall, leading out to the garden, I found a small wooden box that onions had come in, and dug around among the boots and waterproof coats until I discovered a knit cap that was ragged along one edge. Carrying them with me, I went up the back stairs rather than answer any questions about what I was doing.

Making a bed of the cap, I set the box on the table by the window, opened the sash and reached out for the bird. He came to hand easily, and I put him in the box. He settled at once. I closed the window, drew the drapes, and dried my face and hands on the towel hanging on the rack beside the washstand. By the time I'd undressed and crawled between the cold sheets, the pigeon had tucked his head beneath his good wing and gone to sleep. I stretched my feet toward the hot water bottles and warmed them as I pulled the blankets over me.

My last thought as I drifted off to sleep was that Lieutenant Minton had been put off using the laudanum, and perhaps this would be the turning point in getting him well.

My lamp was still burning when I woke with a start, unsure what had brought me up out of a deep sleep. I reached for my traveling clock. The hands were pointing to three in the morning.

And then I heard it again. A man's voice shouting angrily. I couldn't be sure where it was coming from, but I was wide awake, certain that the Lieutenant was awake, feeling stronger, and demanding his bottle of laudanum. Was he willing to take the risk of being poisoned rather than do without the sedative? I couldn't leave Marina to face his anger alone.

I reached for my robe. My slippers were icy as I thrust my bare feet into them and hurried to my door.

I could hear someone stumbling about downstairs, shouting and bumping into things. Catching up my lamp, I went down the passage, dark as pitch save for the light I was carrying. I passed Marina's door. She was standing in it, her face a pale blur above the white nightgown she was wearing.

"I'll see to him," I said, hoping that she wouldn't follow me downstairs.

But she didn't speak, and I hurried on.

Halfway down the staircase, I could see Lieutenant Minton leaning against the far wall below me. He was butting his head against the paneling and crying out in what appeared to be pain.

Experienced as I was with men in the throes of nightmares and delirium, I said as I came down the steps, "That's enough of that. Go to bed." It was the no-nonsense voice of a ward Sister.

He turned to look at me then. His eyes were open, but he wasn't seeing me at all. I wondered then if he was sleepwalking.

But what *did* he see? He went on staring at me, lit as I was by the lamp in my hand, my hair down, my blue robe unfamiliar to him. The rest of the hall was in darkness.

"You turned your back on me then. *Why?* I went back. I couldn't help it if it was too late. I never *meant* it to be too late."

I stayed where I was, watching his face. It was begging me for something, and I had no idea what that was. I considered shell shock, but I rather thought he was lost in the past, reliving something that he couldn't face in the light of day.

"*Say* something," he pleaded, one hand reaching out. "Don't just stand there and judge me. I tried, in the name of God, I *tried.*"

Suddenly he was looking past me—above me—and I realized that Marina had followed me, her pale face and white gown just at the edge of the ring of light from my lamp. She was almost ghostly, standing there. And I thought that he hadn't recognized her, that he was seeing someone—something—else.

Falling to his knees, he began to cry, wracking sobs. Marina started down, intending to go to him, but I put out my hand to stop her.

"I'm sorry," he said, his voice muffled by his hands. "God knows I'm sorry."

I didn't think he was speaking to me now.

A cold draft on the stairs was chilling my feet, all the way to my knees, in spite of my robe. I said quietly as much to Marina as to the man on his knees, "Go to bed, it will be better in the morning."

I looked in her direction, and Marina turned and fled back up the stairs, her bare feet silent on the treads.

Chancing it, I blew out my lamp, plunging the Lieutenant and myself into stygian darkness, even the handsome fanlight above the door barely visible. After what seemed like hours but must have been only ten minutes or so, Lawrence Minton was quiet, only his erratic breathing telling me where he was.

I had seldom seen a man cry as he had done. Whatever was on his mind or even his soul, he carried a burden almost too heavy to bear, and I could understand now why he had turned to an opiate to dull the grief or the pain he couldn't talk about to anyone.

I stayed there on the stairs, afraid to leave him alone.

And then he got shakily to his feet, stumbling once, and then walking erratically toward the door to the parlor. A hand found the newel post of the stairs and then the frame of the door as he made his way to the parlor and the bedding we'd set out by the hearth. I heard a soft *thump* as he threw himself down. I waited, shivering, until I could hear a faint snoring. *The sleep of exhaustion,* I thought as I went quietly down the remaining steps and looked in to see his shape huddled under a blanket.

My first thought was to pull one of the other blankets over him, but I was afraid of waking him. They were close by, if he needed them. I could—should—do no more.

Shutting the parlor door as quietly as I could, I collected my lamp and climbed the stairs, feeling the stiffness of standing so long in the draft. My hand on the bannister guided me, and I could just see the passage to my room as I reached the first-floor landing.

Marina's door was closed when I passed it, and then I was at my own. Fumbling for matches, I was able to light my lamp again and put it on the desk, rather than disturb the sleeping pigeon by carrying it across to the nightstand by the bed.

I kicked off my slippers, kept on my robe, and got back into bed. It was as cold as I felt, and I lay there shivering until I was finally warm enough to sleep.

Who had Lieutenant been talking to, there on the stairs, before Marina appeared above me?

Who had turned his or her back on him? *Was* it a woman? Or had he been unable in his state to realize it was me, seeing instead whatever troubled him. I'd wanted to know what that was, but I was still uncertain, unable to decipher what he'd said. Perhaps it was a part of a conversation he remembered—and as I hadn't been a party to it, I couldn't even guess at the context. And why had Marina's sudden appearance reduced him to tears? It was rather ghostly, he might not have recognized her any more than he'd recognized me. Still, she had triggered that anguish.

In the end, I lay there, watching sheets of rain battering at the window until nearly five in the morning before finally falling asleep.

Marina didn't come down for breakfast.

I made my own, saving the heel of the bread for the pigeon. It was still raining hard. Looking out the window toward the back garden, I could see puddles standing everywhere, rivulets running in the shallow places. A wretched day after a wretched night.

Pulling the shawl I'd found in a drawer in my armoire more closely around my shoulders, I wondered if I should ask the Lieutenant if he could eat a little toast with the last of the tea, but when I looked in on him, he was sleeping heavily. Deciding not to disturb him, I went on up the stairs.

As I was passing Marina's door, it opened and she stopped short at seeing me just outside.

She looked drawn, her eyes puffy. I didn't think she'd got much sleep.

"*Bonjour*," I said. "Shall I make a little breakfast for you?"

"I don't think I could swallow it." Then, as if fearful of the answer, she asked, "How is Lawrence?"

"Asleep. We need to make up the fire, but I thought it best not to wake him just yet." I had to know. And so I said, "Has he had such a—a nightmare before this?"

"I've heard him calling out, moving about. I was afraid—I didn't know what to do. I kept my door locked."

"What did you hear?" I pressed.

"I don't—angels, I think? I must be wrong, he speaks so fast, I can't be sure. And he seems to plead with someone. As he did last night. I don't know who it is. I haven't wanted to ask."

She had brought him here out of kindness, but she hadn't asked any questions. Whether she was afraid to ask—or afraid to know—it didn't matter. I remembered that she was paying a debt, repaying the Lieutenant for bringing her father home.

"No matter," I said, offering a sympathetic smile. "It might be best if you see to the fire. He might not remember that you were on the stairs last night. It will be easier for him."

I walked on. She didn't call me back again.

Breaking up the hard heel of bread into crumbs, I found a saucer that had once had a cup in it, and spread them out so that the bird could get every bit. And then I cleaned the saucer, filled it with water, and brought it to him to drink.

He seemed quite weary, as if he'd searched for some time to find where he ought to return. British and French forces had been moving rapidly in the last days before the Armistice, but it was also possible that he'd been blown off course by a storm, then had had difficulty in finding his masters.

When he'd finished eating, I gently handled the injured wing. I knew almost nothing about bird anatomy, but I could feel the bones in the wing, and none of them appeared to be broken. I thought he'd bumped into something and sprained it.

Pigeons were also the favorite meal for many birds of prey. Whatever had happened to him, he seemed content to lie there in his box, out of the weather.

These birds were heroes and heroines of the war. One was quite famous—I remembered reading about him. Badly wounded, he'd somehow managed to deliver his message. The Germans tried to spot them and shoot them down, even used hawks to go after them.

But homing pigeons had a unique instinct for finding their way. Why hadn't this one?

I searched through the drawers in the armoire and found a scarf to put over his box, so that he could rest quietly. Then I went to stand by the window, staring out at the gray clouds hanging low over the village.

Unable to put it off any longer, I took a deep breath and went down to the parlor. If Marina couldn't ask questions, I could.

But the fire in the grate had nearly gone out, and the bedding on the floor next to it was empty. Lawrence Minton had awakened and made it up the stairs to his room. I was surprised that he'd had the strength.

I went up after him, tapped at the door, and called, "Lieutenant? Are you feeling stronger? Is there anything that I can get you?" It was my ward voice, making rounds, looking at each man and assessing his condition as I asked simple questions. But the response often told me who was feverish, whose fever had broken, who was in pain, and who was making a little progress toward recovery.

There was silence from the room.

"Lieutenant? I only want to be sure you are better. If you can manage a little food?"

His voice seemed to be hollow as he answered in

what was intended to be a growl. "Leave me alone. I'm all right."

He was far from all right, I thought. He needed to eat. Marina had cleaned up his room and changed his sheets. There was nothing else I could offer.

"Some tea, perhaps? Or bread soaked in a little wine?"

"Go away."

Wishing I could see him, judge for myself how he was, I reached out to try the door. But it was locked from the inside.

I turned and went back downstairs.

Marina said, almost defensively, "He wasn't there when I went in to mend the fire."

"He's retreated to his room."

"I understand."

"If you have a tub of some sort, I could wash out my uniforms and aprons," I said, changing the subject.

"You can do them yourself?" she asked, surprised.

"Yes, there was no one else," I told her.

We searched for over an hour before we found an old tin hip bath that had been relegated to the attics. It wasn't as heavy as it appeared to be, and we managed to bring it down several flights of stairs to the kitchen. There I filled it with hot water from the cooker, added some soap powder from my valise, and then hurried upstairs to gather my clothing.

I had just finished rinsing the things I'd washed, when Marina came back into the kitchen to help me wring out the lot and then hang them up on lines we strung across from wall to wall.

The sound of the door knocker echoed down the passage to the kitchen, and Marina turned to me.

"I wasn't expecting—"

Cutting across her words, I said, "It's best if I answer the door. Do you mind?" If it was Lieutenant Bedford, I wanted to speak to him.

Rolling down my sleeves and buttoning the cuffs as I went, I hurried up to the hall, afraid that Lawrence had also heard the knocker and might go down himself, already certain who would be on the doorstep.

I was right, he was just opening the door as I reached the hall. The rain had let up, but a gust of damp, chill air rushed in.

Haggard as he was, his hair in disarray, his unshaven beard dark against his pale skin, Lawrence Minton took one look at the man on his doorstep, and without any warning, swung from the shoulder in a blow that had his weight behind it.

Lieutenant Bedford went down, blood in the corner of his mouth.

The Lieutenant turned, brushed past me without a word, and went up the stairs two at a time, before losing the momentum of his anger and staggering up the last six or seven.

I went out the door and knelt by the injured man.

"What the hell—?" he was exclaiming, then he saw me as his head cleared. "Who are you?"

"Never mind who I am," I said. "Are you all right?" Lawrence's fist had caught him on his chin, cutting his lip and leaving what I expected to be a very visible and ugly bruise. I rose, picking up his cap and brushing off the damp, crumpled leaves.

"What do you think?" he snapped, as he made an effort to scramble to his feet, but he had to hold on to me once he was upright, still too dazed to stand without help.

"The laudanum you brought him on your last visit was poisoned." I handed him his cap.

He stared at me. "Poi—what are you talking about?"

I decided to embroider the truth a little. "We thought we were going to lose him, he was so dreadfully ill. What in God's name did you put in that bottle?"

He pushed away my supporting arm, then said, "He didn't seem to be near death just now." Gingerly touching his chin, he glared at me, angry that I'd witnessed what had happened.

"I think he was rather shaken by his collapse. You

should have waited a day or two before coming back to St. Ives." I was trying not to shiver in the cold air.

"There was nothing wrong with that vial. Or the others." He brushed off the leaves clinging to his uniform.

I smiled up at him. "I'll be glad to let you sample what's left in the bottle."

"What sort of Sister are you?"

"What sort of friend are you, to bring him something that will kill him—more slowly but just as surely?"

"He asked me. He was having trouble sleeping. The war. A good many of us have nightmares."

I heard something in his voice, and asked, "Do you resort to drugs to help you sleep?"

"Absinthe. But I couldn't stand the taste of it."

It had once been a popular drink in France, a mixture of herbs—grand wormwood, green anise, and sweet fennel. It had a high alcohol content, a green color, and tasted like anise or licorice. I'd heard soldiers back from leave in Paris talk about it, even though it had been banned. Or possibly because it had been banned. Some drinkers claimed it caused hallucinations, but that only added to its popularity.

Lieutenant Bedford gave me a mock bow as he wiped the blood from his lip with the back of his hand, said,

"Sister," and was about to walk away when I asked, "Who wanted to see Lawrence Minton dead? Who provided you with these vials of laudanum?"

He stopped at the edge of the street and smiled. "For all I know, it was you. To stop him from using it. Surely you know more about poisons than I ever did."

And he was gone. Some of the swagger I'd seen when last he'd walked away from the house was no longer there. I thought his mouth and jaw ached more than he cared for me to see.

I wanted to follow him—it was the only chance I'd had to see him. But I had no coat, and I had to watch him disappear from sight toward the railway station.

When I stepped inside, I saw Marina standing by the door that led to the kitchens. I shut the outer door.

"How much did you see?" I walked toward her, keeping my voice low.

"Did Lawrence *hit* him?" she asked.

"I'm afraid so. But no harm done. A bruised chin and a cut lip."

"Did he think the Lieutenant had poisoned the laudanum?"

"Apparently. Yes. He didn't say anything, he just lashed out." I shrugged. "We may have seen the last of Lieutenant Bedford."

"It's as well."

We went back to the kitchen, finished hanging up my damp clothes, and then she went to a cabinet and, reaching up, took out a bottle of wine.

"There's no tea. But I think we should celebrate, a little. With no laudanum, Lawrence will be better, he'll be able to return to Paris and his duties." Taking down two wineglasses, she poured some wine in each, then handed me one.

Lifting hers, she said, "To Paris, then." Taking a sip, she added, "I feel rather giddy, and I've only had a taste. I expect it's relief."

"To Paris," I agreed.

I didn't want to tell her that her troubles weren't over, however much she might wish to believe they were. I didn't have the heart.

Chapter 5

I was sitting in the parlor, where I'd added more coal to the small fire on the hearth, warming myself a bit before facing my cold room. Marina had finished in the kitchen and gone up to bed.

The parlor door opened, and I looked up, expecting she had come down again for something. But it was Lawrence.

Surprised, I stood. "I was just going to bed."

He came in, closed the door behind him, and said, "Last night. Did I rave?"

Did he not remember?

I said carefully, "I heard some shouting. Even in my room. Yes."

He put both hands up to his face, covering his eyes,

then dropped them to his sides again. "I can't—I don't remember much."

"I'm used to hearing men cry out in their sleep. Or walk, for that matter, if they can."

He stood there, uncertain. "I expect you are." Then crossing the room, he pulled another chair close to the flames and sat down. "I'm afraid to go to sleep."

"It's hard, sometimes," I agreed, sympathy in my voice, but not accusation. "I worked close to the Front. I try not to remember what I saw there. Still, it's there. And I know it will come back. It hasn't gone away."

He rubbed his eyes again. "What did you see, that gives you nightmares?" It was almost a sneer, as if he thought I was patronizing him.

"Broken bodies. Blood everywhere. Men screaming as they died. Men dying because we didn't have the skills to save them. Struggling not to cry as I held the hands of men who called for their wives or mothers." I hadn't meant it to. Yet in spite of my fierce control, the truth slipped through.

Lawrence stared at me. I realized it had never occurred to him that the nurses tending wounds, holding the hands of frightened men about to have a limb taken off, closing the eyes of the dead, washing the tables where others had bled, emptying buckets filled with filthy cloths and bandaging and worse, might be haunted by what they had seen and done.

"Oh, yes," I said, more harshly than I'd intended. "There are nights when I can't sleep. And I am not alone. I can't tell you how many of us, doctors and nursing Sisters, say nothing."

"I'm—sorry," he said then. "You are always so blood—so cheerful."

But that had been our duty, also, to raise spirits. It was not about our suffering, it was about theirs.

The minutes ticked by, the coal settling in the hearth the only sound in the room. I went on sitting quietly. Waiting. I wasn't certain what for, but I had a feeling there might be more. For the first time since I'd arrived, the Lieutenant was sober enough to talk to me. I could see the stress he was under, and how much he wanted help. But sober, did he know why he needed help? Or did that come out only in drunken or drugged moments when his defenses were down and the nightmares slipped through?

"I've come to dread the nights," he said finally. "It's why I took the laudanum."

"If it would help to talk, what you tell me will go no further."

"Not to my mother?" he asked, giving me a twisted smile.

"Least of all to your mother. Or to Marina. Your commanding officer. I'm a nursing Sister, I am expected to keep to myself what I see or learn in the course of my duties."

He stared into the depths of the fire. The red heart had gone, and the gold, but there was still a blue flame licking at the last of the coal, a lump that had escaped so far.

"I don't remember," he said at length. "That's just it, you see. I had a severe concussion on the coast road as we retreated before the German advance, trying to hold them back from reaching the sea while the French struggled to stop them on the Marne. They couldn't do both, and it was up to us to keep the sea open, it was the only way to supply us or send reinforcements. If the Germans reached the Channel, they could launch an attack on Britain. That retreat was costly, but we'd expected as much. I was told later—by the doctors—that a house had collapsed on top of me. I was in and out of consciousness, but I can remember a little. A German officer who must have noticed my boots sticking out of the debris. I think he must have ordered his men to dig me out. I just had sense enough to stop breathing, hoping they'd decide I was dead. It must have worked, because when they saw my bloody head, they left. Later—it was dark, but how much time had passed I can't judge—half a dozen of my own side appeared and finished the job of pulling me out, expecting to bury me. Instead they picked me up and carried me with them back to our lines. I had been miles inside the German lines, and I had no idea why or even where I was. When they could question me some days later, I couldn't even tell them my name or regiment. They were beginning to suspect I was a German spy."

I said nothing, letting him talk. But I knew how that running battle had been fought on the coast road, and what he was telling me had the ring of truth.

He glanced across at me. "Given the situation, it was very likely I'd have been shot. But my own men had been looking for me, they found me in hospital, and they vouched for me. They even located an officer I'd played cards with in London to identify me. And later there was a Sister I'd danced with before the war. Diana. I wasn't so far gone that I couldn't see how remarkably beautiful she was, but I couldn't bring back her name. There are still wide gaps in my memory. My other wounds healed, and I could function perfectly well, and so I was soon back in the line. I simply lied when they asked if I'd fully recovered. I didn't want to tell them the truth. I wasn't wounded again until late in the war. Almost the end."

I was wondering if the Diana who remembered him was my flatmate, the one who was recently married. She was extraordinary, she turned heads wherever she went, flirting outrageously without in any way leading anyone on, until 1916, when she met the man she wanted to marry. I'd introduced them.

I said, frowning, "And you recall nothing about what you'd been doing before the concussion?"

"Nothing."

But I thought he wasn't telling me the truth there. I wondered if he'd briefly deserted, yet his war after that, his decision to make a career in the military, belied it. If the Army had had any inkling, they would have dealt severely with him. And the fact that his men had searched for him while he was missing spoke well of him as an officer. Just as Major Webb had said.

"And nothing since then has offered you any glimpse behind the curtain of lost memory?" I'd phrased it that way intentionally.

"I wish to God it had."

Again, there was something in the way he avoided my gaze that made me wonder.

"How long have you had these nightmares?"

He got up, and I thought he was leaving the room. But he was only going to the window, staring out at the street. "Will this rain never end?" he said, almost to himself. Then with his back to me, he said, "Paris. Since I came here."

"You didn't have them before?"

"I don't—no."

Remembering what Marina had told me, that Lawrence Minton hadn't come the next morning as promised, I said, probing gently, "Was it Paris that caused them, do you think?"

"No," he said impatiently. "Why should Paris remind me of a house collapsing on me?"

"Someone you passed on the street? Perhaps someone who reminded you of that German officer?"

"No—you're grasping at straws in the wind." He turned. "Don't you think *I've* tried to remember? It's hopeless."

"You told me it was a house that had collapsed. Was it that—or a school—a church?"

"How do I know? They called it a house. Why should they have been wrong about that?" Lawrence was becoming increasingly irritable.

I smiled sympathetically. "Sometimes a question triggers a memory. Not always, of course. You didn't want your supper, but Marina put it away for you. In the event you felt you could eat a little."

"No. Yes. All right." He hesitated. "Are you certain all the laudanum was contaminated?"

"I'm afraid you shouldn't risk it. But yes, why only put something in one vial? Whoever did this couldn't be sure which you might use first." He was having troubles with withdrawal.

Moving restlessly around the room, he asked, "*Was I in danger?*"

What to say? If I told him he was not, he'd go back to using the drug. If I lied and was later proved wrong, he would never trust me again.

Looking for a middle way, I said, "You survived. This time."

"Yes." He thought of something. "Is there any wine?"

"Marina opened a bottle at dinner."

"Then I'll eat something. With the wine."

It wouldn't give him the oblivion he was after, and it might well upset his digestion again. But he was willing to accept food, and that was more important at the moment. I wished for a good, nutritious broth, but that was as elusive as my taste for porridge.

We went down to the kitchen, and I warmed his plate a little, and poured a glass of wine for him. He reached out and pulled the bottle out of my hand, keeping it beside his glass. I gave him no argument.

"It's late," I said. "I'll go up to bed now. But if you need me, please knock at my door."

He glanced at the bottle of wine. "God willing, I won't need anyone tonight.

Well-rested now, the pigeon was eager for his crust of bread, and afterward went to peck at the window glass. But his wing wasn't healed enough to fly very far, and I tried several times to put him back in his box with the scarf over it to block out the light. Finally I decided to get into bed with my hot water bottles and put out the lamp.

That settled the pigeon, but I was too restless to sleep. My mind roved at will—what I was to take as my bride-gift to Ireland when I went to a wedding there next month. The bride had been with me on board *Britannic* when the hospital ship had hit a mine and sunk in 1916. What I was to tell Matron about Lawrence. And how would she take it? Why had Simon gone to Scotland without a word to anyone? Was Iris right, that he had "a lassie" there? Was my father still in Paris— could he possibly find out about Lawrence Minton's war, and most particularly about his head wound?

I looked at my little watch, holding it this way and that, but I couldn't read the hands without the lamp, and the pigeon had settled, I didn't want to disturb him again.

I tossed and turned for another hour, then came wide awake when I heard something fall, the sound echoing down the passage.

My first thought was that the Lieutenant had got himself drunk on wine and fallen down the stairs. I flung back the blankets, felt for my robe, and somehow found my slippers. They were cold from the floor, and I reminded myself to put them up on the bed in future.

I opened the door quickly but as quietly as I could, and went out into the passage. Marina's room was dark, no light showing under the door, and it was firmly shut. I hurried on, my slippers making little sound on the floor.

When I got to the stairs I looked down, but even in the darkness, I could see that there was no one lying on the steps. I went down them, to search the hall. Nothing. Back upstairs I went, and this time turned toward the Lieutenant's room.

I could see the light under the door, and I lifted my hand to knock. And then I heard the voice, swearing in anger and distress.

I hadn't lived with soldiers most of my life not to know what he was saying, but I knew as well that he couldn't have been badly hurt, whatever had happened.

About to walk away, I heard footsteps coming toward

the door. Knowing I was about to be caught out, I fled for the stairs. I had just got myself down the first three or four when the door of the Lieutenant's room opened.

"Go away. I don't need—"

He must have stood there for a whole minute, must have peered up and down the passage, looking to see who had come to his door.

And then he slammed it hard, jarring the portrait in a gold frame just by my ear.

I stayed where I was. For all I knew, he was standing in the passage, waiting to see who would appear once the coast was clear.

The minutes ticked by. And my caution was repaid by the barely audible turning of the latch followed by the soft click of the door being closed as quietly as possible.

Again I waited, but there was no other sound from the direction of the Lieutenant's room.

I made my way up the stairs and down the passage to my own room. Once there I looked back toward the Lieutenant's door.

No one was there.

The morning dawned clear and milder than I'd expected. After breakfast I told Marina that I was taking the train to Paris.

"Are you leaving?" she asked in alarm.

"No, of course not. But I think my father may be in Paris, and if he is, I hope to ask him to find out what he can about the Lieutenant. I didn't want to bring him into this problem if I could avoid it. Now I don't have a choice."

"You could speak to his mother."

"Not yet, not until we know more about his situation and can give her a little hope."

"Did you give him the rest of the wine last evening? The empty bottle and another from the cellar were in the dustbin."

"No. He took it, trying to replace the laudanum. To help him sleep."

She frowned. "I don't know which is worse."

"Do you know, is there a doctor that he saw in Paris?" Madame Moreau had mentioned someone—but her husband's colleague had been suspicious enough of the request for laudanum that he'd turned the patient away. Whether it was Lawrence he'd turned away or someone else, it was best to avoid him.

"I have no idea. The regimental surgeon?"

"He wouldn't—couldn't have felt that he could be honest with him."

"No, I expect not."

I left half an hour later, got to the station in time for the early train, and once in Paris, I went to see Dr.

Moreau. He was just finishing a consultation with a patient when I was admitted by the maid.

I was surprised to see that it was Major Webb the doctor was showing out.

The Major greeted me as if I were a stranger. "Sister," he said, touching his cap. Then to Dr. Moreau, "Thank you, sir. I'll keep in touch."

And then he was gone.

Looking after him as Dr. Moreau welcomed me, calling to his wife to see who had just arrived, I said, "How well do you know that officer?"

"He's been here a time or two."

Madame Moreau was there, greeting me warmly, begging me to stay for luncheon with them. I accepted, but with a smile, I added, "I'm afraid I've come to consult the doctor about a—a former patient." Turning to him, I asked, "If you are free?"

"As it happens, I am." He took me off to his surgery, shut the door, ushered me to a chair, and then said, "This patient of yours. Do I know him?"

"It's better, perhaps, if you don't."

"Ah. Very well, then. Tell me how I may help you."

"The patient in question has had a quite severe concussion in the course of his duties," I began. "For several days he didn't know his own name. Over time—several years, in fact, he's recovered most of his memory, although there are some gaps. Still, he's continued to—to go on with his work. But suddenly he's begun to have night terrors. They must relate to the incident that caused the concussion, but he can't remember how he came to be injured. Nor does there seem to be a sound reason for these nightmares to have begun. Why not immediately, if there was something that he can't face?"

He'd listened carefully to my report then nodded. "Without examining your patient, I can only suggest that something triggered a memory that had been buried so deep in his mind that he could function without remembering it. Therefore, his work must not be connected with this event." He smiled. "If he had been kicked in the head by a cow while milking it, he would be reminded of that when next he had to milk the animal. But if he was hit by a falling limb while walking through a wood, and never went back to that wood again, there would be no trouble in milking his cow. No memory to disturb him."

"So the question is, why was he in that wood, and not on his farm?"

"Indeed, my dear." He closed a file on his desk and slipped it into a drawer. Then he peered at me over his glasses and said, "We are speaking of Lawrence Minton, are we not? Rather than a poor farmer?"

I had to smile, but it was rueful one. "I didn't know how much of his history you knew."

"His mother was concerned about the problem with memory. She consulted me, uncertain whether or not the Army doctors were well enough trained in the subject to help him. But as time went by, and there were no additional problems, it was assumed that he was all right. Would be all right in the future. Some memory loss is not unusual in traumatic wounds."

"Yes, I understand that. But I don't know the details of his case. I can't judge what he might not have remembered."

"There was a brief lull in the retreat down the coast road. Well, lull is perhaps not the right word. The pressure was lifted in one sector as the Germans pushed hard against another. It was discovered that he was missing. At first it was thought he might have been taken by the Germans, but several of his men had seen him the night before, and that precluded being captured. Several days passed, his men were put under the command of another officer, and he was simply listed as missing. Then he was found in a house well north of where he'd been seen last. A beam had collapsed on him, there were other injuries, and for several days he couldn't give anyone his name. You must remember the chaos at the time. Here was an Englishman, but he couldn't answer any questions about what had happened. Some idiot of an officer decided he must be a German spy, but his men were continuing to look for him, and one of them discovered him in hospital. The next question was, had he deserted, but since he was discovered where the fighting had been most intense, that didn't fit the situation either. But Lawrence couldn't explain how or why he had got there. He returned to duty several weeks later, and there was nothing in his subsequent service that in any way caused alarm. It was decided that his men had been mistaken about when they'd last seen him, given the pressures of the retreat."

"Did anyone question them more closely? Afterward?"

Dr. Moreau looked at me. "It appears that they admitted to some confusion, under the circumstances."

In short, they had covered up any doubts.

"They must have cared about him, to do that."

"He got them through a very difficult time. I expect they admired him and were grateful."

I knew the Army perhaps better than he did. Lawrence Minton's men had lied to protect him.

From what?

"How is Lawrence handling these nightmares?" the doctor was asking. He'd taken off his spectacles and was polishing them with a silk handkerchief.

"Not well. He doesn't understand them—the reason for them, anyway—and so he tries to find ways to stop them."

"Alcohol? Opiates?"

For some reason I found I didn't want to talk about the laudanum laced with an emetic.

"Last night it was wine."

He nodded. "He will need something stronger. Brandy, perhaps."

"I don't know if there is any available."

"It's best that I see him. Sooner rather than later."

"He won't come. You are close to his mother."

"But doctors are not talebearers."

I remembered that he hadn't told me why Major Webb had come to him.

But would Lawrence Minton believe me if I told him he could trust the doctor?

"I will do what I can."

"Yes. I'm sure. Thank you for confiding in me. Now we must adjourn for our luncheon or my wife will scold us." He made to rise.

"There's something you should know. I warned you about a Major Webb—that he might come here to ask questions about me. He has rooms in the same house as Lieutenant Minton. It might be best if you say nothing to him about knowing the Lieutenant."

Surprised, he said, "But he didn't ask about you, my dear. Or mention Lawrence at all. He came to see me about an old war wound. A knee. There has been some weakness there of late, and he didn't care to bring it to the attention of the Regiment's surgeon. I gave him something to rub on it at night, and some exercises that might help." He considered that for a moment, then added thoughtfully, "I wonder if that is why he chose to come here. To me."

I was sure that was the reason. *How* many physicians were there in Paris? And yet Major Webb had chosen the one I had mentioned to him only a few days ago.

I said, "At the moment, Lawrence Minton is very fragile. I found him quite by accident, and I could lose him again as easily."

"I will take good care that the Major learns nothing from me. You may be sure of that."

And I believed him. But I was still quite concerned about the Major's reasons for coming here. If there had been a sound excuse, surely he'd have acknowledged me?

Hallo, Sister, you'd mentioned Dr. Moreau—and I'd been considering finding a doctor to look at my knee . . .

It was as ridiculous as it sounded. What then was he doing here?

We walked back into the house, and Madame Moreau glanced from me to her husband as we walked into the dining room, and then said, "Secrets, my dear?"

He laughed. "Hardly. Unless you have a sudden interest in gallstones."

She made a face. "Not at the table."

It was an excellent meal. A parsnip and dried apple soup to begin, fish for the main course, potatoes boiled with herbs, a carrot soufflé, as well as the ubiquitous bread. Madame Moreau apologized for it, all the same.

"Vegetables are not at their best this time of year. But we have made do."

I thought of the meals that Marina and I had had to create with whatever we could find in a village shop. But I complimented her on her skill at making do. There was a custard of eggs and milk to finish with a little sherry to flavor it, and I thought I might be able to duplicate it for Marina.

I had to leave soon after, and quickly found a taxi to take me to the British Embassy, where I asked if they might know where my father was staying.

The secretary who came down to assist me was missing an arm, that sleeve of his coat pinned up to hide the cuff. He was very helpful, gave me the address of an hotel not far from the embassy, and found me a taxi to go there.

Much to my dismay—I'd counted on seeing him— my father was in a meeting, and it was not expected to break up for another two hours. It would mean missing my train back to St. Ives if I waited.

"I'm his daughter. May I leave a letter for him?"

Again, the staff was very helpful, and I was soon ensconced at a small table in the lounge, supplied with pen and paper and ink, and left to write my message.

How to begin? After several false starts, I gave him to understand that I was not presently staying with the Moreau family, but had been concerned about a young officer who had suddenly begun to have nightmares long after his wounds had been healed. This, I wrote, was of concern, and I needed to know more about the wound to his head that had occurred in the retreat from Mons at the start of the war. Then I gave him all the particulars I knew, and asked him to write to me in care of Dr. Moreau. I had closed the envelope and was addressing it when I felt that someone was watching me.

I glanced around the small lounge, saw no one, then noticed Major Webb by the stairs to the upper floors, one hand on the newel post. Rising above his head was a golden cupid balanced on one foot, with a lovely little bow and arrow in his chubby hands.

I nodded in acknowledgment, carried my letter and the other things to the desk, thanking the clerk as I passed him the ink and pen and the rest of the stationery. I said, keeping my voice low, "There's a letter with the stationery. Will you see that it's put in the hands of Colonel Richard Crawford, and no one else?"

The clerk smiled. "With the greatest pleasure, Mademoiselle." He had seen the edge of the bank note that accompanied the letter. Pocketing that quite smoothly, letting the letter fall into the open drawer as he put away the extra stationery, he added, "That officer by the stairs. Is he annoying you? I have observed that he has stood there watching for several minutes."

"Thank you for noticing. His is not an acquaintance I care to renew."

"Understood. Shall I have the doorman find a taxi for you?"

"Yes, please."

He pushed something under the edge of the desk, and while we talked, he kept an eye on the main door. The doorman stepped in, nodded to him, and I was escorted to the door and into a taxi.

As I pulled away, I saw Major Webb step out of the hotel doors and say something to the doorman. The man shrugged in Gallic fashion, as if he knew nothing.

And then we were in the swirl of traffic, and I told the driver where I wished to go.

Major Webb had every reason to be at the hotel where some of the delegates to the convention would be staying, but it was still more of a coincidence than I was ready to believe in, after he'd also appeared at Dr. Moreau's surgery this noon. He had ignored me there, and at the hotel had not approached, although he'd questioned the doorman as I left.

I wondered why. And the only answers I could think of were not to my liking.

I found a shop with a little better selection of vegetables and another scrawny chicken, bought a holder to carry them in, and reached the Gare just in time to make my train. Several people in the carriage eyed my purchases, but they said nothing.

It was a little distance to the Lascelles house, and by the time I was nearly there, my purchases weighed like iron bars. I was happy to reach the door—and to my surprise, I found it locked. No one answered my summons in spite of the sharp rap I gave the brass knocker with my free hand.

I tried again.

Finally someone came, and I could hear the latch lifting.

The door swung open. Marina stood there, frightened and shaking.

"Quickly!" she whispered urgently. "Don't let him hear you."

I gave her the holdall and stepped inside, quietly closing and locking the door.

"Where is he?"

"In your room." She cast a terrified glance over her shoulder, then hurried down the passage to the kitchen, the holdall clasped tightly in both hands.

I ran up the stairs, walked as quietly as I could down the passage, and paused, listening, at my door.

It sounded as if he had been destroying everything inside.

I opened the door to find Lawrence in trousers and shirt, barefoot, standing on my bed and trying to catch the pigeon desperately circling the room but hampered by his injured wing.

"What is the meaning of this?" I demanded in Matron's sternest tones.

Caught off guard, he stared at me as if he was having trouble focusing on my face, and at the same time he was struggling with his footing on the mattress.

"Dinner," he said, making another lunge for the bird, and nearly going headfirst off the bed.

"That is not dinner," I told him harshly. "Now get out of my room."

"It's not your room. It's Marina's. Well. Her father's."

I realized looking at him that he was so drunk he was barely able to keep his balance.

A feather floated down from the frightened bird. It was white, and it brushed against Lawrence's face as it passed.

The change in him was dramatic. He brushed frantically at his face, trying to dislodge the feather, but it had already floated down to the blanket, a white spot on the dark blue.

"*No!*" Completely losing his balance, still brushing at his face, he pitched forward.

Thinking only that he mustn't have another concussion, I rushed forward, trying to break his fall. He was flailing wildly as he realized his danger, and as I reached for him, his weight hit me, knocking the breath out of me, and we both struck the floor hard.

I struggled out from under him as he attempted to scramble to his feet, and as soon as I was free, I slapped him across the face.

It not only startled him, coming so unexpectedly, but it also focused his gaze. Sobering him just enough to let him hear me.

"I—sorry—I'm sorry," he said, rising to his knees and then struggling to stand.

Overhead, the pigeon was still swooping, trying to find a safe place to land.

"Get out," I said, pointing at the door. "Now."

He gestured toward the bird. "Marina came to bring fresh towels—"

"It's a homing pigeon. An Army messenger. Get out." I hadn't thought to tell her not to come in. It was my fault.

Lawrence brushed at his cheek again, more a reflex action than an effort to dislodge the feather. "The war is over," he told me.

"What I do about that bird is my affair. Not yours."

As he made an effort to start toward the door, his feet got tangled in the bedding that had come off the bed with him as he fell, and he put out a hand, catching the nightstand, nearly knocking over the lamp. He fumbled to right it, then lifted his feet with the excessive care of a drunkard, and stumbled to the door.

I was angry with him, not for my sake as much as for the poor bird's, and I slammed the door almost on his heels.

The frightened pigeon kept circling for several more minutes, then fluttered down to his box, too anxious to settle. I stayed where I was, by the hearth, making calming sounds, telling him softly that there was nothing to fear

He jerked his head, blinking his eyes. But after a bit

he calmed down enough that I could pull the scarf over the box.

As tired as he was, I found the overturned chair, righted it, and then lit the lamp.

I was just sitting down when there was a tap at the door. I crossed the room to open it, not wishing to ask anyone to come in.

It was Lawrence, quite hangdog and decidedly even more sober.

"I'm so sorry. Did I hurt you? Are you all right?"

"I am fine, no thanks to you. Go away."

He nodded, turned, and walked off down the passage.

I closed my door. My shoulders were hurting where they had hit the floor with his weight pinning me there. And one hip smarted as well. But no harm done, I thought. Nothing broken, although there might be a few bruises here and there tomorrow. I hoped Lawrence found a few also.

Sitting down, I said to the pigeon, quiet now, "I'm so sorry." And realized that I had echoed Lawrence Minton.

Chapter 6

I woke up just as dawn was breaking, and I couldn't go back to sleep, try as I would. Longing for a cup of tea, I got up and dressed as quickly as I could, washing my face in cold water and shoving my feet into cold shoes. I had forgot to put them on the bed last night.

The house was quiet as I let myself out of my room and walked toward the stairs. I was almost there when I heard a swearing and a thumping coming from below. It was still dark and shadowy in the hall, but when I reached the head of the stairs, I could see Lawrence Minton crouched on the next-to-last step, leaning out, struggling with the heaped edges of the hall carpet. He appeared to be shoving it away, pushing at it as if he loathed it, jamming it down against the floor with some force as it seemed to writhe under his hands.

And then he fought to bring the carpet up to him, where he squatted, grasping at it with both hands, only to lose it at one end even as he worked to gather up the other. Frantic, desperate, he clutched at the rug, moaning to himself as he fought for control of something I couldn't see—but that he saw all too clearly.

I watched him for several seconds, undecided about what to do. How long had he been there? But if he was sleepwalking, it would not be wise to startle him. At the same time, he was in such a state that I wasn't sure what would happen if I left him to snap out of it himself.

An armful of carpet clutched to his chest, he lowered his head and began to rock this way and that, back and forth, the moaning rising and falling, a man in the throes of despair.

I was about to risk quietly calling out to him, when he lost his footing on the stair and began to fall toward the floor. The mound of carpet stopped him, and he jerked as if shot.

"God forgive me."

I could barely make out the words, his voice was so choked.

I stepped back into the shadows as he became aware of where he was. Looking around, still more dazed than awake but gradually taking note of his surroundings, he got unsteadily to his feet. The rug almost tripped him up, and he stared down at the crumpled heap, as if he'd never seen it before. Kicking it out of his way, he stumbled toward the parlor door and got through it somehow before shutting it behind him.

Even after I had heard the door shut and could see—barely—that the hall was empty, I stayed where I was.

The question racing through my mind was, What had Lawrence Minton intended to do with that carpet? It was, I thought, close to six by nine feet. Far too cumbersome to carry anywhere—one usually rolled such a carpet, and lifted it between two people or raised it to the shoulder of one person.

One usually rolled such a carpet . . .

I tried to bring back the image of what I'd seen. It was oddly familiar to a nursing Sister.

The way he was struggling with the carpet, it was almost as if he was trying to manage a body, to lift it and move it, without help. As if it had been a surrogate for the way a body flailed about, the muscles relaxed and no longer in the control of the mind. Before rigor set in.

It was a chilling thought. Was that *truly* what I'd just witnessed?

And afterward—when he'd pulled the rug toward him, holding it fiercely as he rocked and moaned. As if he had been in the throes of grief. Or regret.

But why was he squatting on a step? Reaching down— even jamming the carpet hard against the floor below him? It didn't make sense. He could have managed the carpet more easily from the floor. Yet in his nightmare, he needed to be above what was happening. Like a washerwoman bending over the tub of soapy water.

I wasn't sure why that image had popped into my head. Yet it seemed to fit, somehow. But he wasn't scrubbing at clothes, was he?

I'd considered any number of reasons for Lawrence Minton's behavior, for his insistence on finding oblivion, for his talk about death. Shell shock? Something that had occurred in the war? Something that might have happened since he'd come to Paris?

That last was beginning to seem more likely, since the Moreaus and Marina had appeared to believe that the change in him was recent and sudden. But it hadn't occurred to me that whatever had happened to him, he might have done something so terrible he couldn't tell anyone about it.

God forgive me.

It had been a strangled plea just now.

What had he done that required God's forgiveness?

Somehow this must be the key to everything that had happened to him. But where? Why? And why had he turned to laudanum and not to the police?

I tried to work through it, but there was no answer that made sense.

Had Lieutenant Bedford or Major Webb known about this? Was that why Lieutenant Bedford had been so willing to bring Lawrence laudanum? I couldn't believe that anyone from the regiment would be involved in something like this.

And what about Dr. and Madame Moreau? Would either of them be willing to cover up something sinister, for the sake of their friendship with Matron? Both of them had asked me separately not to tell the other what I discovered about Lawrence's disappearance from Paris.

Then there was Marina? Her family owed the Lieutenant a debt for saving her father's life, but I'd spent time with her, helped her with the household problems and with Lawrence's self-destructive behavior. I was convinced she knew nothing. But her efforts to get him out of Paris might have come at just the right time.

I went over again what I'd witnessed, and there appeared to be no other explanation. Could Lieutenant Minton have *killed someone*? Was that what had haunted him all these weeks since the night he took Marina out to dinner?

The pressing question now was, If I thought that was possible, what should I do about it?

The most logical course of action was to go to the Paris police and ask if they were searching for Lawrence Minton. But I didn't have much faith in them, after an earlier experience of my own in dealing with them. If he didn't remember what he'd done, then he could be accused of any crime that suited the police, and if the facts fit well enough, he could be charged. Whether he was guilty or not.

I could go to my father for advice. He was the former colonel of Lawrence's regiment. Where would he turn for help? I didn't know all the present officers, or how they would proceed. Nor did I know anyone in the Foot Police.

Or I could simply do nothing.

That went against all my upbringing as a child growing up with the regiment. Duty. Honor. These mattered.

If I myself took on the responsibility for finding out the whole story behind these nightmares before acting, would I be putting Marina, and by extension myself, in jeopardy meanwhile?

I was deep in this discussion with myself when I heard the door to the parlor open and then close. And here I was, standing at the top of the stairs, where I'd be seen as soon as the Lieutenant started up them.

The nearest door was down the passage that Lawrence would follow to his room—the next but one to the stairs. I moved quickly and quietly, put my hand on the knob, and mercifully it turned under my fingers. The door swung open silently, and I stepped into the darkness inside.

Closing it all but a fraction of an inch, I listened. He was climbing the stairs now, his tread heavy, weary, as if he was exhausted. And then he was passing my door. He fumbled with opening his own, and I heard it shut a moment later.

He remembered *guilt,* even if he didn't remember the deed. That was clear enough. But why had he blocked it out so completely?

People did that when their pain and the truth were far too heavy to face in the conscious mind.

Had he known the person he'd killed? Someone he couldn't bear to remember?

I waited in the darkness until I was certain he wasn't going to leave his room again. And then I slipped quietly back to mine.

That was the trouble with an empty house, I thought, nearly at my door. Every little sound seemed to carry.

As I opened it and started inside, I glanced back the way I'd come.

Even in the darkness of the passage, I could see the outline of something darker.

And I realized that Lawrence Minton had come back into the passage and watched me walk back to my room.

I shut my door and turned the key in the lock, breathing hard. Which Lawrence Minton had seen me? The sleepwalker, still not completely over his nightmare? Or the awake man, well aware of who I was and wondering where I'd come from?

Would he remember, in the light of morning?

I was tempted to put a chair against my door, and then shook my head wryly at the thought. I'd come through far worse in the war. But somehow that dark shape had alarmed me on the heels of what I'd discovered.

Calming down, I crossed the room to my bed, without lighting a lamp, and still wearing my dressing gown, I took my feet out of my slippers and shoved them deep under the blankets. The hot water bottles were barely lukewarm, and I shivered.

It was quite some time before I drifted off to sleep.

I woke to the light of dawn coming in the window, and I heard the pigeon cooing softly. He needed grain, and I didn't have any, only crusts of bread. I wasn't even sure where I could find feed for him.

Then the night came back to me, and the shape in the passage. As I drifted into sleep, I'd have sworn I'd heard the rattle of the door, as the Lieutenant had come down to test it. But I couldn't be sure if that was real, or part of the twisted dreams that followed.

And how was I to ask questions *now* that would tell him as soon as he heard them what I'd seen there on the stairs? Not to mention how I'd interpreted it.

I stretched, and the cold sheets below the water bottles reminded me that I'd forgot to put my shoes up from the floor. Only my slippers. Sighing, I got up, got myself ready as quickly as I could, and went down to the kitchen.

Marina hadn't come down, and I stoked the cooker, then stared at the kettle, wishing for tea. I made myself a little breakfast before going upstairs again, glad I hadn't had to face the Lieutenant this early. With me I carried a mop and pail and a feather duster. It was actually a smoke screen, although I intended to clean my room. I left the mop and pail outside my door, then quickly went up the back stairs to the floor above ours.

A quick look at one or two rooms told me that this was the nursery floor, with accommodations for the nanny, governess, or tutor, depending on the age of the children. I had removed my shoes, shoved them into my apron pockets, to make as little noise as possible as

I tiptoed down the passage to where I could look over and watch the stairs from the shadows up here.

It was nearly eleven before Lawrence Minton left his room and went down the steps and turned toward the kitchen passage. Marina was already there—I had seen her go down two hours before.

I waited to be sure he wasn't coming back straight-away, then hurried down to the first floor and slipped into his room. I couldn't be certain how long I had to search it, but I didn't need to take particular care, because he had flung clothes and belongings everywhere. If he didn't catch me here, he would never suspect that someone had been looking through his things.

But what was I searching for? If Lawrence Minton had killed someone, he wasn't likely to make a note of it in his journal. Or to keep a souvenir—a lock of hair, a bit of ribbon, a man's watch fob or signet ring. If he felt such intense guilt that he'd blocked the act from his mind, reliving it only in nightmares, there wouldn't be a reminder that he might stumble across in the course of the day.

What I really hoped to find was some indication of the Lieutenant's character.

The clutter and untidiness were at odds with the usual way officers lived, even if they had a batman to take care of their belongings. But this could be explained by the drugs that Lawrence had been using. Still, I could see that while his uniforms were of very good quality, most of them from the better London tailors, they were not extravagant. So why was he unable to help Marina Lascelles buy food and coal?

I found in a drawer of his desk papers that must have been part of his duties at the Peace Conference. I couldn't help but wonder whether it was appropriate for him to have them here. On the other hand, when Marina brought him here to St. Ives, it had been a hasty move, rather than one where there was time to make decisions.

Leafing through the pages, I found part of a private letter in a different handwriting. I stopped to scan it.

It was brief, and it appeared to be a letter about one of Minton's men. The date was October of 1914. The ink was fading, the page had been read so many times that the creases were beginning to wear thin.

Dear Lieutenant Minton,

Thank you for telling me how my husband died. He was a good man, a good soldier, and I am glad to know he served his King and Country to the end. We had a nice service for Harold in the village church, and I asked Rector to read your letter for me. He is taking up a subscription to put up a small brass memorial to Harold in the nave, since there's no grave to mark his death.

He was very proud to be your Sergeant, and I know he was content to die in battle. I am grateful he didn't suffer. Knowing that has put my mind at rest.

And it was signed *Sadie Henshaw.*

Officers wrote letters to the families of those who were killed in action. It was one of the duties they took pride in—and one that also left deep scars of guilt as well. It was not an easy thing, sending men to their deaths, day after day, with no respite. Some officers handled that guilt better than others, but it was still there.

But of all the letters Lawrence Minton had written, of all the responses that he must have received in four years of war, why had he kept this one, and apparently read it over and over again?

God forgive me.

But this was the Mons road in 1914, not Paris in 1919.

What did Sergeant Henshaw have to do with the present?

I slipped the letter back amongst the conference documents, and went on with my search.

On top of the tall chest were a watch, inscribed to Lawrence from his late father, a signet ring with what appeared to be the family crest, and a small velvet case holding a silver picture frame. Inside was a photograph of a couple smiling for the camera, but no identifying initials or names on the back. The man and woman looked vaguely familiar, and I realized that these must have been the Lieutenant's parents, taken before his father's death. In the top drawer was a map, and I recognized it as a stained, battered sector map from the war. A heavy black ink circle marked a crossroads village. I tried to pick out something that might tell me where this crossroads was, and finally decided that it was on the coast close by the Belgian border.

I began to hurry, afraid I'd taken too long already, but a quick survey of the room and its other contents added nothing to what I'd already learned. But I did find there were two brandy bottles by the bed, and an empty one beneath it.

With a sigh of frustration, I slipped back into the passage, shutting the door behind me.

I'd just reached the top of the stairs when I heard voices below, and there was Lawrence, just starting up, still speaking over his shoulder to Marina. I quickly turned and started down, as if I had been coming that way all along.

He glared at me as we passed, and I gave him a brisk "Good morning" even though it was closer to noon.

Marina came to the foot of the stairs, wearing her coat and gloves, a warm hat on her head. "I was just going to market, to see what I could find. You shouldn't be cleaning your own room, Bess. It isn't right."

I smiled. "I've had to clean my quarters wherever I was posted. There was no one to do it for me."

Wistful, she said, "We had maids. I miss them. I wasn't sure where they'd find other employment, but there was no money to pay them here. I try to keep the rooms tidy, take out the cinders, sweep the passages. The ones we don't use I try to keep closed off. I don't know what I'd tell my mother, if she should appear at the door this afternoon."

"How was Lawrence this morning?"

"Not in the best of tempers. He reminded me of my brothers after a night out on the town."

I hadn't had brothers, but I remembered a night in Suffolk when my father and Simon had come back from *reconnoitering*, as they called it, and reeking of whiskey. It had been in a good cause, but a cavalry of elephants wouldn't have roused them from their sleep as soon as they made it to their beds.

That thought reminded me of Simon and Scotland. Pushing it aside, I made myself say to Marina, "Shall I go with you? I could help bring home more coal."

She shook her head. "There won't be any to buy. The supply is dwindling."

"As long as we can cook, we'll be all right."

"I just told Lawrence that we couldn't build a fire in the parlor today. He wasn't pleased. He mentioned something about going back to Paris. I couldn't tell if he was serious or not."

"I expect it was a threat. He didn't look well, on the stairs just now."

"He isn't. And he smelled of brandy. I looked—he's taken several bottles from the cellar."

"Has he?" I asked. "Well, better than laudanum."

"He asked me this morning if I really believed the other two vials were poisoned. I asked him if he remembered how ill he was. He shuddered. I don't think he'll risk it."

"That's one good thing, then."

She went on her way, and I turned back to the stairs. I had just reached the top step when Lawrence Minton all but sprang out at me. He'd been hiding just around the corner.

My first thought was, *I'm here on the stairs, and Marina is gone.*

Our eyes met.

For an instant I froze. I could almost swear that the same thought had occurred to him.

Quickly pushing past him so that I was away from any attempt at shoving me down the steps, I wondered how much of our conversation he'd heard.

Instead, he said, "Have you been in my room?"

I wasn't prepared for the question. Calling on my training, I retorted, "Are you asking me to clean it? You heard Marina, there's no money for maids. I'll be happy to bring you the mop and pail when I've finished."

"I waited. You didn't come down to breakfast. Marina told me you had had yours earlier. What have you been up to?"

Sighing in exasperation, I said, "And what is there in your room that I would wish to see? Really?"

"What did Marina tell you? *She* went in and removed the other two vials of laudanum."

"Should I ask her to bring them back?"

Confused by the tone I'd taken, he said, "They're poisoned."

"What are you so eager to hide from? You came to Paris of your own accord, to work with the conference talks. Your mother told me you were fluent in French and German. I'm sure they're in need of trustworthy translations. Why aren't you there, instead of making Marina shop and cook and clean for you like a scullery maid?"

The unexpected attack brought him up sharply.

He stared at me, suspicion and something else in his gaze. I stepped back, out of reach.

"I didn't ask her to bring me here," he said, angry and no longer hiding it.

"Well, if she hadn't, the regiment would have cashiered you by now. You owe her far more than you will ever be able to repay. That is, if you care about your future."

"Go to hell," he said rudely, and stalked off, slamming his door.

I looked after him. He'd been accustomed to browbeating Marina. That was precisely why I'd chosen to take a different tack with him. And he didn't quite know how to deal with that.

Was that why he'd caught me on the stairs, where I was vulnerable? He had been just above me, he could have sent me down backward, and I'd have been badly hurt if not killed. Then what had stopped him? The fact that Marina would find me there when she came home from market?

The Lieutenant could have carried me to an unused bedroom and left me there, told Marina any story he'd had time to think of, and then urged her to leave with him for Paris. Would she have believed him if he told her I'd already stormed out?

Who would know or guess where I was?

That was something to consider. I'd been told by a policeman long ago that the first murder was the hardest to commit. But after that, all normal human restraint was gone, and the second or third were easier.

My little pistol was in my valise. It was time to carry it with me.

But to be fair, he hadn't tried to push me, had he? Even though I'd stepped out of reach, he *could* have managed it if he'd waited there, intending to do just that.

Then why hadn't he gone through with it?

I went ahead and cleaned my room. The pigeon watched me as I wiped up the droppings from the floor around his box. I thought he looked better. Although I hadn't been trained to judge the health of a bird, his eyes seemed brighter and he appeared to be interested in what I was doing.

When I reached toward his box to touch his head, he bobbed and moved—and his wing was no longer awkwardly held. I had never understood how it was that pigeons could remember their way home, wherever they'd been sent from. Yes, they had a special skill, just as the birds in our garden seemed to know how to find their way back every spring, but these homing pigeons could find not only the county and village, but the specific spot where their box was set up. No matter how far away they were set free.

And that brought me round to another train of thought. *Our garden . . .*

Well, it wasn't really. It was my parents' garden. Before the war, a young woman my age would have married and had the first of her children by now. She would have a garden of her own, a husband, a family, responsibilities.

I'd wanted to stay with the Queen Alexandra's, because there were the wounded who hadn't healed— might never heal—and I hadn't wanted to desert them. But even in the clinic where I'd been posted, several of my fellow Sisters had already been summoned to London to speak with HQ about their future. The Service had grown enormously to cope with the war wounded. Thousands of us where there had been only hundreds before August of 1914. Was I to stay on and make this my future? I was good enough, my skills would be wanted. But was this what I wanted?

I shoved that thought aside. It could wait until I'd dealt with Matron's request. But that brought me an equally unpleasant consideration. What was I going to tell *her*?

And when?

When, I told myself, I could tell her the truth she claimed she wanted to hear. I owed it to her to be sure what I told her *was* the truth.

Chapter 7

Marina's marketing went better than she had hoped. She found cheese and eggs, and some apples that we could stew, a small tin of milk, and half a chicken, as well as some vegetables. The first thing I saw as she came through the door, smiling triumphantly, was the loaf of bread. My pigeon would have the heels tonight.

"A lorry has just come from Paris," she told me as I relieved her of her burdens and led the way toward the kitchen. "There was even a little coffee—the wartime coffee, but it will be better than nothing. I also found three tins of tomatoes and a bit of cheese in a crock." She paused long enough to divest herself of her coat and hat and purse, then caught up with me. "There will be another lorry tomorrow. It's bringing coal, so they say in the shop."

We sorted her purchases rather like children opening gifts on Boxing Day, and chatted as we worked.

The cooker provided the only warmth in the house, and we were content to sit there when we'd finished. She had some mending to do, and I took part of it to keep her company.

Lawrence found us there.

She looked up at him, setting aside the pillow slip she was working with. "There's a little coffee. Would you care for a cup? It's mostly chicory, of course, but it's warming."

"Yes. All right," he said rather ungraciously, and went to stand by the cooker, holding his hands out to the heat.

I declined, but she made two cups and handed him one, with a little milk to help with the strong taste. He wrapped his hands around the cup, took a sip, discovered it was still too hot to drink. Still holding it, he looked at me.

"It would be easier if you left," he said. "Two mouths to feed is difficult enough."

I didn't tell him that his mother's money was paying for what Marina had found.

"Or you could go back to Paris, draw your pay for attending the Conference, and Marina could return to her teaching."

He made a face. "I can't go back to Paris. I've had enough of being spied upon."

Who spied on him there? The police?

When neither Marina nor I responded, he added, "I don't know who to trust. Madame. The others in her house. Dr. Moreau. They tell me they're concerned for me, but all they want to do is spy." He took a deep breath. "Now it's my mother, spying. Why can't they leave me alone?"

I said, "Perhaps they're worried about you. Perhaps they care enough to want to help."

"Help me?" he asked derisively. "I'm past all help."

"As long as you believe that," Marina said gently, "it will be true. There is a priest at the church. He's an old man, he knew my parents when we lived here in St. Ives. Will you speak to him, if I ask him to come?"

"A priest can do nothing for me but damn me. And I've done that for myself."

There was such pain in his voice that I winced. "The Church believes in redemption," I replied quietly. "At least let him come and speak to you."

"Another spy?" He drained his coffee cup, put it by the sink, and strode toward the door. "You'd like that, wouldn't you?"

"The confessional is sacred," Marina began. "Whatever you tell him—"

But he was already gone.

She looked at me, despair in her eyes. "I wish I knew what it is he has done. He was a good man before this happened. How terrible can it be?"

The image of Lawrence Minton grappling with the carpet came vividly back to me. "I'm not sure he knows what's wrong. It's only in his nightmares that he is able to face it."

"Soldiers must do horrible things, everyone knows that. They're sent out to kill. He can't find shame in that."

"You told me he was very much himself one evening—and then he didn't appear the next morning, or the next after that. What do you think happened to him after he left you? What changed him overnight?"

She shook her head. "I wish I knew. It was the end of February. The twenty-first, I believe. We parted as friends, he arranged to meet me in the morning. When I found him a week later, he was like this, distraught, not himself."

"Could he have met someone else, after seeing you to your door?"

"It's possible." She frowned. "He said something one evening—not that evening, but another. I told him we should have an early supper, because he seemed to be so tired. I thought he'd been working too hard, preparing copies of documents for the delegates. And he said, it wasn't that, his duties were supportable. Only, he found it hard to sleep. Then he made light of it, saying that peace always came with a cost. And he made a joke about the French wanting revenge not only for this war but also for the last one, a generation ago, and I knew he didn't want to talk about himself. And I was busy at school, and I gave it no more thought."

Why was sleep eluding him?

Of course it could even have been a lie, something he thought Marina wouldn't question him too closely about. And she hadn't.

But I thought it must be true, even then. What had made it worse now?

"Should I have pursued the sleeplessness?" Marina was asking anxiously. "Was it because I was so busy at school that he didn't confide in me? Perhaps he was being kind, even though this mattered to him very much. If I'd asked more questions, he might have seen that I was willing to help."

"I don't know that it was something he wished to tell you. Or he would have."

Unconvinced, she said, "How can I be sure?"

Whatever it was, he couldn't very well draw someone like Marina into his troubles.

And following his lead, it was also my duty to keep her safe.

"Perhaps it had to do with a woman—a nursing Sister, or someone he'd met in the war. Even when he was on leave in Paris. I can't believe he'd wish to discuss such things with you."

Mollified, she said, "I hadn't considered that."

Rising, she set aside her mending. "I'll be quite a grand cook, by the time I return to Paris." And she rattled pots and pans as she went about preparing the next meal.

I was rather reluctant to leave Marina alone with Lawrence, given his current mood. I wasn't convinced he'd hurt her, but there are more ways to hurt someone than physical blows.

And yet I was in a hurry to return to Paris. I didn't know if I'd heard yet from my father, but I hoped he'd found something to tell me. Now I wasn't quite sure how to go about that without telling him more than I wished him to know at present. I couldn't very well accuse Lieutenant Minton of something, with no more proof than a nightmare. Even if it had been quite so vivid.

What I needed to learn was almost impossible to find out: if there was a police case that hadn't been solved and that might fit into the dates Marina had given me. It was still proof of nothing, of course, unless there was a warrant out for the arrest of a British officer.

And then Marina had a nasty mishap, and all my plans had to be set aside.

She was preparing another stew, the best way to extend our meager resources, and when she turned to reach for some herbs to add to the dish, somehow she hit the handle of the pot. Desperate not to let it fall, she caught the other handle with the cloth in her hand, steadied it in time—and her right arm touched the hot edge of the cooker.

I heard her scream, and not knowing what had happened, I raced down the stairs ready to face whatever was going on in the kitchen.

I found her there alone, clutching her arm, pale, and nearly on the verge of collapse.

Putting my own arm around her shoulders, I guided her to a chair, and as she tried to tell me what had happened, I carefully turned her hand so that I could judge the damage.

It was a nasty burn.

"Do you have anything to treat this?" I asked.

Shaking too much to speak, she pointed to a drawer of the dresser against the far wall. I found ointment and dressings, but realized even as I took them out and went back to her that there was barely enough to use now, much less later. What's more I didn't know how old the ointment was, and if it was still effective.

As the shock began to wear off, the pain set in. I worked as gently as I could.

I was finishing tying the thin dressing so that it wouldn't stick to the raw skin, and I said, "We'll need more for tonight. Is there an apothecary shop here in the village?"

"It—it's still closed up. The fam-family hasn't returned."

I tried to hide my concern. She needed medical care.

"A doctor then. He should be able to supply what we need. But you should rest a little. Let me help you up the stairs, and then I'll finish the stew."

"There's no doctor. He was killed in the war. He was a friend of my father's. And I'd rather stay here. It—it's warmer."

I busied myself with the pot, adding the carrots and onions and potatoes she had already prepared. I said casually, so as not to frighten her too much, "We can travel into Paris tomorrow. There's a doctor. Lawrence mentioned him—he's a friend of Lawrence's mother. He'll see to this."

"No. We can't leave Lawrence alone in the house," she told me firmly. "He might do anything."

"Marina, I must be able to attend to your arm. It will become infected."

"But you have everything—it's where our cook kept things for burns and cuts."

"We need more—and fresh ointment would be best. I have no idea, this could have been sitting there for four years or more."

"No," she insisted. "I'll be fine. You'll see."

But what I could see was how pale she was, and I thought she might soon be sick from the pain. Leaving the pot to simmer, I crossed to where she was sitting, and knelt by her chair. "Marina, you must listen. That's a serious burn, it will leave a scar if you don't take care of it."

Just then Lawrence came into the room, asking if there was any coffee left. As if he hadn't heard her scream.

Stopping short as he took in the scene in front of him—Marina looking ill, the bandaging on her arm, my concern—he said, "What's happened?"

"An accident. She's burned her arm. There's no apothecary in St. Ives, and no doctor. She needs better care."

"I'm fine. Truly," she objected.

But Lawrence was staring at her arm. "She's right," he said after a moment. "You have to be sensible about this, Marina."

Surprised by the unexpected sympathy in his voice, she looked up at him.

His attention still on her bandaging, he said to me, "Could you go into Paris and find what she needs? There's a doctor, Moreau is his name. He'll help. Tell him I sent you."

When I didn't answer straightaway, he said, "It's early enough. You could be home by dark."

It was my turn to be surprised.

"I don't know—" I replied, frowning. I could tell that he was sober this morning. And glancing quickly at Marina's face, I could see that she was taken in by his concern.

"Look," he was saying. "This is partly my fault. I'll keep an eye on her. If you hurry, you could make the next train."

Still I hesitated. This turnabout was confusing. He was neither drunk nor using the opiates. And I caught the faintest glimpse of the man he must have been, at one time. The man Marina was willing to help.

A flush appeared in his cheeks. "What's wrong, why are you standing there?"

"I'm not sure—" I began, but he said, "Look at her. The sooner you go, the sooner you'll be back. That dressing will need changing often, she'll need something for the pain, something to keep the burn from drying out."

He was telling me what I already knew. "If I went to a doctor—if I brought back something for the pain, will you use it too?"

"No! What sort of man do you take me for?" he demanded.

But I'd only seen the selfish, angry Lawrence Minton. I wasn't sure I believed this change.

"It will be all right," Marina said. "Hurry, Bess, you'll miss that train—"

"I'll go. But I hold you responsible for looking after her—and that stew. She mustn't go back near the cooker."

"I swear to you, I'll do what's best for her. Now go."

I came back to the kitchen before leaving the house, looking in on Marina and making certain that Lawrence Minton wasn't scheming to be rid of me. But he had gone back up to his room.

"I'll return as soon as possible," I assured her. "Are you sure you'll be all right?"

"Yes. But hurry. I can't tell you how badly this hurts."

And with good reason.

I went to the stairs, calling up to the Lieutenant, "I thought you were going to stay with Marina?"

I heard a door open and close, and then he was coming down the stairs, his arms full of blankets and pillows. "She can lie down for a while. It might help."

"That's kind of you. Yes. I should have thought of that."

He nodded, rounded the newel post, and headed for the kitchen.

I turned and went out the door.

My first stop was Dr. Moreau's surgery.

He was immediately sympathetic, filling a satchel with dressings, baths for the burn, ointments, even a small bottle of laudanum. Everything I might require.

"I don't need to tell you—if there are changes, bring this friend of yours here. I'll see that she's given the best of care."

I thanked him, grateful that he hadn't asked more questions, and promised him that I'd do as he suggested.

And with the satchel in my hand, I left. But it was still three hours before the next train. I could at least go to the hotel where my father was staying, and ask for him.

I'd just rounded a corner when a man's voice said, "Ma'am? Could I carry that for you?"

I turned to see the American I'd met in Calais.

"Hallo," I replied. "I can manage. But thank you!"

He caught up with me. "Yes, ma'am, but my mother taught me to help wherever I could, and I can't be easy walking beside you, while you're toting that bag." He reached down and gently took it from my hand. Without making a scene, struggling with him over who was to carry it, I let him have his way. "Now," he said, smiling down at me, "where may I escort you, ma'am?"

I gave him the name of the hotel, but he shook his head. "You shouldn't have to walk that far." Turning, he signaled to a taxi, and before I quite knew what I was doing, I was seated next to him inside. "I don't mean to be high-handed, ma'am, but that's a far piece."

"I'm quite used to walking," I said. But in fact, I'd tried to save some money by walking, because I'd used so much of Matron's money to feed us and keep the house in St. Ives warm. Or at least a few rooms where I could.

He had a charming grin, this tall flyer. I could imagine half the women he met were enchanted by it.

I didn't intend to be.

"I insist on paying for this taxi," I told him as we headed toward the hotel.

"No, ma'am. I have standards."

"So do I," I retorted.

"Yes, ma'am, I know you do, but my mother would never forgive me if she thought I'd taken a lady's money."

More than a little amused as well as exasperated, I said, "Do you always have your way?"

"No, ma'am. That wouldn't be either polite or kind. But as I told you, I have standards." He'd taken off his hat when he met me, and he was holding it in his hand now, but he made a little bow of sorts and said, "My name is Clifford Jackson. Everyone calls me Cliff. I'd take it as an honor if you'd do the same."

"Sister Crawford," I said firmly. "And here is my hotel, Captain Jackson. Thank you for escorting me here."

That grin again. "Yes, ma'am. My pleasure."

He helped me out of the taxi, handed me Dr. Moreau's satchel, and watched me safely inside. As if there were heathen hordes waiting their chances of attacking me.

Amused, I smothered a smile, and made my way across the lobby to the desk.

I asked for Colonel Crawford, but the clerk shook his head. "I believe he's out this morning, Sister. Would you care to leave a message?

But I'd left one, and according to Dr. Moreau, my father hadn't replied. So far.

Thanking him, I told him I'd be happy to wait, in the event the Colonel returned.

I sat there an hour or more, without even a glimpse of him. Sighing, I ordered tea, paying for it out of my own funds, and was surprised to be served a cup of real tea. It was such a pleasure, I let myself enjoy it slowly.

When my father still hadn't returned, I decided I couldn't wait any longer, and I left, letting the doorman find me another taxi.

We were just driving away when I glimpsed a news-boy's placard. **ANOTHER DROWNING VICTIM**, it proclaimed in bold black ink.

I sat back in the taxi, staring at nothing. But I could see again what Lawrence had been doing at the foot of the stairs. And my own odd interpretation of a washer-woman bending over a tub, scrubbing linens.

It was grasping at straws, I knew that. But what if—?

I said to the driver, "Are there many drownings in Paris?"

"*Bien sur*," he replied with a shrug. "The Seine is there."

As if that explained everything. But in a way, it did. "Murder or suicide?"

"It makes no difference to the dead," he told me.

But it might to the living.

I asked him to drive me to the nearest police station. It would be close, making the next train back to St. Ives, but I had to know. Now, before I lost my courage.

I walked in and asked the officer at the desk if I might speak to an Inspector.

The man was very polite, wishing to know my business here, and I told him that I'd come to inquire about any drownings that were unsolved.

That surprised him, got his attention, and his manner changed as well.

"Could you explain further, Sister?"

I had prepared my story so quickly, I was afraid it was full of holes. But I was here, now, I had to go through with it and trust that it didn't fail me. "I was sitting on the train from Calais, sleeping a little, as I'd had an early start. And something in the conversation between the two men sharing my compartment caught my attention. They were French, I believe. And I may have misinterpreted what they were saying. But it had to do with someone being drowned in the Seine. It made me quite uncomfortable, and I didn't know what I should do about it. But my conscience wouldn't allow me to let the matter drop."

"Could you describe these two men?"

I had his attention.

"They were not in uniform. They appeared to be quite respectable. I'd put their ages at forty, perhaps, and from the way they were dressed, I rather thought they were respectable men of business. Until I heard what they were saying."

Ten minutes later, I was sitting in the office of one Inspector Martine and repeating my story. He was perhaps fifty, a healed scar across one cheek, and sharp brown eyes that seemed to see right through me.

I was beginning to wish I'd never set foot in the police station. And yet how else could I find out what I needed to know? I folded my hands in my lap, ignoring the temptation to clutch them, and when I was asked, I repeated my story.

He listened carefully, then he wanted to know more about the timing hinted at in this conversation I'd overheard.

I told him it had taken place some few weeks earlier. "They said something about the water being so cold. That it would hasten death."

He reached for a file in the basket on his desk, opened it, and looked at something in it.

"You understand," he said, "that we have any number of suicides. Women who have nowhere to turn. Refugees who have lost hope. Men who feel they have nothing left to live for. This is not a very happy time for many people, in spite of the fact the war has ended. Life must go on, you understand. And sometimes, it simply doesn't."

"Yes, I am aware," I said, thinking of patients, amputees who had come from the Welsh mines and who had preferred death over pity and charity, when there had been no work to return to.

The Inspector looked sharply at me. "Yes," he said after a moment. "I believe you do." Returning to his file, he went on. "We have seventeen men and twelve women who died by drowning in the past six weeks. In five of these cases, there are three men and two women who might have been the victims of foul play."

Five? I'd expected one or two.

"Did the conversation you overheard tell you whether these men were speaking of a woman or a man?"

"Sadly, no. Perhaps earlier in their conversation they had said something. But I wasn't paying attention then."

"I am sorry to hear it."

"Could you tell me the ages of the dead?"

"One of the men was fifty years old. The others are thought to be twenty-five and thirty-two. The women were young, possibly eighteen and thirty-one."

"Have you identified them?"

"The fifty-year-old, yes. The other four, no."

It was proving difficult to know which—or if any— of these five people might have known Lieutenant Minton. Why any one of them might have been his victim, I couldn't begin to guess. I wasn't even sure he'd killed anyone! Still, here were five people who had died violently and been found in the river.

Inspector Martine was sorting through what appeared to be photographs of the dead. He said, "I hesitate to show these to you. They are not pleasant to see. But perhaps since you are in the Queen Alexandra's you will not be too disturbed. And looking might help you remember some detail."

He gave them to me one at a time, allowing me an opportunity to study each face.

I hadn't seen many drowning victims in the course of my duties. But I had seen enough to know what to expect. Pale, flaccid faces, all expression wiped away, the hair wet and tangled, nothing to show how the person might have worn it in life, how it framed the face or was combed away from it. Indeed, it was difficult to tell whether it was brown or black or red, or even fair.

The older man, the one who was fifty, had deep lines in his face, while the young woman, who could have been eighteen, had a bruise on her forehead. I looked at her again. She might have been Marina at that age. Even in death, the drying hair, which seemed to be fair, curled a little by one cheek. Somehow it made her death seem more terrible.

"No families, no information about their killers, or why they had to die?" I asked as I handed them back.

"Nothing. It is disturbing."

"Was there—could there have been a carpet with the bodies? In the river?"

"A carpet?" He raised his brows at that. "No, Sister, there was not. Why do you ask?"

"I believe the two men had been talking about a rug or carpet shortly before."

He shook his head. "None of these victims resemble the two men on the train?"

"Sadly, no." I was beginning to wish I'd never brought up the two men. But how else could I explain why I wished to know about drownings? "Can you give me dates of death? It might help."

He read them from the sheet. There had been two the night of the twenty-first. One of the men and the eighteen-year-old girl. I couldn't imagine how either of them had known Lieutenant Minton.

"How long will you be in Paris, Sister Crawford?"

"I'm not sure. It depends on how quickly I can finish the duties that brought me here."

"And they are?"

"Surveying the last of our facilities here in France. Their needs, the number of patients still there, how soon they can travel to England—how soon each clinic or hospital can be shut down, and how that will be managed." Since speaking to my father, I'd had time to think what my duties might consist of. I had the information ready now, on the tip of my tongue if I should be asked. I didn't care to lie, but I hadn't expected to be put on the spot by questions.

"Yes, I see. Will you think about what you overheard, and if you remember any details that might be of use to us, will you come again and speak to me?"

I promised, thanked him, and left.

Once outside the police station and far enough down the street from it, I took a deep breath of relief. But the question was, What could I do with what I'd learned? It wasn't as if I could sit Lawrence Minton down in the parlor and ask him which of these two he might have killed. I wasn't even sure it was the Seine, or within the city itself. Still, Marina had told me he was making plans to buy a birthday gift for his mother. Whatever had happened, it had taken place over the next few days, if not precisely that very night, after he'd left Marina. That suggested it had happened in Paris. And therefore it had to be the Seine, if he'd drowned someone. There weren't all that many opportunities to drown someone during the war. If only I'd known the exact date and not have had to guess.

Sighing, I wished I could step into a shop for a cup of tea. But this wasn't England.

I walked for about twenty minutes, heading in the general direction of the Gare. The satchel of dressings and medicines was growing heavy, and a wind was coming up, forcing me to put up a hand to hold my cap in place. Turning a corner, I nearly bumped into the person coming the other way.

"*Pardonnez*—" I began, apologizing in French.

"Bess?"

I looked up. It was my father.

"Hallo," I said, rapidly adjusting my thinking.

"I've had the devil of a time at the talks. There's been no opportunity to write to you. My evening is free. Have dinner with me."

Oh, dear.

"I'm so sorry—I have a burn patient I'm attending. I've just got more medicines from Dr. Moreau, and I dare not miss my train . . ." I stopped as I realized that I was all but babbling.

He laughed. I knew that laugh too. How many times had I heard it when I was trying desperately to keep him in the dark about some indiscretion.

Taking my arm, he said, "There's a hotel just two streets away where I could take you for tea. Or what they call tea. God knows what the leaves actually are. You can tell me there."

"My train—" I began.

"I have a staff car at my disposal, Bess. I can take you anywhere. And faster than the train, very likely."

He was already ushering me along the street toward the hotel, and I had no choice but to follow him.

The street was far too busy to carry on much of a conversation, and so I waited until we were settled in the handsome and nearly empty dining room of a hotel where many of the delegates were staying.

My father ordered tea and sandwiches, then turned to me with that affable smile that said, *I'm not judging— but I am curious.*

My mother called it his fishing expression, patiently waiting for the unsuspecting trout to take his line.

"What on earth have you been up to, my dear?"

"As I've told you, I'm doing a survey of clinics still open—"

"None of which, as I understand it, are left here in Paris. Yet here *you* are."

Capitulating—I knew I was going to lose anyway, and a surreptitious glance at the case clock I could just see through the French doors to Reception told me that time was flying by—I said, "I was asked by someone in my Service to handle a matter that required both discretion and nursing skills. I really shouldn't tell you more. I made a promise, you see. But the person who asked me is both respectable and known to you." Remembering that Captain Barkley was in Paris, I added quickly, "I'm not in any trouble." *I'm just living in the same house with a possible murderer . . .*

Our tea and sandwiches arrived, and I realized suddenly that I was famished. And then I remembered how hard Marina worked to prepare what little we could find in the market, and I felt a surge of guilt as well.

It wasn't strong enough to prevent me from eating the sandwiches I took from the plates. Egg and cress and—of all things, thin slices of ham. I couldn't remember when I had last enjoyed ham.

My father said, "Some of the Americans are billeted here. The food is better, they bring it in."

And the tea—ah, the tea was real and delicious and hot.

The delicacies hadn't distracted him from our discussion. He went on, as I tried to enjoy my food, "Is it Helena Minton you've been asked to assist?"

I nearly choked on my cress sandwich.

"I'm not surprised," he said, as he kindly patted me on the back. "We knew Helena in Delhi. Your mother and I. Her husband was attached to the Foreign Office there. A fine man, Minton, I was sorry to hear later that he'd died of the fever that had plagued him for years. I haven't seen her for some time, of course, but I know that her son Lawrence joined the regiment just before the war. Wants to make a career of the Army, apparently. But I've heard—not officially of course—that he's been ill."

My mind reeling, I said, "Is he, indeed?"

My father regarded me sympathetically. "I've retired from the regiment, but that doesn't mean I don't keep an eye on what's happening there. Major Webb is a good friend."

Major *Webb*? Had my father been spying on Lawrence? On me?

I opened my mouth to answer him and took a sip of tea instead.

Then I said, feeling a little less at sea, "I gave my word."

"Yes, darling, which is why I'm telling you what I know instead. So that you won't have to break your promise. But what I need to know is, have you found Lawrence Minton? I can only do so much to save his career, but I'm willing to help in any way I can."

What could I tell him that wouldn't cause more trouble?

Yes, I've found him—he's been addicted to laudanum, but someone tried to poison him by putting an emetic in the vial, and now he's drinking brandy, but I actually suspect he may be riddled with guilt, but I don't have any real idea why . . . just suspicions that may be wrong.

That would really do wonders for Lawrence Minton's future. Not that I was certain he had one, if he was a murderer. The thing was, I couldn't hurt Matron by telling the Colonel Sahib what I believed, not until I'd returned to England and reported to her first.

My father must have understood my dilemma. He'd dealt with men all his life and he had been very good at reading them. Simon Brandon was an excellent example.

Simon . . .

I wanted to ask the Colonel Sahib about him.

While I was still thinking about that, my father said gently, "All right then. You've found him. But you aren't particularly happy with what you've learned." He nodded as an American officer passed through the dining room, then brought his attention back to me. "How can I help?"

"I don't know," I said, keeping my voice steady with an effort. I wished with all my heart I could confide in him and ask his advice. "How can I turn to you when—" I broke off.

"No," he answered quietly. "Of course you can't. Let me ask instead, is there something that can be done? If there is, your mother would insist we try."

He was right, she would.

"However, the question that only you can answer is this. Is there still time? Is it even possible to help him? Whatever it is that's wrong."

"I am trying," I said carefully. "I have done what I could."

He considered me for a moment. "I must know," he said. "Are you in any danger?"

Was I? I remembered standing on the stairs and realizing how easy it would have been for Lawrence to shove me down them. It was likely that if he knew the whole truth, my father would believe I was at risk.

"I don't think so," I said finally. "But if I ever believe that I am, I'll tell you."

"Fair enough." He looked at his watch. "And we must hurry if you are to be at the station in time."

We'd finished our food, I drank the last sip of my tea as he paid for the meal, and then we were out the door, an orderly summoning a taxi for the Colonel and the lady with him.

We made it to the Gare on time. My father wished to purchase my ticket for me, but if he did, he'd know where I was staying. It wouldn't take him long to discover which house it was.

I thanked him, and while he held my satchel for me, I hurried to purchase it for myself. When I came back, he handed me the satchel.

"Was it Minton who is burned?"

"No," I said with a clear conscience on this matter at least, "nor was it anything to do with him. A kitchen accident."

He nodded. And then the train was coming, and I had to go.

"Simon," I called over my shoulder. "He's in Scotland. Army business?"

"In Scotland?" my father shouted back. "I've no idea—"

And then I was aboard and the train was pulling out.

It was only later that I realized that the Colonel Sahib had only to go to the ticket kiosk and ask where this particular train was heading. Of course St. Ives wasn't the only stop on this line. But my father had run a regiment, guided his men into battle, and brought them back again. I didn't think it would trouble him very much to find out which village I'd bought my ticket for.

I sat back in my seat, catching my breath as I tried to remember if I'd said anything else that my father might be able to translate into knowledge—and even worry. There was no way of knowing.

Chapter 8

The satchel seemed to grow heavier with every step as I walked up toward the house.

I was worried about Marina's arm and about Lawrence's haunted memory. And whether or not I was doing the right thing for both of them.

It was late, nearly dusk, and the street was empty except for an elderly priest who walked past me, nodding. And it occurred to me that my presence in the village might not only be whispered about but accepted as regularizing the situation in the Lascelles household. A young single woman, a British officer—did the villagers know that about him?—living together was improper. A nurse in attendance indicated illness, which was more acceptable. After all, villagers saw

Marina at the shops, but as far as I knew, Lawrence hadn't set foot outside the house.

Still mulling this over, I went up the steps and lifted the knocker.

No one came to answer the door.

I knocked again, and a third time. If Marina was in her room and Lawrence in his, it was possible they hadn't heard me.

I was just about to knock a fourth time when the door opened.

Marina was standing there, cradling her arm, her face drawn and tearstained.

Oh, dear God, I thought. *What has he done now?*

Summoning a smile, I stepped inside, and Marina closed the door behind me.

"I've got everything I need to care for your arm, and even something for the pain. I'm so sorry I couldn't have got back sooner—"

She wasn't listening.

"What's wrong?" I asked, breaking off what I'd been about to say. Ushering her into the cold front room, I shut the door behind us and then got her into a chair. "What has he done, Marina? Tell me."

She stared at me. Then said in a whisper, "He's gone."

"What?" The way she'd said it, the look on her face, I could think of only one thing—that he'd somehow found a way to kill himself while I was away.

I knelt by her chair, taking her good hand in mine. "Darling, what's happened?"

"I was in the kitchen, I thought he was in his room. He'd promised to look in on me again, and after a while, when he didn't come back, I managed to warm a little of the stew. It wasn't easy, one-handed, but I managed without spilling too much. He'd been kind, he'd made up a bed for me and put a pillow under my arm—he'd come again, to look in on me—I thought I'd ask if he wanted a bowl."

I braced myself for what was to come. "And did he?" I asked.

She shook her head. "He wasn't there—he wasn't anywhere in the house. I looked. And when I went back to his room, I looked in the armoire. And he'd taken everything with him, valise, clothes—everything. And he had gone. I don't know where. Or even when it was he'd left. I sat there in his room for nearly an hour, hoping—thinking he might come back. That he'd only tried to frighten me. But he didn't."

I swallowed what I was about to say, and instead asked, "Are you sure?"

"Bess—why would I lie?" She looked at me, hurt in her eyes. "Go and see for yourself, if you don't believe me."

"I do believe you," I said. "Of course I do. I'm—just as shocked as you are. That's all."

She nodded. "I didn't expect—he knew you were gone, he knew I was in pain. But I never thought he'd use this opportunity to slip away. Without a *word*."

"Perhaps he's gone back to Paris. To his flat. Perhaps he's come to his senses."

She stared at me, then took her hand away. "What if he hasn't? What if he's done something awful."

I realized she meant that he might have killed himself.

"He was more himself this morning," I reminded her.

"Yes. I saw that. Perhaps that's why he left. He didn't want us to find—him."

"Let me go and have a look." I glanced at the hearth. She was cold, shivering, and there was a little of our precious hoard of coal in the scuttle. "But first we need a little warmth, don't you think?" I got up and began to lay a fire in the grate. When I touched it with a match from the mantelpiece jar, the tinder caught. I watched it for a moment, to be sure, and then stood up.

"Sit here and keep an eye on the hearth," I said. "I'll be back as quickly as I can."

I left her there, went up to his room, and saw that she was right. He'd taken everything. Drawers and armoire were empty, the bed tidily made, the room tidy as well. It was as if he'd never been here . . .

Still, I searched every room on the floor, then the attics, then went down to the kitchen.

The bowl of stew was still on the table, where Marina had left it. The cooker was cold, but when I went to the cellar, I saw that several other bottles of brandy were missing. I made certain the bottles of laudanum were still safely hidden as well. If he'd swallowed the contents of both, emetic or not, he'd be dead before it could take effect.

I didn't know whether to take comfort in that or not. Whether Lawrence intended to use the brandy to numb his mind, as he had here, or if it was Dutch courage for what he'd said all along he wanted to do.

The only room I hadn't looked into was mine.

Was he there?

It might have suited him to kill himself in my room, for me to find his body there, when I came back from Paris. It was the sort of thing he would have considered a final gesture after I'd come here and interfered.

I hurried up the stairs, walked down the unlit passage, and opened the door to my room.

I heard the flutter of wings in the darkness.

He'd frightened the pigeon but hadn't harmed it.

Fumbling for the lamp and matches, I finally got it lit, and held it up.

The pigeon had lit on the bedpost, teetering there as he watched me with his dark eyes.

But Lawrence Minton wasn't there. Dead—or alive.

The lamp's light picked up the white square on the mantelpiece, and I crossed the room to pick it up. An envelope with my name on it.

Setting the lamp down, I tore it open and started to read.

You were right. I'd asked too much of Marina, dear friend that she's been. I see that clearly now. I should have done this from the start, but I just didn't have the courage. I'll find it now. Somehow. Tell her how sorry I am for everything, and get her back to Paris and the teaching she adores. Tell my mother that I love her very much. And that I'm more sorry than I can say for the worry I've given her. She didn't deserve that either. That's just it, you see. I have failed all of them. And so I must make amends.

There was no signature.

I have failed all of them.

Who were these *all?*

Who else was he talking about? Was this, in his own fashion, his confession?

I didn't want Marina to see this letter. And so I put it back into the envelope and buried it deep amongst my clothes in the valise.

That done, I sat down and tried to think.

Would Lawrence come back here? To this house?

Somehow I didn't think so. If he failed at his intent of killing himself in remorse, this seemed to be the last place he'd come to. Facing Marina, facing me.

The more I thought about this, the more I realized what I must do.

Find him, if I could. If it wasn't too late.

And the sooner the better.

But what to do about Marina? And my other patient, the pigeon?

I'd think of something.

I'd been gone for some time. I met Marina starting up the stairs as I was coming down.

"I was beginning to worry," she said.

I smiled for her sake.

"I looked everywhere—to be sure he wasn't hiding, hoping to throw us off the scent, so to speak. And the laudanum is still there. That's a good sign, don't you think?"

I took her back to the front room. The meager fire was taking a little of the chill away, but I had brought a blanket with me and now I draped it around her shoulders.

"I think he's gone, just as you said," I told her. "And I don't think he'll be coming back. For all we know, this is a good sign. We must take it as that."

"If it was a good thing, he would have said goodbye," she told me. Her face was haggard.

"Would he have done? After the trouble he'd caused us? No, I have a feeling he was too ashamed."

Opening the satchel, I began to lay out the contents and proceeded to care for her burn. In spite of my earlier efforts, it was not looking very good.

As I worked, I said, "I spoke to Dr. Moreau. He's concerned about you. I think it might be for the best if I took you to his surgery. He might wish to keep you for a few days, to be sure there's no infection. And then you could return to your teaching."

I was making some of that up as I talked. But I was fairly certain I was on safe ground. Dr. Moreau would be happy to take her in. And I could search for Lieutenant Minton without worrying about her as well.

"But there's Lawrence. Where else would he go, if he can't cope on his own? He might come back here."

"Do you really believe he would admit he'd been wrong?"

She sighed. "I think it would be bad for him to believe we'd deserted him too."

"Then we can leave a message. Telling him that he need only get word to you, and you'd come back to St. Ives."

She wasn't convinced.

I said, "Never mind. There are a few eggs left, and a little cheese. I'll make an omelet for our dinner, shall I? Everything looks better on a full stomach."

I finished what I was doing, stood up, and regarded her arm. "It is very painful, isn't it?" I didn't wait for her answer. "There's something to help you sleep," I said. "Not too strong. Just enough to make it possible to rest." I tried to hide my own sense of urgency—I wanted to go back to Paris. Now. Before it was too late. There was a night train, it might be possible to have us packed up by then. But I could see Marina wasn't ready to give up on Lawrence Minton. That was admirable, I thought it was typical of her kind heart not to want to give up. And the last thing I wanted to do was make her think that he was in danger. After all, what could she *do*? It would only serve to cause her more grief.

It was my turn to sigh, but I suppressed it. "Stay warm. I'll bring your dinner here. You need to rest."

"I feel terrible," she told me. "If I hadn't told him I wished to lie down for a bit—maybe if I had kept an eye on him, he wouldn't have left as he has."

"It's not your fault, Marina. None of this is. You've done your very best. It's just that Lawrence didn't want our help after all. And perhaps he was right, perhaps he needed to stand up and deal with his problems, whatever they were. Who can say?"

I left her with that thought, prepared our dinner, and found her nodding by the fire when I brought it up to her. I'd had a good lunch, and so I gave her the lion's share of the meal. Then watched her eat with more appetite than I'd expected.

After I'd finished clearing away—with an eye toward leaving as early as possible the next morning—I got her to her room and into bed. Then I fed the last of the crusts to my pigeon. He looked healthy, he was using his wing as he should, and so I found a scrap of paper, noted that I'd found him in Paris, healed him, and was sending him on his way. He was nearly asleep when I attached that to the capsule on his leg. In the morning, I thought, I'd open the window and see if he'd go out of his own accord.

It was late when I went to bed, but I didn't sleep, not really. I'd doze, then come awake with worry. About Lawrence, about Marina, about the pigeon, even though I knew that he would not regard this as home, he'd go back to whatever place he knew. He was a soldier, after all . . .

Dawn saw me up and packed. I woke Marina at seven, and said, "There's really nothing for breakfast, but Dr. Moreau will feed us. We can look forward to that."

She had made up her mind not to go. And I couldn't leave her with that burn on her arm. She couldn't tend it herself.

It took me over an hour to convince her I was right, but she was still quite unhappy as she wrote a note for Lawrence and set it on the table by the door.

"How will he get in, to find it?" she asked forlornly.

"He'll find a way, you may be sure of that."

It required two trips to the station, bringing down our luggage, as Marina couldn't very well carry her own. But we made it before the next train, and the stationmaster helped us to board.

My last duty while Marina was writing her letter was to open the window of my room.

The pigeon had looked at it, hesitated, and then with a flurry of wings, flew up to the windowsill. He hesitated again, as if regaining his sense of direction. And after a moment, he flew off, heading east.

I felt a sadness as I watched him go. I wished I'd been able to heal Lawrence Minton as well. But I hadn't. I might well have made matters worse.

And what on earth was I to tell Matron, waiting in London for news?

I found a porter in the Gare, found a taxi outside the station, and soon we were on our way to the Moreau house.

I said quietly to Marina, "These are good people. But they know Lawrence's mother. Best not to mention him to them. His mother doesn't know what has happened, and until I have better news to give her, I would rather not have her upset just now. You understand?"

"You never said—"

"No. But I trust him as a doctor, he and his wife have a warm heart. They know I was staying with a friend, and you are that friend. You suffered a nasty burn and there is no doctor in your village. That's all anyone needs to know. For the moment."

"Does this mean—are you going to look for Lawrence?"

"I didn't wish to raise your hopes, Marina, I don't

even know him well enough to search in all the places he might have decided to use as his escape from us."

"But you believe he's alive? Why didn't you tell me this? It is such a relief, you can't know—"

"I do know that I might not find him, Marina. You must be prepared for that."

"Yes, yes, but you will try." There were tears in her eyes. "How could I return to my school, not knowing what had become of him? This is such a relief," she repeated.

We were only minutes away from the Moreau house. "Just remember, even if they ask, you must not tell them you know Lawrence. This is very important."

"Of course I'll remember." She sat back in her seat. "I hardly slept last night, trying to think what to do. Whether I should stay and wait, or go. I'm not in love with him, but I lost Pierre, my brother, and in a way, Lawrence has taken Pierre's place. Do you understand how that can be? When he was in trouble, I felt I had to do for him what I would have done for Pierre."

"And you did that admirably," I assured her. For she had done. Reaching into my bag, I handed her some francs. "When you are teaching again, you can repay me, and I'll see that Mrs. Minton is repaid as well. But you will need resources until then."

More than a little embarrassed, she took the francs

and thanked me, just as we drew up in front of the Moreau house. The driver helped us with our baggage, and then he was gone.

Taking a deep breath, I went to the door and knocked.

The maid who came to answer it looked at the two of us, looked at the valises at our feet, and said with a frown and French forthrightness, "Is Madame expecting you?"

I introduced Marina and added, "She is a patient of the doctor's. I've brought her here for continuing care."

She reluctantly let us step into the foyer and went to find the doctor. He took the spectacle of two women and all their baggage in stride, welcoming me, treating Marina solicitously, ushering us into his office.

"And this is my new patient?" he said, smiling.

"I must go about my duties, but I couldn't leave her alone. I hope you don't mind if I bring her to you, instead."

He was already helping her out of her coat, looking at the bandaged arm, nodding to me to indicate that he liked what he saw, and then he had her sitting in his surgery, cutting away the dressings, tut-tutting over what he saw beneath, and gently beginning to treat the wound. I watched him work, my professional interest strong, but also personally happy with the kind way he handled Marina.

When she protested over putting him out, he smiled and told her, "On the contrary, my dear, Sister Crawford knows how much I enjoy my work, and she has brought me an interesting challenge. We will do our best to see that this leaves no ugly scar on your arm. And you must stay with us while I do that, so that I can be sure there is no infection."

I was drawing my own breath of relief, when the door opened and Madame Moreau came flying in. "Bess, you have come back to us! I was put out with Michel yesterday when he didn't tell me you were here."

She embraced me warmly, a kiss on each cheek, then turned to Marina.

"And this is the friend, with whom you were visiting? Welcome, my dear. You don't know how wonderful it is to have young people about again." She winced as she took in the arm, which Dr. Moreau was about to cover lightly with gauze. "How painful that must be!"

Once more I performed the introductions, and she began speaking to Marina in French, welcoming her, making her feel at home.

It was almost too much for Marina. After the weeks she'd struggled alone to take care of Lawrence Minton, even the few days with my help, she was tired and very vulnerable. I saw the tears in her eyes, and saw too that Madame had misinterpreted them to mean she was grateful to have a doctor's care.

When Dr. Moreau had finished his work, Madame swept us into the house, leaving the maid to bring our luggage, and carrying us up to the room she had set aside for me. She went away for ten minutes, and then returned to settle Marina in another guest room.

That done, she came back to my room, and said quietly, "That poor child. How did she burn herself so badly? You did well, bringing her here."

"It was an accident. In the kitchen, as she was supervising the preparation of a dish. It happened so quickly, I'm not sure precisely how, but she saw the pot tilt, reached for it, the spoon came out, and in the end, she'd touched the cooker with her arm."

Madame shook her head. "It happens. These accidents. I had a maid once who scalded her foot. It was terrible. But Mademoiselle Marina will have the best care. She's a teacher, I'm told."

"Yes, she's eager to return to the school. Her father has not been well."

"He was in the war?"

"He was badly wounded and taken prisoner."

"The Boche!" she said at once, using the derogatory term for German soldiers. But she had lost her own son in the fighting. "They had no heart."

Linking her arm with mine, she said, "Marina is resting. Come down and have a little tea with me and tell me how you are."

I was eager to get on with my search, but I owed her an hour's conversation, and so we went to the little sitting room that was hers. Tea was brought, and I enjoyed the luxury of a cup while I told her that I was not sure what had become of Lawrence Minton, but I thought perhaps that he was back in Paris. "Staying with friends, possibly. I don't know. I was going to stop at his lodgings again today, to see if there's any news."

"You must let me know what you discover. I owe his mother a letter."

"Yes, as soon as I have news, I'll be glad to send it to her."

We talked about the peace negotiations, and I could see that, like most of the people of France, she felt that the severest possible punishment was the only acceptable reparation for what the country had suffered. "Both the Austrian empire and Germany must be broken up. They should not have the men or the power to attack us ever again."

Trying to be polite, I said, "I'm sure the men at the table will bear in mind what France has suffered."

She went on. "And this American president. He is an idealist, with his peace plan. He does not understand how it is here in Europe. But he thinks, having come in at the end, that he has the right of it, and can influence us."

I let her talk, knowing that nothing I could say would change her mind. But I managed to beg off from luncheon by telling her that I'd promised to dine with my father.

I spoke to Marina before I left. She was still concerned about Lawrence, but the comfort of the Moreau household after the straits of trying to keep a roof over their heads in St. Ives was such a physical relief that she asked for a tray in her room. I thought perhaps the doctor had given her something for her pain as well, although I hadn't seen him offer anything. But then he could have brought it to her room himself once she was settled.

Leaving the house knowing that all was well with her was a relief to me too, but as I walked away from their door, I had to face the search ahead of me, and the truth was, I wasn't really sure how to begin. The streets of Paris were filled with people, and I didn't know the city well enough to find out where a man might go to kill himself.

But there was the river. And the river appeared to have played a role in Lawrence Minton's collapse. That was where I must begin.

For the first time since I'd come to Paris I wished for Simon's help. Reluctantly or not, he'd have escorted me wherever I needed to go. And I could rely on him.

Should I look up Captain Barkley? I hesitated to do that. He had my father's ear, for all I knew, and he'd most certainly try to talk me out of most of what I felt I must do. Simon's approach had always been that I would probably do what I intended to do anyway, and the best way to protect me was to be sure he was there if I needed him.

But Simon was in Scotland.

I shut that thought away.

Who, then?

Major Webb? But I couldn't be sure of his loyalties.

I hailed a taxi, and when it stopped for me, I asked the driver how many hospitals there were in Paris. He told me, and I said, "I'm looking for my brother. I fear he may be a patient in one of them. I need to find him."

I spent the rest of that day and part of the next going to every hospital I could find, hoping that Lawrence Minton was a patient in one of them, either because he'd accepted that he needed help, or because he'd not been able to carry through his decision to kill himself.

I even asked if there was an unidentified man in the morgues who might be the person I was looking for. I had to give his name, but as I went along, I made up various accounts of why I was searching for him.

I've been asked by his mother to find him . . .

He's a cousin, he's been desperately ill, and I'm worried about him . . .

He's my sister's husband, he's been missing for several days . . .

He's my grandfather's ward, and I've been asked to find him . . .

The hospital staffs were usually busy, but because I was a Sister, someone agreed to speak to me. When I gave a description of Lawrence Minton, adding that I feared he might have met with an accident and was unable to identify himself, I was told that there was no patient by that name, and no one of that description in a coma or too badly injured to speak.

In one hospital I was taken to the morgue to look at a drowning victim just brought in from the river. My heart in my mouth, I followed the attendant into the lower regions of the hospital, and waited for the body to be pointed out. And afterward, stepping out into the sunshine again, I thanked God that it wasn't the Lieutenant.

In another, there was a victim of a road accident, and again I was led to view the body. But this wasn't Lawrence Minton either.

I didn't know whether to be glad that I hadn't found him, taking it as a sign that he might not have killed himself after all, or to wonder where he might be, drinking brandy and looking for courage in a bottle. It had been more than twenty-four hours, after all.

Each night I returned to the Moreau house, and each night I had to tell Marina that I'd had no luck. When I'd made the rounds of all the hospitals I could find, I began to walk the bridges that crossed the Seine. It ran more or less east to west through the city. The northern side of the river was where the business of the capital took place, the Rive Droit. The Right Bank. The southern side, the Rive Gauche or Left Bank, was where the artists and writers and students at the university lived, the creative heart of Paris in a way.

Looking over the parapets on both sides, staring down in the swirling current, searching the embankment on the Left Bank, I thought of the many people who had found in the water a place to die. It wasn't a fast-moving river, but by the bridges, it picked up a little speed as it passed through the arches. Even into the evening, when I could see beggars sleeping on the quay, or drunks stumbling toward the murky thread of river, to relieve themselves, I kept searching. A different, dark side of glittering, beautiful Paris. Surely this would draw Lawrence Minton, if he was tired of life.

How many bridges are there? I asked myself as I took up my search the next morning. Twenty? Thirty? A hundred?

It was a daunting task. *Where was he? Where in all of Paris was I going to find this man?*

At midday I stopped at a small café for something to eat, barely recognizing what was in the soup I was brought. Across the street was a bakery, and beside it one of the ubiquitous cinemas in Paris. Some of them were as grand as opera houses. This one was dark, and I couldn't tell whether it was closed up or just had no films showing during the day. It was here that the cinema was born before the turn of the century. But since the war the French government could no longer support it, and there were few new films being made. Later in the afternoon, I crossed to Notre Dame, walking into its shadowy interior, the stained glass casting pretty spots of color on the floor.

There were people praying here, or simply sitting, meditating or taking in the beauty around them. This was one of the churches that began the great Gothic surge of cathedral building, its architects conquering the problems of height and space within, allowing those glorious windows to bring light in.

I didn't want to disturb the others here, and so I sat on the steps of the pulpit, well out of the way, catching my breath, giving my poor feet a chance to rest. Enjoying the silence surrounding me. Then, with a sigh, I rose and began again.

It was hopeless, I knew that. But I couldn't stop searching. Before I called it a day, I found a taxi and asked it to drop me off at the house where Lawrence still had a flat.

But when I'd knocked and Madame came to the door, she shrugged as only the French can, and shook her head, looking sadly at me as she said, "No, I have not seen him, not once since he left here with the young woman."

I thanked her and started back toward the Moreau house. And all the way there, I tried to think what to do tomorrow. Or the day after that. Go back to the hospitals? Speak to the police again? I was running out of places to search, and I found myself wondering if, no more than ten minutes after I'd left one of the hospitals, Lawrence Minton had finally been found and brought in. If he had come down to the water's edge only a half an hour after I'd crossed the bridge that overlooked that quay. I'd asked the hospitals to notify

Dr. Moreau if such a person arrived, either as a patient or as a body. But busy as they were in a city this size, how long would they remember one person's request? By the river there was no one to keep an eye out for a man who might already be dead. Come to that, a body could lie in a fallow field for days before it was discovered, and by then there would be little to help the local police put a name to him.

He could soon lie buried in some pauper's grave, unknown, the plot unmarked.

The proverbial needle in a haystack.

Yet I thought he might be *drawn* to the river—if that was where his nightmares had begun. Was he a murderer? So much seemed to point in that direction, but that didn't make it so. Did it?

I'd been tempted any number of times to go down to the water, to move amongst the beggars sleeping at river's edge, to see if one of them might be Lawrence. But I'd hesitated. There were women of the night in Paris, I'd seen them as well, plying their trade amongst the throngs of men who had come to the talks for whatever reason, personal or official. It wasn't the safest of professions, and some of these women were hard. I'd even tried to speak to them, to ask if they knew where I might find a man who had lost his way. For the most part they'd ignored me, although one had spat at me and called me names in French.

I began walking rather aimlessly on the Left Bank, in streets where students had flats or artists worked, telling myself that I should have taken my father into my confidence as soon as the Lieutenant had gone missing from Marina's house in St. Ives. I was wasting precious time, while he could put the resources of the Army, the Foot Police, or even the French authorities into this search. Yet once I did that, what would the repercussions be of Lawrence's dereliction of duty? Did that even matter now, when he might very well be charged with murder as soon as he was found?

I was turning down another thoroughfare, when someone stepped out of a shop as I passed, and a familiar voice called, "Ma'am?"

I turned to see the American flyer walking toward me.

"Hallo," I said. "You seem to be spending much of your time in Paris."

"Well, I kind of like it here. Truth is, I've never seen this many people in one place before. Where I come from, I see more cattle—or Navajo sheep, for that matter—than human beings. I expect I'll soon tire of it, start to feel crowded, and go home. But who knows?

The way they're going about this treaty business, there may be new calls for my particular talents. So I'll wait a little longer, and see."

"Your talents?" He was teasing me, laying on his bucolic background rather thick. But he'd learned to fly, come across the Atlantic and fought in the air throughout the war, somehow surviving for four years. No mean feat, and it would take more skill and intelligence to do so than he liked to claim.

He flushed a little, not expecting my response. "Shooting down other aircraft. I appear to be good at it."

"You think there will be an outbreak of war?" I asked.

"Well, at the rate these folks are going, the Americans and the French may be shooting it out over terms. Or if they don't get into it, the British and the French might decide to give it a try."

I had to laugh then, his dry sense of humor lifting my spirits.

"Truth is, I love flying. And I don't get much chance at home."

"How did you learn to fly?" I asked, curious.

"In 1911, a man named Charlie Walsh came to the New Mexico Territorial Fair in Albuquerque. He brought with him an airplane he'd built himself, and for three days he had everyone air mad, including me. His craft was a bi-plane, a copy of a Curtiss pusher—the propeller was in the rear, not the front—and I'd never seen anything like it. He took me up on the third day. I was nineteen, and by Christmas, with advice from Charlie, I'd built my own pusher. When the war began in 1914, and I heard about the American pilots going over to fly for the French, I leaped at the chance to join them. My parents were not best pleased, but I was of age, and I wanted to see the world." He hesitated. "I don't think much of their coffee over here, but I don't know if it's polite to ask a Sister to have a glass of wine with me."

"I'll settle for the coffee," I told him, and he gave me that wide grin of his.

"My pleasure, ma'am."

He escorted me to a café not far away. It was still too cold to sit outside, but we walked between the tables to the door, and he opened it for me.

Inside was a surprise. I might have stepped back in time, to the 1890s. The room was bright with lamplight, there were brass appointments and dark drapes, and tables with white cloths and waitresses in black dresses and white aprons.

Most of the other patrons were families or middle-aged couples, and several British officers, although I didn't recognize them.

We were led to a table near a piano. Captain Jackson seated me, then sat down across from me.

"There's music in the evening. I enjoy coming here and just listening. The woman who plays reminds me of my mother. There's such feeling in the way she interprets the pieces."

This was an unexpected side of the man.

"Do you play?"

He looked at his long, slender fingers. "Well, my mother tried, she told me I had great reach, but I fear I've disappointed her."

But I thought he must also play rather well.

He ordered two coffees, and apologized afterward. "It's called coffee, but don't expect much of it." Then he asked, diffidently, "What brings you to Paris? Are there English hospitals here?"

Remembering the convalescent clinics during the war, I said, "Not any longer." And before I could stop myself, I added, "I'm looking for a family friend. He's missing, and I fear he might do something rash, because he hasn't really recovered from the war. I've asked at all the hospitals, and they can't help me. I don't quite know where else to look."

He regarded me sympathetically for a moment, then said, "That explains why you look tired. It can't have been easy, doing this alone."

I smiled ruefully. "There was no one else to ask."

"There are places a lady ought not go. If you'll allow me, I'll do a little searching on my own."

It was my turn to hesitate. He was charming, amusing, good company. But did I trust him? I barely knew him. But he was not in the British Army, and if I didn't trust someone, and soon, it was likely that Lawrence Minton would be dead. If he wasn't already.

And so I told Captain Jackson a version of the truth. That I'd been asked to find Lawrence Minton—I left out his rank and why he'd come to Paris—and that I'd done what I could, to no avail so far.

"You've taken quite a risk," he said frowning, and just then our coffee came. He waited until the woman had served us, then continued. "If you were *my* sister, I'd be lecturing you about propriety. You shouldn't be talking to those women or going about asking beggars their names."

"I didn't actually—"

"But I can see you considered it, ma'am. And that worries me. There are all kinds of people on the streets just now. Not just Frenchmen, but foreigners of all sorts. There's no way of knowing how half of them were brought up."

He reminded me suddenly of Simon.

But before I could say anything, he went on, commenting rather seriously, "If I were *your* family, I'd be downright concerned."

I didn't tell him I carried my little pistol with me. For all I knew, he might not approve of that.

I was just thinking that he now reminded me more of Captain Barkley, when he said, "If you'll accept my help, I'd take it as an honor."

"You hardly know me, nor I you," I pointed out.

"Yes, ma'am, I understand that. But sometimes the rules of etiquette don't match the situation. If I found you wandering around alone in the mountains at home, I'd do my best to help you, whether we'd been properly introduced or not."

I suppressed a smile. "That's true," I replied.

"Then tell me about this family friend of yours, and I'll do my best to help you. Paris can be a forest too, in its own way."

Neither of us drank our coffee. It grew cold and thick, sitting there, as Captain Jackson and I discussed how to begin a serious search for Lawrence Minton.

Chapter 9

Captain Jackson put me into a taxi as we left the café, and I gave the driver my direction.

I didn't know whether to be relieved or apprehensive about his assistance. But I had little choice in the matter. Arriving at the Moreau house, I slipped up to my room and sat down in the chair by the window overlooking the garden. I'd have preferred to pace, but I didn't want to disturb Marina next door to me or Madame Moreau downstairs, who was hosting a tea for one of the American delegates, a doctor from St. Louis. Early in the war, long before the Americans had entered the fighting, the physicians and nurses of that city had provided a base hospital in the old racetrack in Rouen with an invaluable X-ray machine. The number of lives it had saved was beyond counting, particularly in finding bits of shrapnel in wounds where it would have been far too dangerous to probe.

Madame Moreau had mentioned his visit over breakfast this morning, but I had forgot until now, when I'd seen the motorcar outside our door.

Occasionally I could hear laughter from the guests.

There was a tap on my door.

"Come," I said over my shoulder, thinking it might be the maid bringing up the fresh uniforms that Madame had sent to her own washwoman.

But it was Marina.

She was already beginning to look so much better. Proper rest, regular meals, and a warm house were taking away some of the tension, but there were still shadows behind her eyes.

"Bess? Any news?"

"Not so far." I summoned a smile and rose. "A good sign, don't you think?"

"I don't know. Is it? Should we go back to St. Ives, on the off chance that he might have only meant to frighten us into letting him have his way? I can't bear to think that he found the house closed up, and no idea how to find us."

I was tired, more than a little cross with Lawrence Minton, and I wanted to say, *That was his fault, not ours.* Instead, I replied, "Do you feel so strongly about that? Do you want me to go to St. Ives and have a look?"

Her face brightened. "It would put my mind at rest. Dr. Moreau tells me that my arm is healing well, and in two or three more days, I can return to my school. He thinks the danger of infection has passed."

Burns were bad enough, but if the raw wound got infected, there was little we could do.

"That's very good news, Marina," I said genuinely pleased. "All right, I'll go back to St. Ives in the morning. Just to be sure."

That was the last thing I wanted to do. On the other hand, what if she was right, and the Lieutenant had been playing games with us, hoping to frighten Marina at least into asking me to leave? I had to be sure.

We could hear sounds of departure below. Marina said, "They have been so kind. Dr. and Madame Moreau. I wish I could tell them about Lawrence."

"Not until we know something useful. It would worry them, and Madame Moreau is a close friend of his mother's. She'll want to write Matron and urge her to come straightaway. I'm not sure that's for the best." What could she do, if she came to Paris? It would only distress her.

"What if there isn't any news?" Her voice was forlorn. "I thought I was doing the right thing, taking him out of Paris to heal. And it may have done more harm than good."

"We don't know that yet," I said bracingly. But I couldn't hold out much hope even to myself.

And so the next morning, I arose early, found a taxi, and went to the Gare to catch the early train to St. Ives.

As I got off the train and started up the slight incline toward Marina's house, I remembered the times I'd brought what food I could find in Paris to replenish the empty larder here. And the fright Lawrence had given us when we thought the laudanum had been poisoned.

The rush of memories slowed my steps, but I was soon standing at the door and trying the latch, to see if it was still locked.

It was. Taking out the key that Marina had given me, I unlocked the door and stepped warily into the entry. Sunlight filled the front room, but the landing at the top of the stairs was dark. I stayed where I was, listening, my gaze going to the message that Marina had left behind. It was still there, on the little table against the wall. A white square on the walnut top.

I couldn't hear a sound. The house *felt* empty, but I was uneasy. I put one hand into the pocket of my coat and found the reassuringly solid presence of my little pistol. I felt a little foolish as I withdrew my hand—I wasn't about to shoot Lawrence Minton in Marina's family home. But it was a comfort to me, all the same, as I began to search the ground floor. The parlor, where Lawrence had spent so much of his time. The dining room we'd never used, a family sitting room. Her father's study.

Going through the door that led to the kitchen stairs, I paused again, then went down, my footsteps echoing on the bare treads. The kitchen, the servants' quarters, the door to the back garden, all appeared to be as we'd left them. Making sure that no one could creep up on me and shut me into the cellar, I even looked down there.

No new bottles of brandy had been taken.

I used the servants' stairs to the first floor, and the bedrooms. Again they were as we'd left them. In mine, I went to the window, to see if my pigeon had returned. But there was no sign of him.

Marina's room, Lawrence's room, the other rooms on that floor were empty.

He hadn't been back. I'd half expected to find the door to the back garden had been forced. It was the easiest way into the house, and well out of sight of the neighbors. But it too was just as I left it.

Returning to the hall by the stairs, I stood and listened again.

The house creaked. Or was that a door closing? I was suddenly alert. But not on the floor above. More distant, surely.

I told myself I was imagining things. I didn't relish going to the attics. But I had to be thorough, didn't I?

And so I went back up the stairs.

The mattresses were still rolled up, just as they'd been left in August of 1914, in the small rooms with their narrow beds where the servants had slept, women in one wing, men in another.

The attic door appeared to be stuck, but I finally managed to open it. A cold, musty gust of air met me as it swung wide enough for me to look inside.

A mouse fled across the floor, a small dark streak that left a trail of tiny footprints in the dust. And as I glanced around, I saw mouse droppings everywhere.

I stood there, wondering how he lived up here, with no food in the house.

Shutting the door, I listened to the echo of it, and felt an urge to hurry back down to the ground floor.

It had been a wasted trip. He hadn't come back. Lawrence Minton had meant what he'd said in his letter to me. However much I might wish it had all been a trick, he hadn't come back to die in this house alone, with no one to hinder him.

Still looking at the square envelope on the little table, thinking how hopeless it was, I opened the door at my back—and jumped as a male voice spoke just behind me.

My heart racing, I turned.

It was the elderly priest I'd seen a time or two going about his rounds, his hand still raised to knock at the door.

He said again, "Is someone ill here in the house? I have seen you come and go."

He spoke French with a strong local accent, but I managed to understand him and hoped he could understand me.

"I have been visiting the family, Father. But Mademoiselle Lascelles has returned to Paris. I've only come to retrieve something she's forgot to take with her."

He nodded. "So much the better, my child." Despite his age, his brown eyes were sharp.

Taking a chance, I said, "We were expecting friends to call. Has anyone asked for Mademoiselle?"

"Not to my knowledge. There have been no other strangers here except for the young man who came to help her open the house."

"Just the person we were expecting to call and help us return to Paris," I said, finding a smile. "But somehow we missed him."

The next morning I was out in a dismal rain with a borrowed umbrella, and a map of the city that Dr. Moreau had offered me.

I went back to the hospitals, inquiring again for my relative, and again being told that no one of his description had been admitted, either as a patient or in the morgue.

I had so carefully kept my distance from Captain Jackson. If he made any discoveries, he had no way of reporting to me. Amused at myself for boxing myself into such a corner, I kept an eye out for him as well, in my travels.

Back to the bridges, and two days of searching the banks of the river. If I hadn't seen the Lieutenant the first time I'd looked, who was to say that I might not see him today?

Late in the afternoon of that second day, I was tired, I knew I ought to find a taxi to take me to the doctor's house. Overhead dark clouds had settled in, and the foot traffic had thinned around me as people turned homeward. Still, I told myself, I was no more than thirty yards from the next bridge, and I might as well cross there rather than turning back.

Just before I reached the bridge and started across, the clouds darkened even more and a drizzle began to fall. I carried on, hurrying now. But I paused midway across, as I always did, scanning the path that ran along the water on the Left Bank. Below there was a bundle of what appeared to be rags, and as I stared at it, I realized it must be a man wearing a military coat. British khaki, not French blue.

I turned back the way I'd come, all but running now, off the bridge, down the road to where steps led to the lower, water level. It was darker here, and the water to one side of me ran black and menacing to my left.

I was almost in the shadow of the bridge now, and the figure hadn't moved. Could he hear my footsteps over the sounds of the river? Slowing, I took a closer look at him.

I was sure now that I'd been right. That *was* an officer's greatcoat I could see, and Army boots. But the way he was lying there, I couldn't be sure whether he was breathing or just asleep.

I called, "Lieutenant Minton?"

There was no response. I reached the man and put my hand out to find his wrist and a pulse. How many times had I done that in hospital? It was reflex, look at the expression, take the pulse, feel the forehead . . .

I was unprepared.

A hand clamped down hard on my wrist, pulling me

off balance so that I fell against him as he rose to his knees.

Releasing his grip on my arm, he twisted something—a scarf, a pillow slip—I never knew—around my head, knocking off my cap and pulling my hair as the pins came out. Blinded, I fought hard, but I was in such an awkward position that I had no advantage, and he bent me back, inching both of us closer to the river.

As the scarf slipped, I strained to see his face, and I tried to free a hand to pull it away. His eyes were pale in the darkness. Opaque between the line of his brows and the shadows of the scarf.

I was bent over the river, now, my hair already dragging in the current, and I had a sudden vision of Lawrence Minton struggling to push someone back into the water, bending over the stairs in the darkened hall in St. Ives as he grimly brought his weight down on the wadded-up carpet, deaf to anything around him.

With every ounce of strength I could muster, I tried to get my feet under me, but he had the advantage of his weight and it was a losing battle. My knees were hurting so badly I could feel the pain in spite of my fear as he inexorably forced me backward toward the water. Gathering his own strength for the final shove, he drew back a very little, and then slammed his body against mine, and for a terrifying second I thought we were both going into the river. The Seine was deep, my skirts and petticoats would pull me down—

A whistle blew sharply from the bridge just above us, then blew again, before someone shouted in French, "You—there—in the name of the law—"

And we both heard the boots pounding over the bridge, rushing toward us.

The whistle had startled both of us badly—it had been a silent battle between the two of us, I hadn't screamed, saving my strength for the struggle. The pressure on me was suddenly lifted, he rose, got to his feet, and turned toward me for a final vicious kick into the water. If I'd been caught off guard, I'd have gone in. But I had seen that turn, I'd anticipated his blow, and I reached out and caught his foot with both hands, pulling hard. He was off balance, and toppled to the ground.

With a grunt of pain, he scrambled to his feet again, and ran full out, not looking back.

I lay there for a moment, not moving for fear of losing my own balance and going over. Then I inched back to safety, feeling my hair dragged out of the water, pulling at my head.

I was far enough away from the edge to sit up when the policeman came charging toward me, truncheon in hand.

With the other hand, he reached out and gripped my extended fingers, and helped me to my feet.

"Are you safe?"

I nodded.

"Where is he?"

I pointed. "You barely missed him."

He turned and ran after my assailant. By the time he came back, I was standing and trying to pin up my wet hair.

For the first time he realized that I was a nurse, and touched his cap. "What happened, Mademoiselle? Do you know that man?"

"No. I was on the bridge—I saw someone lying down here. I didn't know whether he was alive or dead, but he appeared to be a soldier. I came to see if he needed help. Instead he caught my arm and tried to shove me into the water."

"Are you quite sure?" he asked, staring at me in the dim light of the bridge lamps.

I pulled my wet hair forward, and he could see just how close I'd come. But I was shivering now too, and he saw that as well. The collar of my coat was damp, and my knees were throbbing from being pushed back in ways they were never intended to go.

He led me back to the street level, and under a lamp looked at my right wrist. It was very red, and I had a feeling it would be blue by morning. "I will take you to a hospital," he said. "You understand, I could not find him, but I will report this to my superiors, and a notice will be sent round to watch for this man. Did you see his face?"

My cap was muddy and rumpled, but I attempted to set it on my head. "No. He was wearing a scarf. I tried to pull it down, but I couldn't." Trying to think clearly, I added, "He was dark. Dark hair. And rather tall. But not a heavy build."

We turned, almost in unison, and moved back to where we could look down, to see if there was anything at the scene that might help us, but the quay was bare, just muddy boot prints but none with real definition, smudged and smeared. Nothing useful.

The policeman accompanied me to the nearest police station, insisting that I make a formal complaint. I just wanted to go home, dry my hair, and count my bruises. But good sense prevailed. I could hardly walk into the Moreau house looking as I did, muddy clothes, torn stockings, hair down my back in wet and straggling confusion. At least I could do a little about my appearance there.

I wasn't aware of just how much like a mud lark I looked until I walked with my guardian-companion into the brightly lit police station, and saw the stares of everyone in the waiting room. I could feel myself flushing, and was grateful when the policeman informed his superior that I was the victim in an assault, and I was ushered into a small room to await someone to take my statement.

France has a completely different system of police from the English. For instance, there are the National Police in Paris, and Gendarmes in the rest of the country, although sometimes these two forces overlap. The man who had brought me here was a National Policeman, and the man who came in to speak to me was a magistrate, not an Inspector, as would have happened at home.

But he was quite kind, tut-tutting over my state, and asking me in rather formal English to tell him what had happened and where. I gathered he'd already seen the policeman's report, and knew the details.

I'd had time to think. And that was important, as it turned out.

I gave him the same account that I'd given the policeman, that I'd thought the man lying on the quay was a British soldier—Paris had its share of them during the war and even now—and as my training had been battlefield nursing, I had gone to see if he was alive and if he needed medical attention.

The magistrate was middle-aged, his hair graying and with lines in his face that suggested he'd seen the worst of humanity come through his door. He said as I paused, "That was not very wise, Sister. You should have summoned a policeman to look at this man."

"Yes, sadly I know that now. But there was no policeman in sight, the man was quite still as if he were not well. I've dealt with wounded who were grateful for care, and for all I knew, he needed immediate assistance."

I went on to describe precisely what had happened, stumbling a little only when I could feel the cold water in my hair, pulling at it. Pulling at me.

The magistrate listened quietly, nodding at this or that point in the story, and taking notes as I talked.

"And you did not see this man's face?"

"No. It was hidden." Because I would recognize it?

The magistrate's eyebrows rose. "You have thought of something?"

He was experienced. He could read my expressions. I had to be careful. Walking to the station from the riverbank, I'd been too unsettled to consider anything but what a narrow escape I'd just had, and how I must look with my hair down. Sitting in this little room, waiting to be interviewed, I'd told myself the truth was essential, that I must keep to the truth as far as possible. But who in Paris would want to kill *me*?

And yet I had to accept the fact that Lieutenant Minton might wish to.

I said slowly, "Whoever it was lying there, he was intent on killing me."

I was tiring. Why not just tell this man what I suspected, and be done with it? Why protect a man who had not shown himself to be anything but a killer?

But there was the regiment. And my father.

My interviewer was saying something, and I forced myself to concentrate. "If this was indeed a British soldier, I will confer with the British Foot Police and ask them if there is any information on men who are missing from their posts or have had a history of this kind of attack. We may be able to find him and bring him in for questioning. But I must ask you, if you are still convinced that this was a British soldier?"

I'd been in Lawrence Minton's room in the house in St. Ives. Almost his entire wardrobe was military. He'd owned a few civilian bits of clothing, which is what he usually wore while I was there, as if denying his Army rank and duties. Or perhaps they had belonged to Marina's brother. Who could say? But he'd have had to wear his uniform and greatcoat when he left the house, because it was too cold for a shirt and trousers, even with a jumper. And unless he'd intended to die of cold before he could kill himself, he had no choice in the matter. On that basis, he would still be wearing them . . .

"I can't swear to the fact that he was a soldier. The attack was so sudden and so rough that I was too busy trying to stay out of the river to notice much of anything. But from the bridge, yes, I saw what I thought was a uniform, a greatcoat, and—and—" I broke off. *An officer's boots.* "And I wouldn't have gone myself to see what was wrong, if I hadn't been convinced of that." It *had* been British khaki I'd seen. Not the sky blue of French uniforms. Even in the uncertain light of dusk.

We talked for another fifteen minutes or so. Or to be more precise, he asked questions and I answered them. Finally, he scanned his notes, nodded to himself, and turned to me.

"Sister Crawford, do you have family in Paris? Anyone who could protect you?"

That was unsettling. "Do you think he will—but *why* would he attack me again?"

What had I inadvertently given away, to make him think my life was in danger?

Then I realized what a narrow line I was walking. I said, "He doesn't know who I am—or where I live!"

He smiled slightly. "Forgive me! No. You are in no danger. But you have had a very bad shock. You've answered my questions admirably, without sinking into hysterics. But later tonight, you will relive this attack, and you will feel very differently. It is best that you are not alone."

It was very gallant of him. But I was not likely to dissolve into hysterical tears. Now or later. I'd learned as a nurse to stay calm in the direst situations, to think as clearly as possible, and act if I had to. When a life hung in the balance, there was no time for personal feelings. Training took over.

I'd been shaken, yes, by what had happened, but if I hadn't kept my head, I'd be in the Seine, not here giving evidence. I'd instinctively fought to live, because it was the only option I'd had. Not bravery. Just the will to survive.

Still . . .

I said, meaning it, "You have been very kind, monsieur. I am staying with Dr. Moreau and his wife while I am in Paris. They will take very good care of me. But is there any way to repair my appearance before I see them? It will frighten Madame and worry her unnecessarily to see me like this."

He took me down several passages to a small room with a sink, a mirror, and several towels. Finding me a clean one, he said, "I wish I could do more. I will have one of my men waiting in the passage for you, and he will find a taxi and see that the driver takes you safely home."

I could do nothing with my hair, but I put it up again without all the pins I usually required, set my poor trampled cap back on and then did what I could about my coat. My stockings were ruined, my shoes scraped and muddy, but at least my face and hands were clean, and I would have time in the taxi to think up something to tell the doctor and his wife. And Marina. Poor Marina, she'd be horrified.

The magistrate was as good as his word. A policeman was waiting, and he courteously escorted me to the street and found a taxi.

He spoke personally to the driver—I could imagine what mayhem he was threatening if I didn't reach home safely—and only then settled me into the rear of the taxi. I thanked him, leaned my head back against the seat, and took a deep breath.

Had he hated me so much? Lawrence Minton? To want to kill me?

I didn't want to believe it. But what else *could* I believe? I had no enemies here.

Only then did it dawn on me that the Lieutenant was in Paris. And still alive.

The Moreaus were horrified to see me, just as I'd thought, and they whisked me off to the surgery before anyone else could see me, gave me a small glass of brandy to sip, and demanded to know what had happened.

I told them the truth—as much of it as I dared—and they scolded me for not being more careful.

"The streets are not safe in that district. And the man must have been demented, to attack you in that fashion."

I let them fuss over me, sipped a little more brandy to warm me, then asked to be taken to my room. Madame went ahead to order hot water, assuring me that she would see personally to the cleaning of my coat and shoes. And then she was off, leaving me alone with Dr. Moreau.

"Was it Lawrence? Do you know?" he asked anxiously. "He must have been out of his mind to do such a thing. Are the police searching for him now?"

I set the brandy aside. "I don't know. I didn't tell the police because I couldn't be sure. But who else could it have been? I called his name. He must have known who it was, coming toward him." I shook my head. "If we don't find him soon, heaven knows what will happen to him. Or to someone else," I added.

"Keep this to yourself. For my wife and Marina's sakes. And from now on, I must accompany you when you feel you must search for Lawrence. To keep you safe, and to handle him in whatever state of mind he may be in."

"No. He won't have the opportunity to attack me again. I'll be on my guard. I promise you."

But that took some persuading. When at last he let me go, I could only think of the hot water waiting, and my bed. The brandy, I thought, was having its effect, and I would be able to sleep.

Madame didn't ask me if I thought the man had been Lawrence Minton. I don't think she could quite wrap her mind around such a possibility. And I was glad. I didn't feel like talking to anyone about it now.

She took my damp and muddy clothing, tossed my torn stockings into the fire on the hearth, and helped me wash my hair. And then, mercifully, she was gone. An hour later she brought me a cup of soup, thinking I might be able to swallow a little. I thanked her, and drank most of it to make her happy.

I expected to dream. But I didn't. I slept the night through like someone drugged, not opening my eyes until the first gray of dawn lightened the room a little. But every bone in my body complained vigorously as I tried to move. I only hoped that my attacker was feeling as wretched.

It rained hard that day, giving me an excuse to stay in and rest. But on the following day I began my search again, first close to the bridge where the attack had happened, and then widening the search from there.

I had the odd feeling sometimes that I was being watched. But when I looked, I didn't see anyone whom I recognized. Mostly I searched the streets where artists and students lived, because lodgings were cheap there. The day after that, I was just crossing the bridge below the Pont Neuf when in the distance I spotted Captain Jackson, waiting to cross the street beyond the end of the bridge. Hurrying to catch him up before he'd got too far ahead, I called to him. I hadn't really expected him to hear me over the din of traffic, but he looked around, tall enough to be able to see over the heads of passersby, and then as I called again, he turned and spotted me.

"Just the person I'd been hoping to see," he said somberly. "I think I've found your missing friend. But I can't be sure. And I had no way to find you."

"You've found him?" I repeated, amazed and excited. Then, really taking in his expression, I said, "Captain—are you—is he *alive*?"

"Only just."

All I could think of was that the encounter with me had pushed the Lieutenant over the edge, either in shame or determination to finish it, and I felt my spirits plummet.

My companion was already searching the street for a taxi, found one, and ushered me inside. "The Holy Angels hospital," he told the driver, then turned back to me. "It's a Catholic hospital for the indigent," he said. "They take in those who can't afford to pay, who are old and in ill health. It's in one of the poorer quarters." His lightly teasing manner had vanished, and I was seeing quite a different view of him. Here was the man who had flown countless forays against the best flyers that Germany had in the air, and still survived. "It seems that a priest found him in an alley, terribly beaten. He was barely conscious and yet he kept saying something over and over again. Something about angels. The priest understood him to mean he was known at Holy Angels, but when the ambulance brought him there, he was not someone the nurses recognized. They took him in, anyway."

"Are you sure it's the man I'm searching for?"

"No, ma'am, I'm not. But I think you ought to have a look at him all the same." The drawl was back. "He was wearing an English uniform when he was found, but the condition it was in gave the police to believe he'd bought it secondhand somewhere or stolen it. A good many of the soldiers who chose to stay here in Paris got rid of their uniforms. They didn't want to stand out. British and American."

"But what happened to him? Why was he in a French hospital?"

"They wouldn't tell me. I thought you, being a nurse yourself, might convince them to talk to you. Failing that, I just don't know." The grimness was creeping back in.

Twisting and turning through the outskirts of the city, we found ourselves in increasingly poor quarters, the houses shabby, a few windows broken out and stuffed with rags, paint peeling, and a general air of despair. Even the people, hunched against the wind that had been increasing all morning, seemed to carry the burden of hopelessness on their shoulders. At the end of one street, a dreary stone building stood inside a tall iron fence. It too appeared to be a victim of time and decay. I thought, noticing the grilles at the upper windows, that this might once have been an asylum.

The staff was as worn as the building, the nurses older, with lines in their faces that aged them beyond their years. One or two looked up as they passed by us but didn't speak. After a few minutes an orderly came into Reception and asked our business.

I could barely understand him, and I asked to be taken to the place where I'd been told a man wearing a British uniform had recently been brought in.

We were led down a tiled corridor, and the odor of sickness and dirty bodies wafted out of the doors we passed. And then the orderly stopped and pointed into a room on our left.

Inside were a double row of cots, each one occupied. I looked at the orderly. "Which is the bed we are seeking?" I asked.

"Number seventeen," he told me and I started down the aisle between the two rows, looking for the correct number. All I could see in most of the beds were heads, the men themselves covered by a blanket that appeared to be Army issue, now reverted to civilian use. Old men with tousled white hair stared back at me, and younger men with only one leg, the blanket empty on one side. And beggars from the streets, toothless and gaunt.

How could Lawrence Minton have wound up here?

I found seventeen, and looked at what I could see of the patient. A head swathed in bandaging, only a tuft or two of dark hair showing.

Lawrence Minton's hair wasn't that dark.

I was about to walk on to the next bed, thinking I'd

been given the wrong number, when something made me move closer instead. And I realized that this man's hair was still matted with blood.

Stepping even closer, I said softly, "Lawrence? Can you hear me? It's Sister Crawford."

There was no response. I lightly touched his shoulder, thinking he might be sleeping, and the reaction was shocking.

His whole body lurched away from me in terror, and I fell back, staring at the man in the bed. A wave of pity swept through me. Whatever he'd done, he hadn't deserved this.

Behind me, I heard the Captain suppressing a sound, somewhere between swearing and denial.

I turned. "Can you find a chair for me?"

He looked around the room. "There—at the far end." And he walked briskly toward it.

I went back to the patient. Bending low, so that my voice didn't carry, I said, "Lawrence? What happened, who hurt you this badly?"

There was no movement, no response. And yet I thought there was tenseness, as if he knew who I was, and wanted me to go away. I decided to speak to that.

"I'm stubborn, you know, I find it hard to give up on someone. That's why I was a good nurse, I cared about my patients."

No reaction. And then a thread of a voice I barely recognized said, "The Angel. He—he turned his b-back on me. At M-Mons. Even y-you can't chan-change that."

Whatever it was I'd expected, it wasn't this.

The retreating British forces, struggling to hold the German advance in the first days of the war, had nearly been overwhelmed. And then there was an account of an Angel appearing in the sky, between the Expeditionary Force and the German Army. Giving them time to regroup and hold on a little longer. Combined with the French Army rushing men by taxi to stop the Germans at the Marne River, these men kept the Germans from taking the coast and preventing loss of the ports Britain badly needed to reinforce them. Until then the German onslaught appeared to be invincible. It had in many ways turned the tide of war.

Some claimed the Angel was the invention of newspapers. Others swore that the Angel was there—men who had actually seen it.

But I'd never heard anyone say that the Angel had turned his back on a single British soldier.

Captain Jackson had returned with my chair. I sat close to the bed, not touching it for fear of disturbing Lawrence again.

And then I remembered—remembered standing on

the stairs at the house in St. Ives. When Lawrence was in the throes of nightmare.

What had Lawrence said?

You turned your back on me then. Why? I went back. I couldn't help it if it was too late. I never meant it to be too late.

"Did the Angel turn from you in St. Ives, when you saw him on the stairs?"

There was a different stillness from the figure on the bed now.

I let the silence lengthen.

"How cou-could you kno-know about that?" The voice was muffled, unsteady.

"A priest found you. This is a hospital. Holy Angels, the French call it. How can you think that God has abandoned you?"

I heard the cry of a man in anguish, low and shatteringly harsh.

I turned to Captain Jackson and mouthed, *Leave!* And gestured to the door we'd entered.

He started to say something, then left without looking back until he reached the door. There he stopped and waited for me.

I didn't want any witnesses to Lawrence Minton's reaction. It was a private thing, so deeply personal that he would be ashamed later that others had heard him.

But the breakdown I'd expected never came. Just that one cry. I realized that he must have lost consciousness even as he made it.

After a moment, when I was sure it was safe to leave him, I quietly went to find the nurse in charge of his care. Captain Jackson followed me.

She was busy, tired, her face prematurely lined. I thought she could be in her forties, possibly early fifties—she looked sixty.

"Number Seventeen? *Alors,* he should not be alive, you understand? A concussion, we fear bleeding in the brain. A broken collarbone, a broken arm, bruised kidneys, a broken leg. Internal injuries that we have not yet been able to assess. It was not a man's fists, you know. It was wood or metal, to do such damage to a human body. His assailant wanted him to die in great pain."

"Who could have done such a thing? Someone trying to rob him? An enemy?"

She shook her head. "This was vicious. Not anger, but intent. He was beaten long after he could defend himself. Until, perhaps, some noise, someone, frightened his assailant away. He could still die, you understand? It is still possible." Sighing, she went on. "I have sent word to the British Army, but I had to tell them the truth, that I thought the uniform was not his. No one has replied to me."

"Were the police summoned? Did they take the details of the assault on Number Seventeen?"

"They were summoned, they interviewed the priest, but not the patient. We were too busy trying to save his life." She handed the key to the medicine cabinet to a nurse who had come to ask for it, then said, "Does the poor man have any family, do you know? He can tell us nothing."

"Not in France. I must send to England to find them." I was afraid if I told her about Matron, she would insist on waiting until Lawrence's mother arrived before agreeing to any changes. "What more can be done, meanwhile? Is there a private room where he can be treated? Could I bring in my own doctor to attend him?"

She looked back at the door to the ward. "There are no private rooms here—except for quarantine. And not enough doctors for private care, even if that were possible. We do what we can for these wretched souls. We save as many as possible, and sometimes they die in another way. Too much wine, too little food. An infection from a knife wound or broken teeth. A heart or a liver that can do no more. There is always something. It is very sad."

"I know a doctor here in Paris who is willing to accept a private case. Would it be possible to take him away, to try to save him? If there is any glimmer of hope for him, I must find it." *For Matron's sake.*

She smiled, but it wasn't an encouraging smile. "You will require an ambulance. He cannot be moved otherwise or he will be in too much pain. Even moving could kill him. We've feared for clotting from his wounds. And the stress to his body, just to breathe. And there is more. He flinches from us when we try to change dressings. As if he fears another attack. You must provide for him mentally as well as seeing to his physical needs. Do you realize the task you will be taking on?"

"I worked in forward aid stations, I know how men suffer."

"Very well. I will give my permission. But you must speak to the doctor as well."

I did just that, persuading him that Dr. Moreau could give this patient the care that the ward couldn't possibly offer someone so ill. "I am grateful that he was brought here and that you took him in and did all that you could for him. But from my own experience with badly wounded men, he will require care for a very long time. There must be others who will be in need of his bed, long before he's well."

An older man, nearly gray, he studied me for a moment. "This is true. And I know of this doctor you speak of. If he comes himself, to sign the papers, I will allow the young man to leave. It's highly irregular. But if you are certain he's English, then I see no reason to refuse permission."

I said, "I have heard him speak. I have no doubts there."

"Do you trust this doctor you're sending him to?" the Captain asked later, when I'd finally got the temporary permission I required to begin the removal of Number Seventeen.

"He has known Lawrence for some time. He will see that he's given every care." We'd stepped out into the fresh air, outside the main door. I took a deep breath. "He's going to die in there. Dr. Moreau couldn't be any worse." Looking around at the poor neighborhood, I added, "How do I find an ambulance?"

"That's going to be a problem. They're not at the beck and call of an English nurse."

"I can't leave him here. I won't."

And what to do about Marina?

"Could I ask another favor of you? Will you go to the address I'm about to give you, and ask Dr. Moreau please to find a way to bring Lawrence Minton to his house, where he can be treated? Tell him that there is no hope for him, if *he* can't save him. Ask him if his other guest could be returned to her own duties. It would be for the best, if that was possible. And anyway, he must come himself to sign the papers."

It was all I could do. I was needed here.

I gave him the address and said, "Please do your best, persuading him that I am right. That man was a good soldier. He deserves a chance."

The Captain smiled. "Leave it to me, ma'am. I'll see that there's an ambulance coming for him, if I have to steal it myself."

Well, that was not very reassuring!

I saw him on his way, then went back inside, found my way back to the ward, and sat down again by my patient. Dr. Moreau's, to be perfectly accurate now.

I stayed there, telling myself over and over again that I had done the right thing. And then I felt guilty that I hadn't told Dr. Moreau long before this that there was something in Lawrence Minton's background that was terribly uncertain. He deserved to know, if only to protect his family. If Lawrence had attacked me, I couldn't be sure he wouldn't try to attack the Moreaus.

But, I reminded myself, looking at the patient in the bed, there would surely be time for confessing. For one thing, the Lieutenant might not live. For another, at present he was in no condition to harm anyone. Even himself. I couldn't—wouldn't—accuse him when he wasn't able to defend himself.

And that had been the problem all along. That uncertainty. I was honor bound to find out the truth, and so I had to face the worst possibility, not turn a blind eye to it.

Speaking of truth—there was one explanation for this beating that I would have to consider. That whatever Lawrence had done, *someone* had found him and taken a terrible revenge for it.

Lawrence was quiet again. I tried to assess his mood, knowing I needed to prepare him for the change in his situation, but it was best to leave him to rest peacefully as long as possible. If for no other reason than to keep arguments short. It wouldn't do for him to go into a rage.

I let him sleep until the ward nurse began her next rounds. She made her steady way down the line of beds, speaking to each patient, judging what they might require, ordering fresh dressings for this man, a thin gruel for another, medicines for pain here, or just a kind word there. How often had I done the same for the wounded in my care?

When she reached Number Seventeen, she nodded to me, and I stepped aside to allow her room to work with Lawrence.

He flinched away from her as she removed his blanket, but she made soothing noises, trying to reassure him.

Seeing the dark spread of bruises, the raw gashes, the now-set bones, listening to the ragged breathing as the French nurse gently tended him, avoiding hurting him as much as she could, I felt a rising anger. This was attempted murder. No matter what Lawrence had done, it was the law's responsibility to punish him. Such a beating was unwarranted. Revenge was never warranted.

Lawrence was so exhausted after the dressings and bandaging had been replaced, I couldn't be sure he even heard my voice, much less what I wanted to tell him. In the end, I let it go, for the French nurse had promised to give him a sedative just after the ambulance came to transport him to Dr. Moreau's care.

He came striding into the ward ten minutes before the ambulance arrived. Captain Jackson was nowhere to be seen.

"My dear," the doctor said, kissing me on both cheeks in the French fashion. "You have worked a miracle! Now it is for me to take the burden from you." He turned and looked at Lawrence. *"Dear God,"* he said under his breath, and moved forward to lift the cover-let and study his patient. Shaking his head as he gently lowered the blanket again, he asked, "Who could have done this? It's unconscionable."

I wanted to ask if he thought he could save him, but I dared not. I didn't want to hear despair, only hope. And I didn't read much hope in the doctor's eyes.

Dr. Moreau straightened up and went on, his voice carrying only to me.

"I am sorry to be so late in arriving. But I took Marina to her school and made certain she was settled, and that the infirmary would take over care of her arm. It is for the best, I think, she needs her teaching just now. There is something on her mind, and she is reluctant to speak of it. Her father, I understand, has not been well. He was a prisoner of war."

"They believed for some time that he was dead."

"Yes, I have treated men who were prisoners," he told me somberly. "I have lost some of them in spite of everything I could do." Drawing a deep breath, he said, "I would take Lawrence to a different hospital, but this beating. There is something brutal here. The doctor who first treated Lawrence tells me it was a board or a pipe. Perhaps a wooden walking stick. Do you think his attacker knew it was Lawrence? Or was it random?"

"I don't know," I answered honestly. "I don't know this man's secrets."

Dr. Moreau considered me. "But—you have reasons to perhaps wonder."

"Yes." I couldn't lie.

"Then I will take him to my house. And I will bring in a nurse I can trust to care for him. In a hospital, there are too many people coming or going."

"Are you saying that whoever did this could try again?"

"The nurse in charge of Casualty informed me there have been two inquiries about a man named Minton. But, of course, they didn't know the name of the poor soul who was brought here by a priest. He is listed still as Unknown."

I stared at him. I hadn't inquired at this hospital. I hadn't even known it existed until Captain Jackson brought me here.

"How did you think to ask her?"

"I wanted to know how he had arrived here. Have you told anyone here who Lawrence is? Or that he's English?"

"I had to tell them he was English in order to ask for permission to move him. At the moment he's still Number Seventeen."

"Then when I fill out the papers, I will give his

name as Stephen Ballard. An Englishman. It will do no harm to lie."

He went away to await the ambulance and effect the transfer. I stood there by Lawrence's bed.

If Lawrence had done something troubling, here in Paris—only a matter of weeks ago—what had the Angel at Mons to do with it? That was the autumn of *1914*. This was March of 1919. But then he'd had a concussion, hadn't he? It was the concussion, not the Angel, that had muddled his memory.

But someone else knew he was in hospital here . . .

Chapter 10

Even heavily sedated, Lawrence Minton moaned in his drug-induced state as we moved him to the stretcher, and then to the ambulance. I was given a sack containing the bloody clothing he'd been wearing when he was attacked, and whatever belongings he'd had then. I signed for them, but there was no time to examine them.

Madame Moreau was at the door as the ambulance drew up in front of their house, and she gave rapid, concise instructions to the attendants as she guided them inside and up the stairs to the room that Marina had so recently vacated.

It was spotlessly clean, fresh sheets, fresh coverlet—one would never guess it had been occupied only hours before by Marina Lascelles.

Shortly afterward, he was ensconced in the waiting bed, and the attendants withdrew, leaving only Dr. Moreau and me by the bedside.

Feeling for a pulse, examining his swollen and bruised eyes, Dr. Moreau said, "No worse the wear, thank God." Then turning to me, he said, "I shall hire nurses. We will need to have someone with him at all times. There are several I trust. I will send for them tomorrow."

"I have experience—I can be one of them."

"No, my dear. You must find out for me who did this. You have connections with the Army, surely they can help you in the search. He was at the Peace Conference. They will also be eager to find out who did this."

But I couldn't go to the Army. Not until I spoke to my father. I knew too much—

That reminded me. "The flyer who was here? Captain Jackson. Where is he? I thought he would come back to the hospital with you."

"The young man? He gave me your messages and left. I don't know what has become of him."

Nor did I know. I hadn't properly thanked him for finding Lawrence for me.

Just now, there were more important matters to attend to. I helped settle our patient and organize a schedule of treatment and medicines for the nurses who would be caring for him over the next few days—weeks? I couldn't begin to guess at that.

And there was more to see to—Lawrence's assignment to the conference and writing to Matron. It had already been too long, but what did I have to tell her? Only, it was worse news now. How does one say, *Your son has been nearly killed by an unknown assailant, but Dr. Moreau is treating him now, and we must hope and pray that he recovers . . .*

She would be on the next crossing to France.

I stopped folding fresh bandaging on a tray and spoke quietly to Dr. Moreau, who was standing by the window, his expression strained with worry. Outside dusk had become night, and I hadn't been aware of it until now.

"What do we tell his mother?"

"I've been thinking about that, yes. I have come to no conclusion. He is her only child, her son. She must be told. But how?"

"I wish I knew."

He took a deep breath. "Well, then. Let us see what the night brings. He is in our care, it can be no worse than what he has had until now. We will take it by turns, you and I, to stay with him. I will have a cot brought up. We must conserve our own strength. It will not help him if we collapse from fatigue."

Of course, he was right. But I wasn't feeling tired. Not yet. It was like those frightful moments at the forward aid station when we could hear the battle going on and the first of the wounded began to trickle in. Knowing that very soon it would become a flood, and we would be hard-pressed to save all of them. Adrenaline flowing because one had to be at one's best, one's self and one's own needs set aside, until the last of the stretchers and walking wounded came into sight. There were times when we didn't eat or sleep, times when a quick cup of tea was all that we had to sustain us, and the ground beneath our boots was slick with blood and our aprons stiff with it.

I said, "I must go out. There is someone I must find, to see about speaking to the priest who found Lawrence, and the police in that quarter who must have been summoned. They may be able to tell us something more than the hospital staff knew."

"At this hour?" Dr. Moreau shook his head. "No, it's not wise. This can wait until morning. Do you know where that young flyer is billeted? We can send round for him tomorrow."

But it was my father I wanted to find. If he was still in Paris.

There was a tap at the door.

I turned around to open it. Madame Moreau, her face anxious, was standing there.

"Please, tell me something. I can't bear the waiting."

I glanced at the doctor, and he nodded. I let her in, and she went at once to the bed, tears filling her eyes as she looked down at Lawrence Minton. But I thought she was seeing her own son, wounded and dying on some distant battlefield. She reached out to brush his face, what little we could see of it, the swollen eyes and cut lip.

The doctor leaned forward and caught her hand. "Best not to," he said. "Not just now."

Madame Moreau nodded. "Shall I write to his mother tonight?"

"Tomorrow will be soon enough. Let her rest tonight, not knowing. She can do nothing until morning."

"Yes. True. I will go to the kitchen and start making jellies and soups. He will need nourishing food. I can do that much. I'll scour the markets for anything that we can use."

"You must tell no one he's here," Dr. Moreau warned. "Not until we know who did this. The staff must be sworn to secrecy as well. Will you bear that in mind?"

She stared at him. "You are speaking to *me*. Your wife." With a last glance at Lawrence, she turned and left the room.

He grimaced. "I don't mean to be harsh. But I had not told her the entire truth about what happened."

There was a sound from the bed. We moved in unison to see Lawrence's eyes open, his lips moving.

I quickly realized that he wasn't seeing us or speaking to us.

Instead, his words were incoherent. And then he said, as clearly as if he were awake and in his right mind, "Damn you! Kill me, then. Or I'll kill you."

In the silence that followed, heavy in the already quiet room, I could feel Dr. Moreau's gaze turning to me.

"Who was he speaking to?" he whispered, fearing that Lawrence could hear us.

"I don't know. I wish I did."

Was it his assailant he was speaking to? Or a memory of murder? I didn't know. And I couldn't tell Dr. Moreau what I *did* know. Not yet.

The doctor took the first shift, as it were, and I went down to find that Madame Moreau had kept a dinner warm for me. I didn't feel like eating, but she had been kind enough to think of me, and I couldn't disappoint her.

While I was finishing my soup, she sat down across from me and said, "I've been told nothing. Only that he was found, terribly injured. Someone from the streets had attacked him. What do the police have to say?"

"I don't know," I admitted. "I spoke only to the staff at the hospital. A priest found him in an alley, that's all they appeared to know."

"That's a quarter of thieves and murderers. Was he robbed?"

"Truly, I don't know. There's a sack in the room with his clothes and other belongings. I've been too busy setting up his care for the nurses who will be brought in tomorrow. I will do that, when it's my turn to watch him."

"Then we don't know why he was attacked? By whom?"

I didn't know just how much her husband had decided not to tell her. And so I answered with care. "I wasn't told any more than that there *was* an attack."

She threw up her hands in frustration, a very French gesture. "He protects me. As if I am too fragile. Yes, I nearly had a breakdown when word came that our son was killed. It was different for me, I'd given birth to him, I'd watched him grow, and I couldn't be there when he died, to offer comfort, hold his hand and close his eyes. It's a mother's feelings. You have a mother, you must know that it is different, what she feels. I fought my own way through darkness, because my husband couldn't help me. He was too lost in his own grief, you see, but *he* had his work to support him. I had this empty house, and memories. Of a child's laughter, boots muddy from the garden, toy soldiers underfoot, favorite dishes for his supper. So *many* memories—"

I put out my hand, and took one of hers. She clasped mine tightly as she fought back the tears.

"Ah, well," she said finally, keeping her voice level with an effort I could see. "There is nothing you can do about loss, is there? What is gone is gone. I must think what to say to Helena. Is it—will he survive, do you think? Should I ask her to come?"

"Dr. Moreau has told me to wait until morning. He will assess the patient then."

"He can't face the truth, not tonight. That's why."

She was very likely right.

"Don't let him die," she whispered. "For my sake as well as his mother's." And she got up hastily, to bring me the next course. But she was in the kitchen far longer than it took to dish up vegetables and meat. When she came back again with my plate, her eyes were suspiciously red. But she smiled and questioned me about the Captain who had come to the door to summon her husband to the hospital.

"Do you care for him?" she asked, tilting her head conspiratorially.

"I hardly know him."

"He is quite handsome. But an American, I think, although his French was good. Would your mother care to see you married to someone in another country?"

"I—I haven't even considered the subject myself." But an Australian soldier had proposed to me at war's end. I hadn't thought about what my parents might have felt if I'd accepted him. I just knew somehow that, fond as I was of him, I wasn't ready to think of marriage. I still had work to do.

But would I have that work to look forward to when I got back to London? I'd hoped that this mission for Matron might persuade her that I should return to clinical nursing. And until now I hadn't considered that there might be nurses who wanted to stay with QAIMNS because they had nowhere else to go. Remembering the nurses at Holy Angels, middle-aged, committed to the care of whoever was brought to their ward.

Was that my future? Or was I one of the lucky ones who could go home? With the hard-won skills I'd learned in the war, perhaps I *should* teach. Pass on to others what the battlefields of France had taught me. Was I being selfish, not to want to?

I must have been silent for longer than was polite, because Madame said lightly, "Ah, there *must* be a young man you care for. Where is he now?"

Without conscious thought, I nearly replied, *In Scotland.*

My face suddenly felt the heat of a blush, and Madame laughed. "I was right, I think?"

Why on earth had I thought of Simon? Because I was worried about him, I told myself. Off to Scotland without telling my parents why, when they cared for him as the son they'd never had? That was cause for worry.

"I was just remembering all the proposals I'd had during the war," I said lamely. "They were sincere at that moment, and then they were sent back to the war." Or had died, but I didn't add that.

Changing the subject, I asked, "How is Marina? Was she upset about this sudden move?"

"I think she was glad to be back in her school. She left all sorts of messages for you, thanking you for what you had done for her. She's a lovely girl. So kind, so considerate."

"I'm glad all will be well for her. I was afraid that if we brought Lawrence here, someone so badly beaten, it would worry her to have him in the next room."

"It was kind of you to think of that. And her school welcomed her back, the Head Mistress embraced her, the other teachers clustered around her. It did Michel's heart good to see how she was cared for."

I finished my meal and was about to rise to go back upstairs, when Madame smiled at me.

"Don't let Lawrence fall in love with you while you nurse him," she said, teasing. But I realized she actually meant what she was saying.

"I'm afraid that's not very likely," I replied, suddenly feeling my hair being swept by the Seine's current as I fought him for my life. "Keeping him alive is far more urgent. For your sake and Matron's."

She nodded. "Please do that, for all our sakes."

What if I was saving his life only for the courts to hang him?

This was France. I winced as I tried to remember if they still used the guillotine for murderers.

The nurses arrived, competent, quiet women who took over the patient without comment, listening carefully to the instructions about his care.

I was tired after a long night with little sleep, the sounds of labored breathing coming from the bed keeping me awake, alert for any change. Lawrence moaned from time to time as he tried to shift positions to something more comfortable.

But after breakfast, I put on a fresh uniform and set out to find my father.

The clerk at the hotel desk reluctantly gave me the Colonel Sahib's room number. He was not the man who had helped me before, and I thought it was only my uniform that persuaded him that I was respectable and might in fact have business with one of his guests.

Amused, I found the lift and gave the operator, a thin man in the hotel's livery, the number of my father's floor.

The cage rattled up and the gate opened. The operator reached out to push the heavy door open for me. I thanked him and walked down the wide, carpeted passage to room 22.

I stood there for a moment, still uncertain what I should say to him, but I rather thought he would see Lawrence Minton as an Army problem, not one for the Paris police. And that would be troubling.

But I needed my father's help, there was no way around it, whatever happened.

I tapped lightly at the door, and after a moment it opened.

Major Webb stood in the doorway, staring down

at me. A slow flush crept up his face. In spite of it, I could see a cut on his cheekbone, barely beginning to heal.

My suspicions flared, but when I looked down at his hands, I could tell he hadn't been attacking someone in the last few days.

"Sister," he said.

I smiled. "Hallo, Major. Is my father in?"

"I'm sorry. He's got a breakfast meeting this morning. Something to do with one of the lesser parties wanting their pound of flesh." He hesitated. "Is there something I can do?"

"How much does he know about Lieutenant Minton's disappearance?"

"I don't know."

"Of course you do, Major. Remember, you offered to help me find him. I can't quite believe you were acting on your own."

"You'd better come in."

"Thank you, but no."

"Sister Crawford—Bess—we need to talk. And we can't do that here in the passage."

"I don't think we have anything to discuss."

"Look, I happened to be staying in the same house where Minton had a flat, and when he went missing, Madame Periard, who owns the house, was quite upset, and all for calling his commanding officer. That would have been the end of his career, and I persuaded her to wait, telling her it was a brief romance, either marry the young woman or come to his senses. I spoke to your father, and he was concerned, he knew Minton's mother, and he asked me to keep an eye on the flat. I did just that."

Oh, dear. Had my father known even when he encountered me in Dover that Lawrence was missing? Is that why the Major had tried to befriend me when I appeared at the Periard house? The Colonel Sahib had surely put it all together, and was keeping an eye on *me* as well as on the Lieutenant.

When I didn't immediately answer, the Major asked, "Have you found him, by any chance? Minton, I mean? The regiment is beginning to ask questions. If you can persuade him to come back sooner rather than later, it will make a difference."

I had no intention of confiding in the Major. He was far too glib, far too eager to help. I was rather surprised that my father had trusted him. But until I could be sure, I intended to keep my own counsel.

And so I said lightly, "I came by to ask my father to take me to lunch, if he was free today. I wish I could tell you where Lieutenant Minton might be. I've still to deliver the messages from his mother."

He flushed again. "If you're angry about seeing me at the doctor's house, I didn't know Moreau's name. And I wanted to be certain you'd given me the right address. After all, I was a stranger to you. You might have been wary of telling me where you were staying. How else could I be sure you were safe?"

"How, indeed. Good morning, Major."

And I turned and walked back toward the elevator.

He didn't try to stop me or to follow me.

I found a taxi just after leaving the hotel, still put out by my confrontation with the Major. *Did* my father trust him? Could I?

And the answer was, I couldn't be sure until I'd spoken to the Colonel Sahib. And at the moment, that didn't appear to be likely anytime soon.

I kept seeing the Major's face, flushed with what appeared to be guilt. For what? For misleading me?

Out of nowhere came the voice of the ward nurse at Holy Angels.

He was beaten long after he could defend himself.

If Lawrence had fought back, then surely his attacker was marked too?

I leaned forward, urging the driver to go faster, but he ignored me. The streets just here, in this part of the city, were busy, we'd need wings to move any faster. It was nearly thirty minutes later when I walked through the door and took the stairs up to what had become the sickroom.

Lawrence was sleeping. And it was healing, sleep. But now I would have given much to find him awake and lucid.

The day nurse, nodding silently to me as I stepped into the room, whispered in French, "No change. He hasn't spoken again or indeed opened his eyes."

His breathing was still labored, as if his chest hurt with each breath. There was a pillow under his broken arm and another under the broken leg. Bones ached abominably. I knew that from personal experience, having broken my arm during the frantic escape from the sinking hospital ship *Britannic*.

I moved closer to the bed, gently lifted the coverlet, and looked at Lawrence's right hand. Amongst all his terrible injuries, his hands had got short shrift. But the knuckles were swollen, bloody, and I thought it was possible that one of the bones in his hand was broken.

Dropping the coverlet, I went to the other side of the bed and did the same with his left hand. It too was discolored with bruises, and one of the knuckles was still oozing a little fluid. I set the coverlet back in place.

Lawrence Minton *had* defended himself! And well. Or the damage on his hands wouldn't be so extensive.

And that meant that whoever had done this would be clearly marked. Not just a cut on one cheek.

I smiled for the nurse, and slipped quietly out of the room.

I found myself remembering Captain Jackson's face when I'd met him and heard the news about the Lieutenant. He couldn't have attacked Lawrence. His face was unmarked, his hands as well.

There was Lieutenant Bedford—they'd fought once before. Had this attack been revenge for the bruised chin and cut lip?

I found another taxi and gave the driver the address of Madame Periard's house.

Clouds had thickened overhead and the first few heavy drops of rain were falling as I went to the door and knocked.

Madame answered it shortly afterward, and I asked if I might speak to Lieutenant Bedford.

"He has taken a chill and is in his room recovering from it," she told me. "Is there news of Lieutenant Minton? I have worried for him."

"Alas, no, Madame. I wish I could give you good news," I said. "Is it a chill, or was Lieutenant Bedford in a fight with another officer?"

"I do not gossip, Mademoiselle. He has asked me to turn away visitors, and so I do just that."

I couldn't be sure whether that meant he had—or he had not. And so when she had closed the door, I walked a little distance away, crossed the busy boulevard at the nearest corner, and came back on the opposite side of the street. I stood in a recessed doorway where I could watch her house but where I wasn't plainly visible. And I waited as the rain came down.

It was falling even harder when the Periard house door opened finally. I held my breath. And there was Lieutenant Bedford stepping out and then pausing. He looked for a passing taxi, gave up, and put up the umbrella he was carrying as he started down the street. I matched him step by step on the opposite side, ignoring the rain. And then he crossed over, and I picked up my pace to catch him up.

He stopped at the next corner, and I was just behind him. Reaching out, I tapped him on the shoulder.

He wheeled, as if expecting an attack, lowering his umbrella and planting his feet to fight back.

And I saw his face for the first time.

One eye was swollen, there was a cut on his lip, and a fresh darkening bruise on his chin.

When he realized who was behind him, he recovered quickly.

"Well, then," he said. "Come to gloat?"

Chapter 11

I stared at him, at the fresh visible damage.

"Gloat? Hardly. You nearly killed him. I want to know why." My voice was as cold as I could make it.

"You should be asking me how to hide this"—he gestured at his face—"from my commanding officer. What would you like me to tell him? That I fell down the stairs? Or didn't see the door?"

"I really don't care. If Lawrence Minton dies, you'll be court-martialed and your career will be over."

"*Dies*? He's got a longer reach, damn him. I only landed two blows. Hardly enough to matter." Then he added bitterly, "I thought he was a friend."

"You have a strange way of showing it. You put emetic into the laudanum you brought to him in St. Ives."

He was angry now. "You're both mad, mad as hatters. Why should I do such a thing? He was raving mad then too. I've washed my hands of him."

He made to turn away, then swung around again. "Tell him to keep his distance, do you hear me? If he jumps me again, I'll be prepared. And he won't like what he gets then."

"You've already beaten him so badly he may not live. There might not be a next time."

I thought he was about to swear at me, then he shut his mouth with a snap. Finally he had recovered control enough to say, "Is that it? You're to be his witness? I'd thought better of the Queen Alexandra's."

And he walked away, his face a thundercloud.

I watched him go, my mind working furiously. And then, ignoring the rain, I hurried after him.

"Lieutenant Bedford—"

"Go away."

My cap was wet, pulling against my hair. "No, it's important. I must talk to you."

He rounded on me, still angry. "If you don't leave me alone, I'll find a policeman and tell him that you're hounding me."

I thought he'd rather knock me down instead, but was too much of a gentleman to say so.

This time as he strode off, I let him go.

Was he lying to me, when he told me that he'd barely touched Lawrence Minton? It wasn't very likely that he'd admit to such a severe attack. But his face was evidence that he'd been in a fight with *someone*.

Nearly wet through, I found a taxi to take me to the Moreau house.

I should have followed him, I told myself. *Made* him speak to me. But how I was to do that was another matter.

Madame Moreau fussed over me and how wet I was. She sent me up to my room, and hot water and hot water bottles quickly followed. The maid took away my wet clothing, promising to see to it. And my hair was so wet I had no choice but to wash it and dry it by the fire, a blanket over my shoulders.

Finally warm again, I looked in on Lawrence. The day nurse was preparing to send for her dinner, but I sent her down to the kitchen instead, promising to sit with him until she got back.

I couldn't tell if he was better—or worse. His breathing seemed as labored as before, but his body appeared to be more relaxed, not tense in anticipation of more blows. And the nurse had mentioned that he didn't flinch from her when she changed his bandages.

There was a pot of gruel on the hearth, a broth of vegetables and chicken. I poured a little into a cup, worried that he hadn't had any food for two days. Carrying it to the bed, I said, "Lawrence? Can you drink a little broth? I'll help you."

There was no response at first, and then he struggled to lift his head from the pillows. I carefully helped him raise himself a little more, enough so that he wouldn't choke.

At first I got more on the cloth I'd draped across his chest, under his chin, finding it difficult to hold the cup and take his weight as well. In the war I'd have had an orderly help me. And then we both seemed to get the hang of it, and he swallowed the next several spoonfuls.

But the attempt had tired him, and I felt his weight grow heavier as he slipped back into sleep. At least, I thought, he'd got something down. And if he kept it down, we could try again in a few hours.

I had a feeling he didn't know where he was, or who I was. He'd been wounded in the war, and it was possible he remembered that rather than what had happened to him in the alley. And so he was responding now to what appeared to be familiar.

I came back later that evening, after dinner with the family. The night nurse had arrived, a large woman with kind eyes, and with her help, I was able to feed our patient a little more of the broth. Setting my internal clock, which had served me well throughout the war, I came back at four in the morning to try again.

But this time, he was too heavily asleep to help us help him, his mouth sagging open and his ability to swallow just as lax.

We made him as comfortable as possible, and I went back to my bed, falling into a deep sleep myself.

The next two days were critical for Lawrence Minton. And I hadn't heard from my father. I couldn't help but wonder if the Major had given the Colonel Sahib my message. To complicate matters, Marina came by late in the second afternoon, to thank Dr. and Madame Moreau for their care.

I had seen her coming in the very nick of time to disappear up the stairs and out of sight. She couldn't ask Madame about Lawrence, but she could ask me for news.

Madame Moreau told me afterward. "She asked for you. Why did you not come down?"

"I was asleep, I'm afraid," I told her, hating the lie, even though it was necessary.

We'd decided not to send for Matron. I'd been of two minds about that, but Dr. Moreau felt now that we could wait a little longer.

I couldn't tell whether or not *he* was lying to *me*.

On the fourth day, Lawrence opened his eyes, stared around the unfamiliar room, and then closed them again. "Marina?" he called a few minutes later.

I was not there—the day nurse hurried to find me. I was dressing for breakfast when she knocked.

"I don't know who this Marina may be. If he woke, I was to say that he was in the house of a friend. That he was not to worry. I don't know how to answer him."

"She's a friend," I said lightly, setting my apron aside, pinning up my hair but not bothering with my cap. Following the nurse into the passage, I added, "Why don't you go down to your breakfast. Let me settle him."

She hesitated, then set off toward the back stairs. I waited until I was sure she was out of hearing, then went into the room.

Lawrence was lying there with his eyes closed. But not, I thought, in sleep.

Pulling a chair to the bedside, I sat down and spoke quietly, calmly. "Good morning, Lieutenant. Could I bring you a little warm broth?"

"Any more and I'll drown," he said, and opened his eyes.

The old Lawrence was back, I thought, suppressing a sigh.

"Who are you?" he asked, then, frowning. "Marina told me she'd let the staff go."

"Sister Crawford." I waited. "Bess Crawford."

Recognition came back slowly, and he flushed a little, turning away. "My mother's spy." A flash of pain went through him as he moved. Looking at me with alarm, he demanded, "What have you done to me?" He began frantically to assess his body, his hand going first to his head, tearing at the bandages he could feel there.

I reached out and stopped him, taking his hand in mine as he struggled briefly, then gave in to the pain.

"Oh, God," he said then. "What have you done?" He pulled his hand free.

"Lieutenant? You were in a fight with someone. Do you remember?"

"There was no fight. I never—" He broke off. "Bedford. I knocked him down. But that was—" He stopped again. "I was poisoned." He looked around the room. *"Where have you taken me?"*

There was anger and pleading and fear in his voice, and he reached out and gripped my hand.

"Lawrence, listen to me. You're safe. This is Dr. Moreau's house, I didn't know where else to take you. You were found in an alley and taken to a hospital where I found you. You're badly hurt, but with good care you'll recover. But you must stay quiet."

"Dr. Moreau? Oh, God, he knew my mother—he'll send for her—she can't see me like this."

"We haven't sent for her. Not yet."

I let him absorb that for a while, then I said, "Do you remember who attacked you?"

He started to shake his head, then quickly stopped. "Why are there all these bandages? Why can't I move my leg? My arm—"

I told him how badly he was injured, and he just lay there, staring at the ceiling. I was concerned that I'd told him too much, too soon.

Silence filled the room, only the ticking of the clock on the mantelpiece and the crackling of the fire broke it.

"Marina?" he asked at length.

"She's all right. She's back at her school now. It's for the best."

"Yes. For the best."

And he shut his eyes, shutting me out, shutting out the present.

I wasn't sure when he slipped from consciousness to sleep again. I stayed by his bed for hours, waiting, but I didn't think he was ready to face anything more. The nurse brought up a soft omelet with cheese, hoping he might be hungry, but I finally ate it rather than waste it, remembering how hungry Marina and I had been in St. Ives.

Dr. Moreau came up shortly after the nurse came back from breakfast, looking at our patient, lifting an eyelid, checking his pulse, listening to his heart.

He tried to persuade me to go out into the sunshine and take a walk, but I wanted to be there when Lawrence woke again.

Madame Moreau came to sit with me for a time, reaching out to touch his face gently before she sat down. "If he woke up in his right senses once, he will again," she said, trying to reassure me. But I thought it was more than that. She was trying to convince herself that he would survive.

It was after two in the morning when Lawrence Minton came back to us. The night nurse tapped on my door, and I was already flinging back the covers, reaching for my robe, and fishing for my slippers on the rug by my bed.

I hurried into the bedroom, realizing that the nurse had turned down the lamps and only the fire was burning. I asked her to wait outside and stepped in, shutting the door before she could answer me.

"Hallo," I said quietly, and walked toward the bed.

"I expect you think I ought to thank you."

I brought the chair forward and said, "Not really. It was a priest who found you. If you feel like thanking anyone, it should be him."

"I thought you said I was found in an alley?"

So he remembered that? A good sign.

"But not by me. It was a doctor at Holy Angels who prevented you from dying. By the time I found out where you were, I could see that you needed more care than the overworked staff there could give you. Dr. Moreau was willing to have you come here."

"You always were a busybody. You should have let me die."

"That would be too easy," I retorted, refusing to let him sink back into that frame of mind. "If you were meant to die, the priest would have been too late. The doctor would have been unsuccessful. I wouldn't have found you. No, I think God would rather have you survive and suffer." It was cruel, but it had to be said.

And from the expression on his face, I could see that if I'd slapped him, he couldn't have been more surprised.

Rallying, he retorted, "I thought nursing Sisters were supposed to heal the sick, not torment them."

"You left Marina in that cold, empty house, alone and in pain, after she'd been badly burned. That was callous and selfish."

He defended himself. "I did everything I could for her, I knew you'd be back soon, and she'd be looked after."

"I hardly call that repaying her for her many kindnesses to you."

He had the grace to look ashamed of himself. The bruises on his face were slowly fading, mostly green and yellow now, and ghoulish against his pallor. "I'd kept back a little money as well. I'd hoped there was enough to take the train to Paris, but I was wrong. I walked. I couldn't beg, I was wearing my uniform. Three nights ago, I found a room in a working-class district. I was too tired to think."

It wasn't three nights ago. He'd lost nearly a week. Still, it explained why I'd searched Paris for him, and hadn't been able to find him. He hadn't arrived—

Three nights ago—had he been sleeping in the rough, just arrived in Paris, the night I thought I'd found him sleeping below the bridge? And had nearly been drowned by the man lying there?

I turned away so that he couldn't see my face.

If he'd attacked me—had he known who I was? Or been so startled by my presence that he'd lashed out, thinking someone was robbing him of what little money he had left?

But I'd called his name. Identified myself . . .

I wanted to pursue it there and then, to bring it out into the open. But my better judgment told me it could wait. What was important now was to learn what I could while he felt like talking.

He sighed. "I gave the *pension* the last of my money to do something about my uniform. But it was hopeless. I couldn't resign from the Army, looking as if I'd slept rough for days on end. And so I set out for Madame Periard's house to see if there was a uniform in my flat. My valise was stolen one night as I slept, somewhere on the outskirts of Paris. But Madame wasn't in, and I couldn't find my key. I was afraid I'd run into someone else, and so I went across the street to wait, out of sight, for her to come home."

I thought, *It was where I'd stood, waiting for Lieutenant Bedford. Or very close by.*

"Go on," I said, when he appeared to have stopped.

"Bedford came down the street. He saw me, there was no place to hide, and he made some sneering remark about my condition. I was at the end of my patience. I said something about the laudanum, and he denied having poisoned it. He said he'd bought it on the street, he wasn't responsible for the quality. I hit him then. I didn't intend to, but I was tired, hungry, I needed to find that uniform. I don't think I hurt him very badly. But I regretted it almost immediately, and I turned and walked away."

"Why does he dislike you?"

"I didn't think he did," he said, his voice reflecting how quickly he'd begun to tire. "He held a battlefield commission, and he's sensitive about that, sometimes too much so. I tried to overlook it, tried to befriend him." He took a deep breath. "But then there was the laudanum."

If he'd cared about you, he wouldn't have supplied it in the first place. He'd have done something to help instead. The words were almost out of my mouth, but I caught them in time and asked instead, "Did he follow you, do you think? To get his own back?"

"I—I can't remember. I walked away, knowing I should have asked him to let me into the house to look for my uniforms. And telling myself I was a fool. The next thing I recall is standing outside a café, smelling the odors of cooking, and realizing I hadn't eaten anything that day. And not much the day before. After that it was just plodding, trying to get myself back to the *pension.* And I kept seeing his face, flushed and angry, after I'd hit him. I couldn't believe we'd brawled in the street like drunkards. Knowing that if he reported me, I couldn't resign with that on my record."

"What else do you remember about walking to the *pension?*"

"I—I think there was a beggar, but I didn't have anything to give him, and he cursed me. I told him he had more to live for than I did. At least I think there was a beggar. I can't really be sure now." The fingers of his good hand were plucking restlessly at the coverlet.

"Why did you intend to resign? You'd asked for this assignment, or so I've been told."

He gave me an angry glance. "I won't disgrace the Regiment."

And I knew what he meant. If he intended to kill himself, he couldn't do it until he'd left the Army behind. That was why he'd left the house in St. Ives. To resign, while he was still sober enough to do it.

"It would be better, don't you think, to live and to atone somehow? That often takes more courage than dying."

"You don't know anything about it." He resolutely shut his eyes, and I couldn't reach him after that. Whether he was really asleep or just avoiding me, I really didn't know. On the whole, I thought he'd been too exhausted to go on.

After a late breakfast, I went back to my room for my coat and after hesitating over it, chose to wear my wool hat and my Welsh scarf. For though the rain had gone, the wind had risen with the clearing of the skies, and there was a chill in the air.

I walked toward the boulevard, hoping to find a taxi, and instead encountered Captain Jackson standing on the corner chatting with a friend. He saw me, said good-bye to his companion, and hurried to catch me up as I hailed a taxi.

"I haven't seen you for a while, ma'am. I hope all is well with our patient?"

He got into the taxi with me before I could answer him, and added, "You appear to be on a mission. Maybe I should tag along?"

I'd actually planned to find the priest who'd discovered Lawrence in the alley. Did I want the Captain to stay with me?

The driver of the taxi turned impatiently and said, "Where to?"

I could hardly ask the Captain to get out. But I was beginning to wonder at how handy he was becoming. Still, he'd found Lawrence for me, hadn't he?

I gave the address of Holy Angels hospital, and the Captain leaned back against the seat. "What takes you there, ma'am?"

"I must talk to the staff in Casualty. I want to ask if they remember the name of the priest who had called for an ambulance."

"Well, then, I'm glad I came with you. That's not a part of Paris a lady ought to be walking around alone."

Shades of Captain Barkley! Trying to recover my sense of humor, I said lightly, "Women and children to the lifeboats first?"

He laughed. It was a pleasant laugh, deep in his chest, rather like Simon's.

"Seeing that I can't swim, I might have to push you aside for a seat."

We drove the rest of the way in a companionable silence.

And he did prove useful, asking the porter at the entrance to Casualty if we could speak to someone about a patient who had come in recently. His French was far more fluent than mine.

The porter looked us up and down, then allowed us to enter the busy Casualty ward. I felt right at home in the bustle and confusion. It reminded me of the early days of my training. There were accident cases, with broken arms, bruises, even what appeared to be the results of a knifing, an appendix, a woman with heart problems, a child limp with fever, his body covered in the telltale red rash of measles. A nurse saw us and came over to ask which of us was ill. I said quickly, "There was a man brought in here some days ago, terribly beaten. A priest had found him and summoned help. The man's family has asked me to find this priest if possible, to thank him."

She was about to turn us away when an older nurse, passing by as we talked, stopped and said, "The priest? He stayed to offer last rites. We expected the man to die."

"Do you know him? This priest?"

"Father Ambrose. He's something of a legend, he scours the streets for those in need. But his church is several streets over. Notre Dame de la Miséricorde."

Our Lady of Mercy. I thanked her, and we hurried out of their way.

Outside, Captain Jackson pointed. "That could be the church." And I could just see the tall roof he was indicating, in a gap between tenements.

We made our way there, followed by a throng of children begging, an ex-soldier asking us to take pity on him, and a vegetable vendor. I looked at him twice— too clean-shaven for a vendor, although he wore the habitual smock. And his shoes were of better quality than most of those I could see around me—scuffed, down-at-the-heel, toes peeling away from the sole.

He saw me staring, touched his greasy cap, and moved on.

I watched him go, thinking his face was familiar, but then Captain Jackson was saying, "Look. Over there."

And I saw a priest near a shop just down the street from us, his black hat and soutane hardly visible amongst the four or five black-clad women surrounding him. I realized he was speaking to them, asking questions. And then they nodded to him and moved on. He looked after them, his face sad.

When we were close enough to speak, I saw that he was about fifty, his hair iron gray, what I could see of it, and only a little taller than I was. But there was a subtle energy about him as well.

"Father Ambrose?" I called in French, and he looked away from the women and turned toward us.

"Good morning," he said in French, then switched to passable English. "Sister. Captain."

"Could we beg a little of your time, to ask about the man you found dying in an alley? And rushed to Holy Angels?" I asked.

"Ah. Yes. Of course." He moved forward, and I saw that he limped. "Are you his family? We didn't know his name, I feared he would die without our learning it."

I saw a café close by, and I said, "Could we offer you a coffee, perhaps?"

"That would be very kind."

It was obvious that his clothing was worn, with a patch at the cuffs. We walked as far as the café, took the chairs around one of the three tables there, and moved them a little, out of the wind.

Captain Jackson went inside to order three coffees, and I said, "We aren't related to the man, but I am in France in place of his mother, who has been worried about him. We'd been searching for him, you see. I had nearly given up hope of finding him."

"How is he?" the priest asked. "I have not been to inquire. You understand, there are so many in need. Widows. Children. Soldiers who have nowhere to go."

"He is in private care. There is hope, now. In the beginning, like you, we feared he might not live."

"Ah. That is good news. Yes. Good news."

Captain Jackson came out with a tray and our coffees. He set them down in front of each of us. Then he joined us. He was so much taller than Father Ambrose, and even seated, he seemed to loom over us.

"How did you come to find him?"

"There is a widow who lives in the house two doors away from the alley. You can see it from here—just there?" He gestured toward a dark space between two houses across the road.

I turned to look. Until now I hadn't realized how close we were to the place where the beating had occurred. I felt a shiver of revulsion.

"It is full of rubbish, an unhealthy place. *Alors,* I had brought this widow her medicines, explaining to her how these powders were to be taken. When I was certain she understood, I left her. I had walked by there—the alley, you understand—on my way to the widow's house. It was empty. I notice these things. An alley is where the desperate go to die. When I passed it on my way to my next call, there was something in the shadows. I saw a foot—a boot. I went in, and there was a body. The uniform was English, but so untidy I wasn't sure it belonged to the man. I thought he was dead. I began to give him last rites, and he moaned as I touched his forehead. I ran to the corner, found a policeman. I knew him, I sent him for an ambulance, then stayed with the man all the way to the hospital, because I expected to be required. But he did not die. Only God knows why."

"Who did this to him?" I asked. "Surely you must have seen something?"

"I was in the widow's house for twenty-five minutes. No longer. But there was no one close by the alley when I walked back past it."

"Did you see anything in that alley that could have been a weapon?" It was the Captain who spoke.

Neither of us had touched our coffees, but the priest had drunk some of his, as if he liked the warmth if not the taste. I had the impression he couldn't often afford to indulge himself.

Setting his cup down again, he frowned. "I never looked for a weapon."

"The doctor told us that something had been used besides fists," I said.

Father Ambrose shook his head. "There was no time, you understand. His life was ebbing quickly."

Captain Jackson glanced at me. Then he asked, "Are you sure there was no one nearby who could have done this?"

Father Ambrose sipped his coffee, thinking back. "A butcher's apprentice crossing the street. Two women were standing by the corner, talking. The policeman. A beggar with one leg. A soldier in a greatcoat just going over the bridge. I saw no one else."

"British or French soldier?" the Captain asked.

"I can't be sure."

Lawrence's attacker would have been covered in blood. Surely someone would have noticed?

But there was that butcher's apprentice—he would be wearing a bloody apron—and no one would have thought anything about it. I couldn't imagine why a butcher's apprentice would want to kill a stranger. Unless he knew Lawrence somehow?

I said, "Could the man on the bridge have been an English officer?"

Captain Jackson looked sharply at me.

But the priest was adamant. "I couldn't tell. It was the merest glimpse, you understand."

"The apprentice then. Is there a butcher's shop close by?"

"Not in this street."

Captain Jackson rose. "Excuse me, ma'am." And he walked off, that long stride quickly carrying him to the corner and across the street, threading his way through the peddlers and vehicles that were passing by. We watched him disappear into the shadows of the alley—we could see signs of movement, but not what he was doing.

A few minutes passed, and then he came out of the alley. In his hands he carried something, holding it gingerly. But it was hard to see just what it was. We went on watching him as he walked to the corner, crossed the street again, and came toward us at the café.

And then I recognized what it was he was carrying so carefully. A rolling pin. Something that could be found in any kitchen in France or England, or anywhere else in Europe. It was a long one, wooden, tapered at both ends in place of handles. A baker's tool. I'd used a smaller one with the usual handles at home, helping our cook make pastries for a party.

Only this one wasn't white with flour, it was dark, with even darker patches to it.

Father Ambrose crossed himself as he realized what the patches must be. Lawrence Minton's blood.

Chapter 12

Captain Jackson brought it to our table, holding it up so that we could see it more clearly. As I'd thought, it was the French style, with those tapered ends. This one was larger than most, and a little longer, as if for shop use, rather than at home. In effect, a rather nasty weapon.

A very handy one as well, for it would extend the reach of the assailant and bring more force to bear than a fist, as well as save the attacker's knuckles.

We stared at it in silence, the Captain and I.

"Why would a butcher's apprentice carry a rolling pin?" I asked.

They turned to look at me.

"His bloody apron wouldn't have attracted attention, would it? That's to say, someone couldn't have walked out of that alley with fresh blood on his clothes, his face, his hands. Even if he wiped away some of it, he couldn't do much about his clothing."

"How would a butcher's assistant persuade the Lieutenant to follow him into that alley? Minton was in the war, he could defend himself." It was the Captain who asked the question.

"I don't know," I admitted. "For all I know the man could have asked his help to rescue a child or a dog."

But the uncertainty hung in the air.

Defending my position, I said, "Only a few minutes ago, there was a vegetable vendor, he was carrying a tray with a few moldy turnips, shriveled potatoes, and wilted cabbages. They could have come from a dustbin, thrown out by a greengrocer. He was clean-shaven, and his boots weren't down-at-the-heels like most people in this quarter—" I stopped. The priest also wore scuffed, down-at-the-heels boots. "He didn't look as if he belonged here," I ended, a little embarrassed.

Father Ambrose smiled, but added, "This quarter is the last place for those with nowhere else to turn."

But I wasn't convinced. My training had taught me to *look* at a patient, observing his condition, any changes, anything that was unexpected, worrying. I didn't think twice doing it—it had become a habit with me over the years. But I couldn't explain why a man with clean boots and a butcher's assistant with a bloody apron stayed with me, even as Captain Jackson changed the subject.

"This was a vicious beating. In your parish have you come across such a thing before? Do you know anyone capable of doing this?"

"Even the poor steal from their brothers. I have seen every kind of cruelty and meanness. But if I'd suspected one of my flock, I would have said as much to the policeman. Still, I have been watchful."

We had barely touched our coffee, but Father Ambrose had drunk his own to the dregs. I asked if he'd like another.

"Thank you, but no. I must be about my duties. If anything new comes to my attention, how will I let you know of it?"

I was about to give him the address of Dr. Moreau, but the Captain stepped in quickly. "My name is Jackson. I'm staying at the Hotel Royale. You could leave a message at the desk."

He thanked him and was about to rise when I reached into my pocket and drew out some francs. "Father? A donation? To help those like Lawrence?"

He took them gratefully and graciously. We sat there, watching him limp away, watched people passing him acknowledge him with a little bow of the head.

"A good man," the Captain said. "What shall I do with this weapon?"

I hadn't thought about that. "Could you keep it? I know, it isn't very nice to have in your rooms. But I don't know that the police will find it very useful. Not yet." I didn't want Madame Moreau to know what had been used to attack the Lieutenant.

He looked around, saw a crumpled newspaper in the doorway of the shop next to the café, and carefully wrapped the rolling pin in it. "Much better, don't you think?"

"I'd like to find that butcher shop in the next street," I said. "Or failing that, the vegetable vendor."

The Captain grinned. "You don't give up easily, do you, ma'am?"

"I do wish you'd call me Bess," I said as we walked toward the corner.

"I try not to presume, ma'am." But there was a decided twinkle in his eyes.

We found the butcher shop easily, although one would hardly know what it sold, for the trays in the counter were mostly empty.

I let the Captain ask him what we'd come to find out, but the man pointed to the trays.

"I have hardly enough meat to open each morning. I can't afford an assistant. My wife helps when she can."

His manner was brusque, and watching him, I couldn't be sure he was telling the truth. Yet there was no way to prove he was lying.

Captain Jackson thanked him, and we left the shop.

And although we went up and down several more streets, we never saw the vegetable vendor again.

Dissatisfied, wanting to do more, and not really sure how to go about that, I finally said, "I must go back to the house. I don't like to leave Lawrence alone for very long. The doctor has his surgery hours."

"Surely his care isn't all on your shoulders."

"No, there are other nurses, but I feel better if I can keep an eye on his condition."

"That's admirable of you, ma'am. Is there no one else who can help?"

"We manage well enough. For now."

He found a taxi for us, but we had to cross to the Right Bank first. And then I was home, thanking him for his help.

"Don't worry, ma'am. Answers have a way of popping up when you least expect to find them," he said, seeing me to the door as the taxi waited. And then he was gone.

I lost track of time, watching over the Lieutenant's care. His recovery was slow, painful. He slept much of the time—or pretended to—but at the end of the week, it was obvious that not only would he live, if there were no surprises like infections or blood clots or even brain damage, but he was also sleeping less.

But he refused to respond to questions, or even talk to either the nurse or to me about such simple things as what day of the week it was, how long had it been raining, whether it was ten o'clock or eleven in the morning. He still looked like a man who'd been beaten within an inch of his life.

We ought to summon Matron. She was a nurse, she'd seen severe beatings before. This was her son.

But there was more to it than her feelings when she saw what had happened to her son. She would have to be told what else I knew, and I wasn't sure of anything at the moment. I had begun to realize that Matron must have her own suspicions too. She had not written to ask for a report on my progress.

It did occur to me one night in the dark hour before dawn that his beating had been retribution for what had happened to me on the brink of the river. But somehow I couldn't see Captain Jackson finding a man he didn't know and had never seen before, and nearly killing him. It didn't hold up to scrutiny.

I toyed with the idea of the nonexistent butcher's assistant and the clean-shaven vegetable vendor, and got nowhere. I'd felt I'd seen the vendor before, but where? I went over all the places I'd been, but of course it was impossible to remember the faces of everyone I'd encountered on any given day. I tried to remember faces from the train, or shops where I'd looked for food, or anywhere else I could think of, but it was hopeless.

I walked into the room on a day when the nurse was having her meal downstairs—now that the patient was out of danger—and Lawrence was lying there, pretending to sleep. But I'd thought I'd seen him looking at the door as I stepped in, before closing his eyes and changing the rhythm of his breathing.

It was only right to find out what sort of person he really was, before his mother came to collect him. The question that had been worrying me of late was what I would do if he confessed to attacking me. Or harming someone else. I couldn't just let him go home to England, could I? If there was a dark streak of violence in him? What if he blacked out, as a result of that earlier concussion, and had no memory of what he'd done to me or anyone else?

I said, in a ward Matron's voice, "You aren't asleep. I'm a nurse, remember? I know the difference. Sleep isn't just closed eyes and steady breaths. So you might as well stop playacting."

His eyelids tightened. But they didn't open.

I pulled up the day nurse's chair, and sat nearer to the bed.

"There is a lot I don't know about you. Probably will never know. You can keep secrets. I've seen how well you do that. But there is one question I'm going to put to you, and I won't give up asking it until you answer me."

There was silence from the bed. But I saw the toes move on his good leg. He was bracing himself. For what? My question? Or—the question he was afraid I was going to ask?

"Did you try to drown me?" I asked him.

He opened his eyes then. His lids were still puffy, his eyes bloodshot. "No."

It was short, unequivocal. I didn't know whether to believe him or not.

Finally I said, "It's time to tell me the truth. I have to know what to do about you. Whether, as soon as you're well enough, to hand you over to the French National Police or the Foot Police. *Are* you a murderer?"

Taking a deep breath, he said, "Do whatever you have to do. I don't really care."

"But why don't you care any longer? You asked to be sent to Paris, you wished to stay in the Army. And then you've walked away from the conference, you've abused Marina's trust, you've disgraced your regiment. There has to be a reason why."

He turned away from me. "You should have let me die in that hospital ward. I would have been buried in a pauper's grave, without a name, forgotten."

"And what do you expect me to tell your mother? That you were too much of a coward to face the consequences of what you'd done? Did you *hire* someone to beat you to death because you didn't have the courage to kill yourself?"

That was terribly harsh, I wanted to call back the words, but somehow I had to break through his wall of silence. And he still wasn't well enough to hand over to the police.

Something flared in his eyes, then died away, almost a recognition of what I'd called him. A coward. Then he simply shut them, shutting me out as the lids closed. He completely withdrew, as if I didn't exist.

Defeated, I went away, after trying to find a way through the wall he'd thrown up, blocking all my efforts.

Later that evening, my mind made up, I went downstairs to look for Dr. Moreau.

He was just winding the case clock in the parlor before going up to bed. I said, "Could we talk?"

Turning, he glanced at me, then his gaze sharpened.

"Yes, of course, my dear. Let me finish here, and we'll go into my surgery. We won't be disturbed there."

I stood in the doorway until he'd put the key away and shut the case, then I followed him to his surgery. Neither of us spoke on the way, but when he'd settled me in a chair and given me a blanket against the chill—there wasn't enough coal to keep this part of the house warm all night long—he took the chair opposite me rather than going behind his desk.

It was a signal that this conversation was to be personal, not professional.

He said quietly, "Now then, tell me what is worrying you."

"It's Lawrence Minton. I don't quite know what to do. Or where to turn."

"Begin at the beginning."

But I couldn't, not really. After a moment, I said, "Let me report to you, a Sister reporting her findings about a patient of yours."

"Very well."

"There's something that happened to the Lieutenant some weeks after he came to Paris. I don't know what it was. But it appears to have changed him almost overnight. The capable career soldier was gone, and in its place, he was lost, unable to regain control, wanting oblivion. Peace. I don't know what it was. I have my suspicions. But I don't think he will be well again until he accepts it instead of running from it."

"Had there been any symptoms before this change?"

"I—don't know, you see. But there *was* a medical condition. That concussion in the early days of the war. There were serious gaps in his memory then. There may be other gaps now that he doesn't wish to remember. And it's the gaps that worry me. There are no witnesses to these gaps."

"He was separated from his men during the retreat, and he was thought to be missing, most likely captured," Dr. Moreau said. "Do you believe that he was taken, and it's this experience as a prisoner that changed him? In that advance the Germans did some appalling things, but I have not heard that they tortured prisoners."

"He was an English officer. He could provide valuable information they could use. There was some suspicion that he'd been a spy, remember." Many Germans had lived in England, gone to school there, spoke excellent English. "He does speak the language. What if it was more than a suspicion?"

"After he was released, Helena wrote to us about the strange, rather terrible dreams he'd had as a result of the concussion. But that's not unusual."

"What if they weren't dreams, but memories he couldn't accept?"

"My dear. As far as I know, he went on to have an exemplary career. Mentioned in dispatches, given a medal in the aftermath of the Somme for bringing back three of his men who'd been wounded before they'd reached the trench. Even I would have to say that he was completely recovered."

I realized, sitting there, listening to Dr. Moreau, that perhaps Matron, Lawrence's mother, had sent me to Paris because she wasn't certain he *was* recovered, and she wanted a nurse to find him and evaluate him medically, and report to her before the Regiment learned of it. That it wasn't the fact that he hadn't written in some time that made her uneasy. She feared something else. But what was it?

I'd only had glimpses of it in St. Ives. *Something* haunted him.

"What if in those missing hours, when no one could find him, something terrible happened? Something real, not imagined. And he shut it away so tightly that he went through the war without remembering. Then here in Paris, something unlocked those events. And now he thinks he knows what happened."

"Are you suggesting he broke under the stress of the

retreat and surrendered to the enemy? Betrayed the positions of his own men?" Dr. Moreau took off his glasses, vigorously polishing them on a clean handkerchief. He was looking down, I couldn't see his face or judge whether he knew something that I didn't. Something that Helena had confided in him?

And upstairs, I'd accused Lawrence of being a coward . . .

Had he encountered someone who was here in Paris, someone who knew the truth about him? The city was filled with people who had come to confer about the terms of the peace treaty. Someone from his past could have confronted him.

I remembered the carpet as he knelt on the staircase. Had he tried to drown that person? And half asleep, had he tried to drown me as well, thinking it was the *same* person? Was that person the one who'd found him again and beaten him nearly to death?

Clutching at straws, I asked, "Surely there is something we can do, to get at the truth? Before his mother comes to Paris? Dr. Moreau, she ought to know what is wrong with him."

There was a silence. He put his glasses back in place before saying, "The truth is, I have known Lawrence for some time, and I haven't seen anything that would make me suspect him of doing anything—disgraceful.

He's not that sort of man, there's no weakness of character to explain it."

But Dr. Moreau hadn't been in St. Ives. He hadn't seen the bouts of laudanum and then brandy, the way Lawrence treated Marina—the incident on the stairs when I watched him with the carpet.

The doctor sighed. "I must confess. I've written to Helena—I know, we had discussed when best to do that. In my opinion as Lawrence's doctor, the time had come. She is presently arranging matters at the Queen Alexandra's, so that she can spend as much time with Lawrence as necessary. She could be here tomorrow. Or the next day."

I was horrified.

But this was his house—Matron was his friend. I was here as a guest. There was nothing more I could do. Frustrated, I said in despair, "If only we could open up his head, as we might probe a wound—or do exploratory surgery in the abdomen. If only we could somehow search his memory."

"Is it truly so important to you?"

"I should think it would matter to his mother."

He looked at me, and I thought he was about to ask me to walk away from this problem, to let Lawrence go back to what he was before. But he couldn't. I couldn't.

Then to my shock, Dr. Moreau said, "There is a way."

———

I couldn't quite believe it when he told me what he had in mind. Dr. Moreau had learned how to hypnotize the wounded when they were in great pain.

"It has helped them in situations where opiates couldn't be given in high enough doses or not at all. In Lawrence's case—if you are correct—it isn't the physical pain that is so upsetting to him." He fiddled with his glasses again.

I was beginning to realize that it was a habit he wasn't aware of, a way of hiding his own uncertainties.

"If he can accept what happened to him, bring it out of the darkness into the light, so to speak, it will lose its power over him. That at least is the theory."

"Does it always work?"

"No."

"Have you ever had it fail, and leave the patient worse than before?"

"If done by a responsible person, it is safe. We are not asking him to make a fool of himself onstage, for the amusement of the audience."

"And what if he says something while in this trance that horrifies you—disgusts you?"

He took off his glasses again and rubbed his face with his hands. Putting them back on, he looked at me straightly. "I cannot believe that of the young man I know."

It was late, well past midnight. But Dr. Moreau urged me to start now, because Lawrence would be more vulnerable, awakened from sleep.

That was a risk in itself.

"Surely we need his permission?"

He turned, gazing at me for a moment. "He will not answer what he doesn't want us to know. We cannot make him act against his will. As his doctor, it is my duty to do whatever is in his best interest. Treatment is not always a powder in solution."

But I thought he was convincing himself, not me.

The house was quiet as we walked back into it from the surgery. I led the way up the stairs and down the passage to the door of Lawrence's room, and opened it as softly as I could.

The night nurse looked up, surprised to see us.

Dr. Moreau whispered to her, "I would like to sit with him awhile. Why don't you go down to my wife's sitting room, and rest until I call you?"

It was unorthodox, and she looked from one to the other of us before rising, collecting her bag of knitting, and tiptoeing to the door.

The only sound in the room now was the regular breathing of the man on the bed. But I thought to myself that it was his way of keeping us at bay, that he couldn't be that deeply asleep.

We waited until we were sure she was gone, that she hadn't forgot something, and then Dr. Moreau began to speak quietly to the man on the bed.

I watched from the nurse's chair by the hearth, listened in the semidarkness of the room, lit only by the spirit lamp on a table by the window. Lawrence didn't know I was there, he hadn't opened his eyes. I prayed it wouldn't break the spell if he saw me.

"Can you hear me, my boy? Of course you can. And you are glad of my company after having to deal with the nurses. You feel safe with me here. And you find you are very relaxed, hearing my voice. You can sleep in peace, a deep, healing sleep that will free you from fear and despair . . ."

The low voice went on, seeming to float in the dimness, coming from nowhere in particular, its resonance soothing, drawing me in. I blinked, willing myself to fight against the spell of the voice, reminding myself that he was speaking to Lawrence.

The tenor of the voice changed slightly. "You want to talk to me, don't you, my boy? To lift the burden that weighs you down. I won't judge. I am just here with you in the night, and your secrets are safe with me. Can you hear me, Lawrence?"

"Yes. I hear you."

"Are you comfortable? No pain? Relaxed and calm of spirit?"

"Yes."

"Does the past disturb your sleep, my boy?"

There was a slight movement from the bed, and I thought surely it wasn't working, that Lawrence had realized what we were trying to do. I could feel the tension rising in my own body, dreading what might come next.

But what else were we to do?

And then he answered. "Yes."

"Let us look back then, to see what troubles you. Back to the retreat from Mons?"

"I don't like it." There was denial in the tone of his answer.

"But this is hindsight, and you are safe from it, even as you remember it. It is a memory, now, and can do no harm."

And a few minutes later, the story came spilling out. Slowly at first, and then in mounting fear as he relived it.

Chapter 13

He was back on that road, night was falling, and the Germans were still pressing hard.

"What do you see," Dr. Moreau asked softly.

"There's been no panic. We've retreated in good order. But the longer we can hold them the sooner reinforcements will get here. I'm proud of them, by God I am."

They must have encountered a party of Germans, because he startled me with his cry, "Take cover!" And the rate of his breathing increased as he gave order after order, encouraging his men to hold. But they must have understood very quickly that this was no scouting party, it was the probing advance of a German Army, and they were facing overwhelming odds. He began ordering a retreat. "Go on, the two of us will cover you from that cellar over there. Where the outer door has been ripped away. They can't get to us."

A pause.

"God, it's black as pitch in here." Then, "Look out! Damn it, is it bad?"

The other soldier with him must have been hit. He said, "Sergeant? Can you hear me? Hold on, I'll reach you." His breathing was heavy again, as if he was struggling to drag his wounded Sergeant to safely. "Here, this is better. They won't think to look here. Hold that dressing to your chest. I'm going up into the house, I can see better there."

I tried not to stir. But that letter—from Mrs. Henshaw. Was this her husband?

"Gentle God!" Lawrence was exclaiming next, almost to himself. "What the bloody hell are they doing here?" Then raising his voice a little, he said, "Madame, take your children and get down in the cellar. Hurry. My Sergeant is already down there. Do something for him if you can."

There was silence, with only grunts and curses punctuating it as he relived the action. And then he said, "That's the last of them, thank God."

In a more natural voice he called quietly, "Madame?" And then, "They're gone. You and your children should leave as well. Go south along the back roads. You'll encounter my forces some seven miles from here. Can you manage? Yes? All right, Sergeant Henshaw, let's get you—"

His words stopped short. There was silence after that.

Dr. Moreau asked softly, "What do you see, Lieutenant?"

"He's bled to death. Damn it, damn it, *damn it!*"

"Who has?"

"Sergeant Henshaw." His voice was curt.

"What else do you see?"

"Madame and her family. They're too frightened to go out into the road. And I've got to get back to my men. I'm trying to reason with them, but the little boy is exhausted, and she can't carry him and the little girl too. The older girl isn't strong enough. I don't think they've had any food for several days."

"Who is Madame?"

"I don't know. Never seen her before. She tells me her husband was working in Liège, when the Germans crossed the border into Belgium. He sent them on ahead, but the children couldn't keep up with the stream of refugees. They'd hoped to find a little food here in the house. Then the fighting came this way." He sighed. "There's nothing for it, I shall have to leave them here. I promised I'd come back for them. I don't think they believe me. The smaller girl is crying, the older one is trying to comfort her. But there's nothing I can do. *Nothing.*"

"Describe them for me."

"I don't know. There's no time. Madame is in her thirties, the lad is four or five, his sister around two, and the older girl is perhaps ten? She's small, I can't be sure. They're French, not Belgian. They are only here because of her husband's work."

Liège had held out for nine terrible days, with a tenth the number of men the Germans had. No artillery. Just courage. And they'd held on until we could get the first of our forces, the Expeditionary Force, to France and then north to stop the German advance down the coast in a pincer movement to hold the ports and cut off the French Army as it raced to the Marne.

Lawrence went on. "I've got to go. They'll be all right, now, the Germans are gone or dead. And I'll be back or send help as soon as I can." But you could hear the doubt in his voice, as if he already knew the odds were against him.

"Madame, no, I'm not deserting you. I must go, you'll be safe until I can get back to you."

And then, quietly, "Now she's crying. She's afraid they'll find her, rape the girls, and kill them all. I had to walk away. I had to go. They are safer here than on the road with me, I'm already behind enemy lines as it is, the Germans were moving fast, they won't come back until they've pushed us to the sea."

"Did you get back to your own lines, Lieutenant?" the doctor asked after a time.

"There were several German scouts—it was a fluid position, none of us had a clear idea of where the other side was. But I made it. I had to tell Franklin that Henshaw was dead. That he was Sergeant now."

I was beginning to realize that we'd thought we were in the right place, but there was no Angel here. I wanted to say something to Dr. Moreau, but I didn't want to break the spell.

I realized Lawrence was talking again. "We've got to catch up with the rest of the regiment. And we'll have to move fast. If the Belgians could hold out nine days, surely we can give London more time."

There was a long silence.

"What do you see?" Dr. Moreau asked again.

"We can hear firing up ahead. Don't know whether it's a skirmish or a battle. But we've got to go around it. Then attack from the flank. We don't have enough men to take them on in a frontal assault. Let me see that map again."

His voice was very tired. To my astonishment, Dr.

Moreau brought him out of the trancelike state, telling him to rest and awake in the morning, refreshed.

Then he beckoned me to follow him out of the room.

I said anxiously as soon as we'd reached the passage and shut the room door behind us, "It's not finished. His account. We haven't got to the Angel."

"He was tiring. And what he's told us so far doesn't seem to indicate cowardice. Far from it."

"Then it isn't here. Whatever happened. It must be closer to the time he was concussed. We started in the wrong place." I'd lived with a regiment, I could follow the action.

But I could clearly see that Dr. Moreau was upset, anxious. We had just heard Lawrence Minton exonerate himself, and I couldn't understand why it had been necessary to cut off the session. Searching for a reason, I remembered that his son had been killed in a battle. And the vividness of Lawrence's descriptions must have brought that back. He couldn't open that wound.

"Go to bed, Bess. You need your rest as well. I'll go down and ask the night nurse to return." He could see that I was on the point of arguing still, and he went on. "My dear, it isn't safe to push too far too fast. Let me be the judge."

And I had no choice but to do as he said. But instead of going to bed, I sat by my window and watched the watery sun rise over the rooftops of Paris.

He was right. There was nothing so far to explain such a drastic change in Lawrence Minton's life. He had been worried about the family, he'd watched his Sergeant die. But the retreat from Mons had held every imaginable horror, and even these seasoned forces had had to deal with them. The death of comrades and the plight of refugees were not isolated incidents, they were every day's nightmare with no end in sight. Sometimes they must have had to put feelings aside and concentrate all their energy on holding, surviving. As the Bible said, there would be a time for that. Or so they must have promised themselves. There had to be more. Or else the Mons road had nothing to do with the present.

In the morning I came downstairs to learn that Dr. Moreau had left the house early to visit a patient in hospital. Or to avoid me? Madame was evasive.

At ten o'clock there was a knock at the door, and the maid came to find me in the sitting room.

"It's the American officer, again," she said. "Will you see him, Sister?"

Captain Jackson had called often during the past week. I'd made excuses not to see him, asking the maid to tell him I was caring for our patient. I knew that was unfair—after all, he'd found Lawrence for me, I knew I ought to be more grateful. And so I reluctantly agreed to speak to him in Madame Moreau's parlor.

He came in, dwarfing the room somehow, tall as he was. I wondered how on earth he'd ever fit himself into the cramped confines of an aircraft's cockpit.

His hat in his hand, he said, "I've been worried, Bess."

I'd given him permission to use my name, but as a rule he called me *ma'am*, and I thought it was on purpose to tease me, reminding me that I wasn't his sister. *Bess* meant he was truly concerned.

"I'm so sorry," I said, and found I meant it. "I've been worried too, and afraid to leave the Lieutenant for very long."

"There's a night nurse and a day nurse. I've seen them come and go."

"Yes. They are here to watch him. I assist the doctor in caring for him."

"Could I see him?"

I blinked. "Do you want to?"

"I do."

I couldn't refuse. Not after what he'd done. And so I said, "You must be very quiet and not wake him. And you mustn't stay."

"I'm just fine with that."

And so I led him up the stairs to the sickroom, and allowed him to walk in after making certain that Lawrence was all right. I hadn't looked in on him myself since the hypnosis session.

Lawrence was asleep. We'd removed the bandages around his head, as the cuts there began to heal, and his hair was rather ragged where it had been cut short at the hospital. It looked more like a monk's tonsure growing out around an untidy bald spot. But his face was still discolored, the cut along his jaw an angry red line, still puffy. Even under the blankets and coverlet, the splints on his left arm and his leg were clearly visible, and the knuckles of the right hand, lying on the coverlet, were still swollen, bruised, and cut.

Captain Jackson whistled under his breath. "It's still appalling, what was done to him. I don't know how he survived," he said softly. Then he studied my face. "No offense, ma'am, but you look tired. Are you sure you aren't working too hard, not letting the other nurses share in what's needing to be done?"

"Well, it appears he'll live now. I can rest." I felt myself blushing a little under his scrutiny. Hoping he couldn't read more in my face than was safe. For instance, that I'd had little sleep last night, and not from worry over my patient's condition.

"Shouldn't you inform his Colonel that he's been set upon? I mean, the Foot Police should start looking into what happened to him, since he's getting better."

"Dr. Moreau feels that it's too soon to interview him. A few more days?"

"I expect he knows best. Still . . ." His voice trailed off as he turned to go. I followed him into the passage, shutting the door behind us. And he said, "Someone wanted that man dead. I'd not be happy if whoever it is found out where he's being cared for, and decided to pay a little visit. It's not safe, ma'am. You must think about that. There's the doctor, but the rest of the household are women. Not very much protection for your patient. Or you."

"I'm hoping he won't know. Whoever he may be. But thank you for the warning. I'm grateful." We walked on down the stairs, and I offered him coffee, but he smiled and said, "We live north of Santa Fe, that's where my grandfather went after the War Between the States. Texas was a little too hot for him, since he'd been an officer on the losing side and made a few enemies. He was worried about my grandmother and his two sons. Just as well, they came to burn the house down one night, those enemies. Only he'd already secretly sent his family away. He had to take the law into his own hands, there was no one to come and help him out when it happened. Do you know how to handle a revolver, ma'am? Because if you do, I have one I'd like to leave with you."

I was on the point of telling him that I already had the little revolver that Simon had given me once, then I thought better of it, and replied, "I'm quite a good shot."

He actually grinned at that. "Glad to hear it. I feel better already." Glancing around to be sure they were alone, he went to the rack in the entrance hall where his coat was waiting for him. Reaching into the pocket, he handed me a very business-like revolver. "It's a Colt, ma'am. I was given it on my twelfth birthday, so it's on loan. But it shoots straight, I've never had trouble with the sights." He reached into the other pocket. "And here are extra cartridges. Just in case you had to hold off a posse."

I wasn't quite sure what a posse was, but I gathered it was more than one or two men. I felt the balance of the revolver in my hand, liked the feel of the grip, and then accepted the extra ammunition.

"Thank you, Captain. I'm truly grateful. Let's hope I won't require this extra protection."

"No, ma'am."

He said good-bye then, and left. I felt rather badly about putting him off on his earlier visits.

I took the revolver and the box of cartridges up to my room and hid them where they wouldn't be found when my room was cleaned. And I thought it best not to mention them to Madame or her husband. I didn't know how they would feel about a weapon in my possession.

That night Dr. Moreau wanted to put off another session of hypnotism, but I reminded him that Matron was on her way. "She'd have the right to move him—take him back to England, even. And we'd never get at the truth."

"Do we need to know the truth?" he asked. "As to that, I don't know where to start."

"Ask him about the Angel. He'll know what that is. And with any luck at all, he will tell us."

I wasn't certain that I'd convinced him. But the doctor tapped on my door at midnight, and we repeated our visit of the night before. When the nurse had gone, I moved to the hearth where I was not as visible, a silent witness, and Dr. Moreau began his quiet one-sided conversation with Lawrence Minton.

When he was certain that the hypnosis had worked, and Lawrence was once more back in the war, he said, "Tell me about the Angel."

There was sudden movement from the bed. "No. I don't want to go there."

"It can do you no harm. And in the morning, you will not remember telling me. You'll feel only refreshed, at peace."

There was a silence.

And then, his voice so low I had to strain to hear it. "Our section was relieved, the worst of the fighting was west of us, closer to the sea. I'd made a promise, I had to go back to where I'd left the refugees. I thought I had a better chance of succeeding if I went alone. And that sector had been quiet. No reports of activity. I set out, taking the map, telling my men to rest while they could. I was very tired, but I made it safely back to the village, and even in the dark I found the cellar. I couldn't find *them* at first. Just my Sergeant's body. The street was quiet, and I went upstairs, hoping they'd listened to me and got out while they could. But I had to be sure, you see. I found a stub of candle in the kitchen, lit it, and made my way from room to room. I didn't have to go far. They were in the dining room, under the table, trying to hide. And they'd been shot where they were. *Shot*. The mother and the two small children." His voice was ragged. "The older girl wasn't there. I looked everywhere, every room, the wardrobes—cupboards—then went back to the cellar, thinking she's been hidden and I'd walked straight by her. There was no sign of her. No body. I didn't know whether the Germans had taken her with them or if somehow she'd escaped and got clear. I searched the neighboring houses. I even went to the church. Calling to her. I *did* try. I swear before God that I did." He was shaking, and I could see the strain in his face as he stared at Dr. Moreau in the dim light from the fire.

"I believe you. And it's all in the past, Lawrence, you needn't fear it now. It's just a memory. Tell me what happened after that. Just as if it was in the past."

The man on the bed began to calm down. At length when questioned, he picked up the story again. "The Germans had brought up artillery. They began to shell the sector, only ranging shots. I got back to the cellar, on my way to collect the Sergeant's body and take it back with me. The next shot fell short, well short of the fighting, and hit the church, the one after that hit the house squarely. And the whole thing came down on me. It was blacker than black for a split second and then something collapsed on top of me. The next thing I remember, I could hear the sound of voices, but not what they were saying. I didn't know where I was or even why I was there. I couldn't see for the blood caking my eyelids shut, and my head was thundering. I could hear them talking again, and realized they were German. I don't know how they saw me. But one of them was kicking my boot. I tried not to breathe. They started digging me out, but then they stopped. I think the dried blood all over me made them believe I was dead. The voices faded. I don't remember anything much after that except that I was so thirsty."

"Who found you?"

"I don't know. A patrol. They thought I was dead as well, until I managed to croak something. My mouth was bone dry. They dug me out, tried to get me to swallow water, but I couldn't. I don't know how they got me back to our lines. I was in and out of consciousness, in pain. And then there was a doctor asking if I could see him, and I realized he must have washed my face. He said something about our being in a tight spot, and he'd send me back as soon as he could. Then I was alone, and I could hear the fighting. It was fierce, and finally the doctor came back to say they were about to be overwhelmed, and he'd have to leave me. Shortly after that, I saw the Angel. Above us in the night sky, and there was a brightness that hurt my eyes. I shut them, but not before I knew, looking up, that the Angel had his back to me. I couldn't see his face. And I felt a wave of grief sweep over me, and a bitter sense of failure. When I looked again, the doctor was there. "My God," he was saying, "we're going to make it. Can you stand?" But he had to shout for another soldier to come up, and between them they got me back. I was put on a stretcher and taken to hospital, or so I was told later. When I woke up again, I didn't know what had happened to me or what my name was. It was several days before I remembered anything."

"You didn't remember the family dead in the house?"

"No. I dreamed about them. I thought it was only a dream. That it hadn't really happened. The Sisters told me not to worry, that nightmares were common with severe head injuries. By then I knew who I was."

"Did you recall seeing the Angel?"

"No. Only a very bright light, blinding me."

"Why can you remember these events now?"

"Because of what happened in Paris."

"While you were recovering?"

"No. Later. Much later. A few weeks past."

"Tell me about it."

"No, don't ask me."

"It's important to me to know, so that I can help you. Nothing will happen to you. You are safe now. Do you believe that?"

"Yes."

There was a longer silence that followed.

"Where are you now?"

"Walking back to my flat. Approaching the bridge."

"Which bridge? What time of day is it?"

"The bridge near Marina's school. It's late, I'm going back to the Periard house. Not a soul in sight. I can hear my own footsteps. No—wait—there's a girl standing in the middle of the bridge. She's speaking to me, asking me to help her. She thinks she knows me, but I don't recognize her. It's more likely she's a prostitute, they're quite clever sometimes. They're starving—they need money to pay for a doctor for their mother or sister—whatever story works."

A pause. "She's asking if I remember her. If I was there when her mother and the other children were killed. Asking why I didn't stop it. I don't know what she's talking about. Now she's telling me what happened to her. Reminding me that she was only ten. It's a worse story than usual. She's telling me that the Germans kept her for a week, until they were tired of her. God, she's showing me a scar on her shoulder. It's where she was shot. I'm not sure what to do. If she's mad, or something."

Another pause. "I've told her I don't remember her or her family, that she's got the wrong man. But she's telling me over and over again that I am responsible for those deaths. I tried to give her a few sous, then walk away, leaving her standing there. She couldn't be more than eighteen, I feel sorry for her. I'm almost off the bridge now. Oh God, she's screaming at me! I'm turning around—there's a man dragging her away. He's moving fast, they're already on the Left Bank, and he's pulling at her, and she's screaming. I'm starting after them, racing back over the bridge, not knowing what's wrong, but the screams aren't false, they're real. They're on the quay now, and she's calling my name. It's odd—he's stopped, they are just standing there, but she's still struggling, begging me to help, begging me not to let her die the way her mother and brother and sister died. I'm yelling for the police. I don't understand any of this, but she's in some sort of trouble, and there's no one else. I'm running full out, and they're only thirty feet from me—twenty—they aren't moving."

He cried out, "He's got the girl by the shoulders—he's moving away from me now—he's closer to the water—*he's just shoved her into the river!*"

His voice was breaking. "He catches me before I can get to the river, reach out for her. We are struggling, he's hitting me, but I'm stronger, and I finally knock him down. I'm at the river's edge, leaning out—all I can see is the cloak she was wearing. I'm reaching out as far as I can—*I can't swim!* Oh, lord, I've got the edge of her cloak—but she's slipping out it, it's in the way now, and I'm shoving it aside, nearly falling in, just as she comes up a few feet away, just beyond my fingertips. She's staring at me, but the current is pulling at her clothes. *She isn't coming up again.*"

Dr. Moreau spoke then, his own voice more than a little ragged. "It's all right, Lawrence, it's only a memory. It has no power over you in the present."

But I could see the tears streaming down his cheeks as he tries to get to the drowning girl.

"I'm floundering after her. Dear God, there's her *hand.* I think I can reach it. I've got her fingers, they're cold—I've almost got her hand, I'm going to be able to pull her in."

He cried out in pain just then, and my first thought was, he's lost her hand. But he was mumbling something. I realized it was *No, no, no!*

This time, the silence lasted so long I thought the shock had brought him out of the trance.

"I don't know how long I was unconscious," he said, his voice dead, almost too low to be heard. "I'm awake now, it's cold, my arms are wet. I'm holding on to something, and I try to lift my head, to see if she's all right. But it's only her cloak I'm clutching. And—and there she is, lying on the other side of me. She's cold too—dead. I can't rouse her. And that's when I remember the cellar. The—the Angel. He seems to be there again, his back to me. But it's only the man who had been with her. He's on the bridge, looking down, and the bridge lamps are hurting my eyes. And he's saying something. I think it's *Now she's dead too. Or ought to be. They're all gone.* When I could focus again, he's gone, the Angel is gone. But the girl is still dead."

"Are you quite sure it's the same girl?"

His voice became a wail of anguish. "How could it not be? Who else knew about her, about that family?"

"And who was the man with her?"

"I—I don't know."

"Why would he drown her?"

"How do I know?" He was sobbing now, reliving that night over and over again, even as Dr. Moreau tried desperately to calm him.

And I sat there like a stone in the chair by the hearth, remembering the staircase in St. Ives, and Lawrence Minton struggling with the Turkey carpet from the hall.

He wasn't trying to drown someone, even though the heavy rug in his grip had made it appear that way. *He was fighting her heavy cloak and trying to save that poor girl.*

Dr. Moreau finally managed to break the trance, and Lawrence fell back against his pillows. He was crying and saying over and over again, "Why can't I use my arm? I need my arm, if I'm going to save her. Let me go, I tell you, I have to reach her before it's too late."

"I'm afraid to give him anything," Dr. Moreau whispered to me. "It might not be safe."

And so we stayed there with him until he was quiet again, his breathing regular, and this time, not a ruse to make us think he was asleep.

When we were back again in the passage, Dr. Moreau said, "You were wrong. We didn't need to know any of that. We've put him through torment for no reason."

But there *was* a reason. I'd found out the truth. And I was so grateful I had waited until I knew the entire truth before I'd called in the police. Grateful that I hadn't jumped to the wrong conclusions. Heaven knows I'd come close enough.

Dr. Moreau opened the door of my room for me. "Good night, Bess. We'll talk in the morning. I had no idea—"

"*Could* he have failed to remember anything about the Mons road, after he'd been so severely concussed? And then remembered it again, so much later?"

"Yes, it's possible. With the right stimulus. I think it's entirely possible." He shook his head, still affected by what we'd heard. "I wish I'd known. I might have helped." He nodded, and walked on, his shoulders slumped in shock.

But he couldn't have helped.

Shutting my door, I leaned against it. Spent, but my mind reeling.

Who was that dead girl? And who had tried to make Lawrence Minton believe she was the one from the Mons road? Because the girl the police had found was eighteen. And from what I'd heard while he was hypnotized, Lawrence had said the girl in that house was only ten, and small for her age. That would make her barely fifteen now . . .

The only two people who knew that story about the dead family were the Lieutenant and the ten-year-old daughter. They were the only two survivors. If Lawrence hadn't told anyone, then the girl must have done.

How could she have lived through that nightmare? And who would she have confided in?

I remembered what the police report said. She was lying there beside the quay, but no mention of a cloak. And she'd been dead some time.

Lawrence, dazed, must have wandered off.

I took that question to bed with me, and worried it like a dog with a large bone for the next two hours until I finally drifted into sleep from sheer exhaustion.

Sometimes sleep heals, and sometimes it's stolen away by fear or worry or unhappiness.

Last night. The shocking story of the family, of the girl who'd drowned. It came back to me in a rush, before I was fully awake. If it affected me so strongly, how must it have affected a mind already concussed and unable to think clearly. Lawrence's guilt over what had happened to that family, his inability to save them or find the older daughter, had haunted him even when he couldn't remember any of it. How he'd seen the Angel reinforced his failure. When he asked about his dreams, the only way he could recall what had happened, everyone, including his doctors, had told him that strange, unsettling dreams were natural in a concussion. And eventually he must have believed them.

But now—now that we knew the truth, we could help him. That was to say, his mother could. She was an experienced nurse. She would take him back to England as soon as possible, and use her leave to help him mend.

That brought up another matter.

Would Matron recommend me for more clinic duty, now that my mission for her was complete? It was selfish of me even to wonder. But once she arrived, I would be expected to return to England—there was nothing to keep me here. Lawrence was improving and no longer needed special nursing. Was I to report to headquarters in London, or was she bringing my assignment to me?

As I began my morning tasks, I took particular care as I dressed, pinning up my hair twice until I was satisfied with it, standing before the mirror as I set my cap in place, making certain that my cuffs and apron were spotless.

It mattered so much, working with the wounded. Marina loved teaching, I had seen it in her eyes and in her voice as she talked about her school. And I'd slowly become aware that I didn't have the same passion for it.

The war was over. If Matron asked for my resignation, I would have no choice but to give it. And then what?

I knew what my parents would say: Come home. Marry, have children, be happy.

But I didn't think I was ready for that either.

I'd been on my own throughout the war, and much as I loved my parents, coming home again as their daughter would be difficult.

I'd considered this before—and was no farther along in my thinking than I had been earlier. It was just that now a decision was looming nearer and nearer. And I found myself wishing I could talk to Simon. He'd faced just such a change when my father had retired from the Regiment, and Simon could have stayed, if he'd chosen to do so. Instead he'd resigned.

What would he do with himself if he did? How would his life change? He too had been young enough to need to make choices. How had he found his way? Had he asked my father for advice? Or muddled through? Or been unexpectedly wise at the crucial moment?

Had he been happy with his own decisions? Or had he come to regret living in the cottage through the wood just beyond our back garden?

I suddenly realized that it hadn't occurred to any of us—the Colonel Sahib, my mother, me—that Simon might wish to go his own way. Leave the family circle and make a new and different life for himself. Had it occurred to *Simon*?

This was an unexpected, shocking thought, that once the war was over, he might finally choose another path. Was it Scotland? Was that the reason he'd gone there, without telling us why? He'd spent some time there during the war. He might have found it a place where he could put down roots of his own.

I'd always seemed to know what I wanted from my life. And now, suddenly, I didn't. It was such an uncomfortable, lonely feeling.

Shoving such thoughts away, I glanced in my mirror, not completely satisfied with the stiffness of my collar. And for the first time, I noticed the dark circles under my eyes from sleepless nights. The face looking back at me as I pinned my cap in place seemed to be chiding me.

I wished I knew what that face in the mirror knew that I didn't . . .

Breakfast was not the comfortable meal it usually was. The doctor excused himself early, to attend a patient who had worsened overnight.

And Madame Moreau was absorbed in readying her house for Matron's arrival, making notes on the sheet of paper beside her place as she ate.

Glancing up as the door closed behind her husband, she tried to make conversation for my sake. "I look in on Lawrence as often as I can. It's terribly painful to see him. I think of André, dying alone and without our comfort. Is that selfish of me?"

"I think it's natural for a mother," I told her frankly. "Is there room enough for all of us, when Matron comes? She'll want to be close to her son. I'll be happy to move, or even go to an hotel. You've been so kind to have me here for this long."

But she wouldn't hear of it. "Helena wants a cot put in her son's room. We will soon be able to dispense with the nurses, and she can take over his care."

Still, I couldn't help but feel I'd be in the way.

That reminded me. "Have you had any word recently from Marina?"

"Such a lovely girl," she answered. "I'd have liked André to find someone like her. She did come to thank us for her care, and she brought a lovely gift—unnecessary, of course, but sweet of her. Her arm is healing well. My husband says she will very likely have a small scar. It could have been far worse without your quick thinking and care. I believe she's busy at school, but I have asked her to come again to visit as soon as she can."

"I'm glad you like her. She needs someone in Paris to keep an eye on her. She isn't able to visit her parents as often as she'd like. They too lost a son in the war."

"Yes, she told me how her mother faced the news. I felt for her, having been through the shock myself." She looked away. "We gave so much to France."

The day was damp, with a wretched mist that felt as if the river was over its banks and drifting through the air. But I needed to walk, to get out of that house for a time, and think a little. I borrowed an umbrella from the stand by the door, and set out at a brisk pace that matched my mood.

I'd been wrong about Lawrence. He had been as much a victim as that poor family. But he had made it difficult for me or anyone to understand him, wanting oblivion, so buried in his own troubles that he ignored everyone else's needs. He had talked about his guilt, and what I'd seen on the staircase appeared to support his claims that he had nothing left to live for. His sleepwalking, his nightmares, were too vivid to be just imagination or bad dreams. His callous treatment of Marina and resentment of me had painted a portrait of a man who had changed for the worse.

And yet, because I had wanted to know why that change had happened, we had finally got to the truth.

Dr. Moreau had been certain that the hypnotism worked. I myself had become convinced of it too. I didn't think Lawrence was well enough for him to invent such a tissue of lies.

Therefore, if his story under hypnosis was true, then why would he have wished to kill me?

That was before he'd been beaten so badly. And who had done *that*, pray?

He claimed he didn't know who had attacked him. Was he lying?

I stopped short, nearly colliding with a woman pushing a pram. Apologizing, I stepped to a window display of baby clothing, and listened to what had occurred to me, out of the blue.

His Sergeant had been killed in the village where he'd found the woman and her children. He'd even debated carrying the dead body back to his lines but had had to leave it there, just as he'd had to leave the family. At some point, another German party had come through the village, discovered them cowering in the dining room, and killed them.

The ten-year-old daughter was missing. Lawrence had searched for her, but never found her. It was the reason he was so ready to believe she was the girl on the bridge.

Someone had set that scene in motion.

Certainly not Lawrence. And certainly not the German patrol.

Who else had known about her?

Had the woman's husband come after them, finding them too late?

But even if he had, he couldn't have known about Lawrence, or that he'd tried to save the family.

Unless he'd found his older daughter. Somehow, somewhere? Only she could have told him about the English officer who had walked away. And her memory might have been unreliable, even as it was convincing.

But there were hundreds—thousands—of English officers in France. How could the girl's father have learned it was Lawrence?

The body of Sergeant Henshaw was still there. The

father had only to look at his insignia to find out which regiment the officer had come from. Even so, it must have taken years, and an iron determination to track him down. And then, finally, Lawrence had come back to Paris.

Was the beating given Lawrence Minton revenge for a family's murder?

I'd been facing the window, blindly staring at the display of baby clothes and gifts for the newborn, an array of tiny shoes and blankets and caps and bibs.

And then something distracted me, and I looked up to see a man's face reflected in the glass, just over my left shoulder. He was staring back at me as he was crossing from the far side of the street.

It was the vegetable vendor. I was sure of it. Only he was wearing a dark suit, the flash of a gold chain across his middle. And in that brief glimpse, I remembered where I'd seen him before. On the train that took me to St. Ives. *Surely that was where—!*

How many other times had he been there, and I hadn't realized he was following me?

We stared at each other for several seconds, and I saw again the eyes over the top of the scarf with which he'd tried to conceal his face. They had been light too, I remembered that now, they were like holes in the darkness because they were so light.

I whirled, preparing to confront him, already starting toward him.

I stopped abruptly as an omnibus came rattling down the wet and muddy street. I hadn't even heard it coming, I was concentrating so hard on that man. It noisily passed me by, a blur of windows and faces, cutting off my view of him as it passed.

When it was gone, he was nowhere to be seen.

I searched.

The shops, in the nearest café, in doorways, everywhere, but I had no luck. He had disappeared. As if I had imagined him. But he'd been there. Somehow he must have used the omnibus to conceal his movements—he could even have walked along beside it until he was well away, and I would never have known.

So clever . . .

I stood by the shop window again, trying to see where he might have come from. But it was a street of cafés and shops, it could have been any of them. I looked up at the windows above the shops. Surely there were rooms to let there? But I couldn't find a doorway with stairs to them.

He knew me. He'd recognized me in the poor streets around Holy Angels, and he'd recognized me today. It would have been easy. My coat and my cap were clearly distinctive, even with the umbrella over my head. When had he begun to follow me? When I called at Madame Periard's house? Had he lost Lawrence after that night on the bridge, and had to search again for him? Only, I'd unwittingly led this man to his victim.

But who was he? That tragic family's husband and father?

I was walking back to the Moreau house, when Captain Jackson caught up with me.

"What brings you out in such weather?" he asked chattily. "Errands for the patient?"

"I needed to think, and the house was feeling as if it was closing in on me," I said, then instantly regretted telling him that much.

But he didn't ask why. He just matched his longer stride to my shorter one, and kept pace with me. He was too tall for the umbrella to cover him, but the broad-brim hat he wore seemed to be impervious to the damp drizzle.

"Does it rain in New Mexico?" I asked, quickly changing the subject.

"It does, ma'am. Sometimes in buckets. But it's mostly dry country."

Thinking in terms of a dry English summer, I said, "What do your cattle eat?"

"They manage quite well. The Navajo, now, they're smart enough to run sheep. But we raise horses too."

"What is a Navajo?"

"It's a native tribe that lives in the countryside. Nice people. Quiet."

We walked on for several streets, and then he said, "You looked more than a little upset when I saw you. Anything I can do to help?"

"I just saw the vegetable vendor a bit ago, crossing the street by that shop where you saw me. He recognized me. And I recognized him."

"In this part of the city? Selling vegetables?" He turned to look at me, incredulous.

I suddenly realized that I'd been so intent on the man's face that I had paid no attention to his clothing. I tried to bring back the image from the reflection. "I— he was wearing a dark suit of clothes. Respectable. Not at all like the vegetable vendor. The only reason I noticed him was his reflection in the window glass, just over my shoulder. I realized I knew who he was."

"And who is he?"

"I don't know," I said slowly. "But I'd seen him before, you see. On a train. I'm quite sure of that now. In a ward full of wounded, one quickly learns faces. Not just their number."

"And you don't have any idea where he might have gone?"

I told him about the omnibus.

"That was clever of him," he commented thoughtfully.

"Why would he have been on the train, then where Lawrence was attacked, and then here, staring at me?" We had nearly reached the Moreau door.

"You can't be sure he was staring. Can you?"

"It's—suspicious," I said. I really didn't know what else to call it. "Unlikely that the same man was in my vicinity on three separate occasions. And wearing such different clothing each time." And how many more had there been? Occasions when he was there and I was distracted, and never noticed him.

"Still, you must be very careful, and stay where there are other people around. I am not happy about the way you walk all over the city, Bess."

Now that Lawrence had been found, and it appeared that he was going to recover, I needn't roam all over the city of Paris. I needed to find my father, all the same, and I didn't know if he was in England or France, at the moment.

The captain doffed his hat as usual, pausing at the steps of the house. Courtesy demanded that I ask him in for tea or coffee, a sherry. I was about to do that as I opened the door and stepped into the hall.

My boot stopped short, bumping against something, and I put out a hand to catch myself. I'd been looking at the Captain, but now I looked down.

There was a collection of luggage just at the door, and in the distance, the raised voices of people happy to see each other.

Oh, dear.

Matron had arrived.

Chapter 14

After a hasty good-bye to the Captain, explaining who had arrived, I left my umbrella and coat in the hall and followed the sound of voices to the sitting room where Dr. and Madame Moreau were standing, greeting Matron. It was apparent that she had only just arrived, for she was removing her coat and talking as she did.

"It wasn't too bad. An easy crossing, and then the train. Very different from the war. I hardly recognized Paris. Coming from the station—"

She broke off as I came to stand in the doorway.

"Sister Crawford," she said, frowning. Beyond her, out of her line of sight, I could see Dr. Moreau shaking his head slightly, as if he expected me to start telling her immediately about her son's problems.

Smiling, I said, "I'm glad you've come. Lieutenant Minton will be happy to see you." Even as I said the words, I wondered how true they were.

"Why didn't you send for me sooner?" she asked, as if this had been on her mind since she'd got the letter from Dr. Moreau.

"Medical decisions had to be made. It was possible he was going to die before you could even leave London. The first order of business was to save his life. It was touch-and-go, even so."

Behind her, a look of relief spread across the doctor's face.

She turned to him. "I'm a nurse, Michel, I could have taken turns nursing Lawrence."

"All is well, Helena. Be glad that he's safe. Please, sit down and let me fetch you a glass of wine. It will refresh you, and you'll be prepared for what you see. Remembering that he is healing. Despite how he may look to you."

"I'd rather go straight up."

But Dr. Moreau had already turned to the little drinks table and was pouring glasses of wine. "You have just arrived after a long journey. Five minutes more, and you'll be ready to start nursing Lawrence." He brought forward two glasses, which he gave to Matron and then to his wife, finally pouring his and mine.

As a guest in their house, she could hardly refuse the wine, but she sat on the edge of her chair as he lifted his glass and said, "To Lawrence, and a full recovery."

After sipping mine to seal the toast, I set the wine aside. "Perhaps I ought to prepare him. We hadn't told him you were coming because we were afraid to raise his hopes too soon."

Before anyone could object, I smiled and got myself quickly out of the sitting room. Then I all but ran up the stairs, not knowing how long Matron could be persuaded to be polite.

Opening the door of the sickroom, I nodded to the nurse. "You might wish to go down to the kitchen for a bit. There are guests in the sitting room. I'll keep an eye on the patient."

She nodded and left.

Lawrence was lying in the bed, staring at the ceiling.

I didn't know what to say to him. Not after last night. But it had to be done, and so I walked forward, taking up his hand and feeling for a pulse. It was quiet, regular.

"You have a visitor," I said cheerfully.

"If it's Marina, I don't wish to see her."

"Actually, it's your mother."

"Damn it," he said, jerking his hand free. "Why did

you send for her? You knew that was the last thing I needed. Or wanted."

"She has come because Dr. Moreau sent for her. It's what doctors do when there is an illness. They send for the patient's family. You can be nasty to her, of course, but the nicer you are, the sooner she will feel she can safely leave you."

I didn't think he was listening. But after a moment he said, "You don't know her. She'll want to stay, take care of me. I can't bear it."

"She's still with the Queen Alexandra's. I expect she only has a few days' leave."

"What have you told her?" he demanded suspiciously.

"Nothing except that you had us quite worried in the beginning, but you are slowly healing."

"Is that the truth? That's what you told her?"

"You'll be seeing for yourself soon enough. Why should I lie?"

He lay back, closed his eyes, and said, "I'd never have let you bring me here if I'd even guessed this would happen."

"Well," I said, striving to sound practical, "for one thing, you were barely conscious. Dr. Moreau had to make a medical decision without consulting you. Of course, you could have stayed in that ward. But if you'd managed to live, most likely you'd have been crippled for life. They didn't have time to give you proper care. There were too many patients as it was."

"So you say." He didn't open his eyes.

"Surely you remember something about that ward."

"It's foggy. Bits and pieces."

"If you begin by telling her you'd rather die than live, she will believe you, and she won't let you out of her sight."

I could hear footsteps now on the stairs. Dr. Moreau was bringing Helena up. They hadn't lingered over their wine.

I moved away from the bed, saying softly, "She doesn't deserve to be hurt."

There was a tap at the door, it opened, and Matron came in, her face schooled not to show what she expected to see. But I watched her flinch a little as she took in her son's condition, and she turned quickly to Dr. Moreau, as if in understanding, before smiling and saying, "Hallo, love. They told me I would be shocked, but you look far better than I'd expected. I'm so glad. Dr. Moreau has taken great care of you."

I slipped past her as she walked toward the bed, carefully coming to the side where he could use his arm.

And as I went out the door, closing it quietly behind me, I heard him say gruffly, "Hallo, Mother. I'm glad you've come."

I sat in my room until time for our supper. I heard the day nurse make her farewells, and the cot being made up for his mother. Lawrence would hate that, but there was nothing he could do about it. When I went down to the dining room, Dr. Moreau was preoccupied and Madame was trying to persuade him all was well. I was glad to escape to my room again.

I was in bed and nearly asleep when there was a tap at my door. Pulling on my robe, I went to answer it, and found Matron standing there, still fully dressed in her uniform.

"May I come in?" she asked.

I could hardly say no. "Please, do. The fire is nearly out, I hope it isn't too chilly in here."

She came in, looking around, then took one of the chairs by the hearth. "Who did this to my son? Did he tell you?"

"I've asked. He doesn't remember much about it. We think he was lured into an alley, and then set upon."

"And what have the police done about it?"

"What can they do? They had no witnesses, and no evidence. Paris is full of strangers, Matron. Anything could happen here. I myself was set upon one evening. I had a lucky escape. The police interviewed me, and I've heard nothing more from them."

"It isn't England," she said with a sigh.

I said tentatively, "Something happened in the war. Something to do with his concussion in 1914. I don't think he remembered it for a very long time, but it came back to him here in Paris. Suddenly and without warning. He has to heal from that as well as the blows in that alley. It will take some time."

"Do you know what that was?" she asked, intent now.

"I—he hasn't really told anyone as far as I know. Not wittingly. I wouldn't press. Let him tell you in his own good time."

"Then how do you know so much?"

"Bits and pieces, put together. He was delirious in the beginning."

"Thank you for telling me." Then she asked what had really brought her here. "Why didn't you contact me sooner?"

"Truthfully? I didn't know where he was in the beginning. And I didn't want to report him as missing. Neither London nor the Regiment would take that lightly. He should have been here, at the conference. He even has papers in his possession from various meetings. I felt it was much better to find him myself. I was hoping to save his career."

"That's very kind of you. But *I* should have been told."

And I saw that nothing I could say would change her mind. The laudanum, the brandy, his disappearance, and then the beating—not even the skills of a Matron in the Queen Alexandra's would have saved him from these things. And I could hardly tell her that perhaps the beating that she found so horrible had actually saved his life by putting him in hospital before he could do anything rash. Let Dr. Moreau set the past in perspective. If Matron even gave him a chance before whisking the patient back to England.

She rose, and I stood as well. "I have all the documents you gave me in London. I'd like to return them to you now. I've spent money searching for him. But I've kept a record of every penny or sou. It's all there." I turned to my desk, picking up the folder.

Matron took it with a nod. "Good night, Sister Crawford."

"Good night, Matron."

And she was gone.

I sat there by the dying fire for another hour, rethinking our conversation and wondering what I could have—should have—done differently.

In the post the next morning was a card from Marina inviting Dr. and Madame Moreau to a dinner given by the school to parents of the students.

He looked at it, passed it to his wife, and she read it aloud.

"I think we ought to attend," he said. "It was kind of her to include us."

"Yes. Perhaps Helena will feel like joining us, if she's still here."

"If she hasn't brought anything suitable, perhaps you could take her to buy something here in Paris."

"Of course, I'll speak to her later about it."

Nothing was said about my attending. I was beginning to think it would be best for me to find an excuse to return to London. Since my father knew Matron from India, I hoped he would join us for dinner one night and provide that excuse. If he was still in Paris.

After breakfast, Dr. Moreau took me off to his surgery. There were no patients at this hour, and he said as we sat down in his private office, "I have been thinking about what was said in the two sessions of hypnotism. Lawrence is clearly blaming himself for what happened to that family on the retreat from Mons."

"Yes. I think we've got to the bottom of what haunts him."

"It wasn't his fault. But his concussion made it impossible for him to deal with what happened. Was that Angel real? Do you know?"

"There's been some discussion about that. Whether it was true or contrived by the newspapers. But the men I've spoken to really believe it."

"And shocking as it must have been, he was not responsible for what happened to the young woman who was drowned."

I wasn't sure just where he was taking this.

"Who was that man who killed her? Do you have any idea?" he went on.

"The only person it could possibly be was the father of the family. Looking for revenge." Another reason for me to leave.

Shocked, he exclaimed, "He wouldn't have drowned his own daughter."

"I don't believe she was his daughter—just a poor young woman he dragged into this, to drive Lawrence mad. A sham. Somehow the girl was tricked into helping the man, not knowing she would die." I shook my head. "If the death of that family affected Lawrence as much as it did, imagine what it must have done to the father's mind. I'm beginning to wonder if the daughter survived. Surely she could have told her father the truth about the Lieutenant."

"He's a monster. And he must be found."

He had made up his mind. There was no point in arguing over it.

"I don't know if the police can do that."

"Then we'll insist. If the National Police aren't capable, we'll call in the Gendarmes. When he is brought to justice, Lawrence will be rid of this nightmare."

"But it was clear that Lawrence didn't know who the dead woman was. Nor do the police. How would the police ever go about searching for this man? No name, no description?"

There was the man I'd seen—as a vegetable vendor—on the train in my compartment going to St. Ives—reflected in the glass of the shop window. Where else had he been? Marina had answered the door one day to a soldier looking for work. Was that the same man too? Hunting for Lawrence, half mad with grief, blaming the wrong person.

"For Lawrence's sake, we must try. After my surgery hours, we'll go to the police, tell the magistrate everything. Put it into their hands."

"First I think it would be best if his mother took him to England as soon as he can travel. Safely out of the country." Remembering what Captain Jackson had feared, I said, "If he discovers that Lawrence is alive, he may just be mad enough to try again to kill him."

"He will be safe, once the police do their work. And travel just now is out of the question. We'll speak to the police this afternoon. Be ready, please."

And that was dismissal.

I waited until Matron had gone down to have lunch with Madame Moreau, and slipped into Lawrence's room. They had moved his bed a little, so that he could look out one of the windows, and he was watching pigeons on the roof next door. I was reminded of my pigeon, and I hoped he'd made it safely back to wherever he belonged.

"Hallo. Would you mind terribly if we talked for a few minutes? While your mother isn't here?"

He turned his head on the pillows. "I don't have much choice in the matter."

I smiled. "I suppose not. Lawrence—" I hesitated, afraid to tell him about the hypnotism. I didn't know how he would feel about it. "Lawrence, you've been talking in your sleep. And I desperately need your help."

Alarmed, he tried to rise against his pillows, struggling to face me.

"No, it's all right. The other nurses never guessed. I was in the war as well, you see, and I could piece together what troubled you."

"Go away—leave me alone." It was almost a cry, and helpless as he was, I knew how he must have hated me at that moment.

"Hear me out! Please! I think I know who attacked you, and I know why." He was staring at me in anguish, as if I was about to shout out his sins to the world. I put out a hand to comfort him, and he lunged away. "You had nothing to do with the deaths of that family. If you had been there when the next wave of the German Army came through to relieve the coast road, you'd have been shot too. They must have been trying to keep their movements secret, trying to overwhelm the Expeditionary Force, make a breakthrough. And there was no room for prisoners."

He put his good arm over his eyes, shutting me out. "If I'd got there sooner, before the Germans came through, they would have lived."

"But you couldn't know that. You had your own men to think of—your duty was to them as well." I paused. "I think the father must have found them before you did. And he got the older daughter to safety. But she was only a child, she'd watched her mother and brother and sister die. She may even have been badly wounded herself. How much do you think she could tell him? That one soldier had come, and then many more? Would she be able to tell the difference between a British officer and a German one? I think he's been hunting you since that day. How he found you, I don't know. But he did, and he wanted to kill you. He beat you with a wooden rolling pin, to do the most damage possible."

He lifted his arm. "How could you possibly know that?"

"It was found in the alley. Afterward."

He didn't answer.

"And the girl he pushed into the river couldn't have been his daughter. She was used to pull you down to the water. I expect he wanted you to drown."

"I couldn't—I *couldn't reach her.*" There were tears in his eyes.

"It was a cruel deception. She was around eighteen years old. The ten-year-old would have been closer to fifteen."

"How do you know that?"

"The police found her body. But they haven't been able to identify her." I stopped, wondering if he was ready for more. "Lawrence. I think the same man tried to drown me. Pretending to be you. I think he must have found you—and didn't want me to keep searching all over Paris for you. It's the only explanation I can imagine. And if a policeman hadn't come along, I'd have gone into the Seine as well."

He lay there, trying to absorb everything I'd told him. But the clock on the mantelpiece was ticking away the minutes, and his mother would be back before I'd finished.

"What have you told my mother?"

"Nothing about the past. It isn't my place."

"Who else knows?"

"Dr. Moreau. Some of it. I don't think he's even told his wife."

"Why should I believe you?"

"You don't have to," I replied. "But if you give it some thought, it makes sense."

I waited. Then I said, "Did the mother tell you anything about her husband? A name, what work he was doing in Liège. Anything we can use to find him."

He frowned. "There wasn't time to ask questions. I was worried about them. They were better off out of there, and the sooner the better. I showed her how to go."

I could hear voices on the stairs.

"Lawrence. Please try to remember."

"Is any of what you told me true?" He needed reassurance, he needed to know he wasn't the man he'd thought he was.

"I swear it."

And then I had to go. I was walking toward the stairs when Matron and Madame reached the top. Madame said, "My dear. You missed your dinner. I have put it back for you."

"I'm so sorry. I was writing a letter to my parents, and I fell asleep."

"Well, Matron is here. You can make your report about your mission for her, and then enjoy Paris a little before you go back to England."

"Yes, thank you!" I smiled at both of them. "He's showing progress every day now."

"Indeed."

And I went on down the stairs to eat my meal in the kitchen with the staff.

There was one part of the matter that I needed to clear up. And after I'd eaten, I slipped out of the house and went in search of Lieutenant Bedford.

I found him quite by accident. He was sitting in the window of a café, a glass of wine in front of him, and healing bruises on his face. I only noticed him because several women came out together just as I was passing, and I'd moved closer to the window to let them go by.

He gave me a sour look as I opened the café door in my turn and crossed the room to his table.

"I'd rather drink alone," he said rudely.

I gave him my version of Diana's smile. "I have come to apologize."

ere he got the
if I told them

v of his wine,

was in the
ou'd prefer to
too."

ve not spread
proper back-
rly if he's got

ined his dis-
help himself
more used to
fe, playing a

a time or two
here in Paris
was dressed
greasepaint
ff. We began

: the only patrons
staff here. It was a

enant Minton, you
supplied him with
it wasn't helpful.
ances. They gener-

it, it would be safer
to find it. Drawing
ay from me, out the
e of the bottles was
's true."

made him quite ill.
ne." I thought it best
t yet. "But where on
"

If Minton wants to
be ready for him this

business. Someone
d nearly succeeded.

'The police?"
ou. He was attacked.

The police are going to want to know wh
laudanum. And I thought it was better
rather than involving you."

He digested that, took another swallo
and said, "Why would you do that?"

"You're a British officer. My father
Army." I made to rise. "Of course, if yo
talk to the police yourself, that's all right

"No—wait."

I sat down again.

"Before the war I was in the theater. I'
that around, mind you. Not quite the
ground for a British officer, is it? Particula
a battlefield commission."

Listening to him, I thought that expla
tinctive swagger. He was playing a role, to
fit in. The brave, gallant soldier. He was
being someone else on the stage. He felt s
part.

"Were you an actor?"

"Yes. Repertory, but I'd been in London
as well. I was sitting in a bar one evening
when a man came in and sat next to me. He
in dark clothes, but there was a smudge o
behind his ear. He hadn't quite got it all o

to talk, and one evening when I was free, I went to see
him in a play. My French wasn't good enough to understand all of it—it was a farce, double meanings to
everything, kept the audience laughing throughout. He
was really quite good—better in fact than many of the
other players. I ran into him later, and I told him what
I thought. We'd meet occasionally, and I discovered that
he'd been in the French cinema. Gaumont, one of the
biggest filmmakers. But there was no work during the
war and it hasn't picked up yet. He was doing theater,
meanwhile."

"And so you became friends."

"Not friends." He finished his glass of wine. "But
we enjoyed talking theater, you see. Meanwhile, Minton was drinking too much, and he came in drunk one
night. He told me that brandy wasn't doing anything
for the pain he was in. Wounded late in the war, hadn't
healed. He was looking to try something stronger, but
the doctors weren't helping him. I asked Paul where
laudanum was to be had, and he told me he could find
something that was safe. I paid him, then Minton paid
me. He left Paris right after that, but when he ran out,
he told me where to find him. I wasn't happy about it,
but he wanted more. Until he was poisoned. And then
he was angry with *me*."

"Did you tell Paul where Minton was?"

"No. He had made me swear not to tell anyone. He'd told the Regiment he was going back to England to see about that wound. I didn't want anyone to know it was a lie, I'd be in trouble as well, for not reporting it."

Paul couldn't follow Lieutenant Bedford very easily—and then I came along. I led him straight to Lawrence. I felt cold. What if he'd broken into that house? Or set it afire in the middle of the night? Perhaps he'd even planned to. Then Lawrence left suddenly, and Paul had it to do all over again. It explained the multitude of disguises.

"What sort of person is Paul?"

"Like the rest of us. We're only alive when we're onstage."

That wasn't helpful, tracking him down. "Why did you stay in the Army? Why not return to the theater in London?"

"Half my old company had been killed or maimed. And the Army pays regularly. I'd have to revert to my old rank if I left now."

"Does Paul think the cinema will flourish again?"

"Yes. I'd like to be a part of it."

And that explained the friendship.

"I saw a lot of cinema before the war. Some here in France. What sort of parts did Paul play?" It wasn't quite true, but that didn't matter.

"Mostly the hero. But he'd older now. If the cinema business doesn't pick up soon, he'll be too old for the best roles."

I tried another direction. "Has he ever been part of a film made outside France? In England, possibly?"

"He was doing one in Belgium when the war broke out. Tried his best to get back and enlist, but he was captured once, then escaped, finally made his way back to friendly territory and joined the French Army. He has several medals for bravery."

I wondered if he really did—or if that was more stagecraft on Paul's part.

"What's his full name?"

Lieutenant Bedford glared at me. "Oh, no. You aren't going to turn him over to the police."

I couldn't persuade him that that was not true, that it was a matter of murder, not laudanum that interested me, and I did my best to infuse enthusiasm for the cinema into my voice as I begged.

But before I could ask the color of Paul's eyes, the Lieutenant got up, tossed payment for his wine on the table, and bade me a good day.

I sat there after he was gone, upset with myself for failing. Had I pushed too soon? Too hard? When the waiter came over to my table to ask what I'd have, I got up and left.

Paul. It was more than I'd had before. And the fact that he was an actor and currently playing onstage, somewhere in Paris. There was no time to visit every theater in the city. But when we went to the police this afternoon, at least I could give them clues they could more easily follow up.

I wasn't at ease with that, either. I'd had a run-in with the police once before, and while they were very good, I was the foreigner, and they would listen to the French witness first.

From what I'd heard from Lieutenant Bedford, and what I'd gathered myself, Paul whoever-he-was would be a far more accomplished liar than the usual run of accused that the police dealt with. And I had every reason to believe he could talk his way out of everything.

Not a very happy thought.

It was five minutes past the hour when I finally reached the Moreau house. I rushed directly to the surgery to look for the doctor, already preparing my apologies.

He wasn't there.

I hurried to the sitting room, where Madame was writing a letter, and I asked, "Has the doctor already left?"

Surprised, she looked up at me. "Yes. It was an emergency. Was he expecting you to accompany him?"

"Ah. Er—no, we were going to have a look at Lawrence's leg." It was the first thing that popped into my head.

"I believe Helena has already spoken to him about that. She's lying down in my room, just now. I don't think she sleeps very well on that cot."

"I'll look in on him, shall I?"

"That would be a good idea. Let her rest if she can. She'll make herself ill, if she doesn't take care."

I excused myself and climbed the stairs as quietly as I could. Tapping lightly on Lawrence's door, I stepped into the room.

"Hallo. I'm told your mother is resting. Is there anything you need? There's some of that nice broth in the larder, if you'd care for a cup."

"I've been waiting for you." His face was drawn, and my immediate thought was, *there must be infection somewhere*—

And then he said. "I don't know whether to believe you or not."

Crossing to the bed, I pulled up a chair. "Concussions are rather nasty, you know. They can muddle your thinking, your memories can become quite confused—or they may not come back at all. Sometimes your dreams are frightening, more like nightmares. On top of that, you'd been through more than your mind could accept."

He rubbed his eyes with his good hand. "The doctors told me that as well. They told me I couldn't remember who I was when I was brought in. And so it wasn't surprising that I couldn't remember the house collapsing. I only knew that because the men who found me told me later that they'd had to finish digging me out, once they realized I was alive. My men thought I'd gone back to retrieve Henshaw's body."

"It was logical, after all."

"Yes. And then on that bridge, seeing that girl—watching her drown—it all came rushing back. I couldn't believe I'd pushed it out of my mind. I felt twice as guilty. There was no one I could tell, I had to bury it again, as best I could, and pretend."

"How did you come to be on that bridge?"

"I was walking back after having dinner with Marina. There was a half moon, and it was not as cold as it had been earlier in the evening. We were going to pick out my mother's birthday present the next day. Afterward—I couldn't very well face her. Not with what was on my conscience. I went home and drank myself into oblivion. And I did it again the next night, and the next, but it wasn't enough. It was never enough. I went to a doctor, told him my shoulder wound was hurting again. He gave me laudanum. I slept for the first time in days. It was the only thing that helped, that laudanum. When the doctors refused to give me more, Bedford found a vial for me. I didn't ask where. I didn't care. It numbed what I was feeling, and that was all that mattered. Without it, I kept seeing that girl's cloak in the water, and her face just below the surface. Or those dead children lying under the dining room table in that house on the Mons road."

"You must stop thinking about that. It's what he wanted you to do."

"And he did a damn—a very fine job of it."

I left him a few minutes later, but I was still worried for him. One didn't get over such shocks easily. And he still wasn't very strong physically.

In my own room, I tried to think what to do about the information Lieutenant Bedford had given me. Who was Paul? It occurred to me that Madame might know, but when I went to the sitting room, she shook her head.

"We've never cared much for the cinema. We do attend the ballet and the opera when Michel has the time. Why do you ask?"

"I overheard a conversation today, about the cinema before the war. I had never heard of the actor they spoke so highly of. Paul something. I didn't quite catch the last name. I was curious."

"I can't help you there. André could have told you who he was. He was mad about the cinema." A shadow passed over her face. "I thought it was foolishness. I wish now I'd shown more interest."

A dead end.

Chapter 15

Short of hiring a taxi to carry me around Paris to look at the marquee of every theater in the city, in the hope of finding Paul's full name listed amongst the cast members, I wasn't sure how to track him down.

And then a possible solution occurred to me. There was no way I could speak to the police about Lawrence's attack or even the drowned girl. I hadn't been present at either crime, and I couldn't explain that the only evidence I had came from a patient who had been hypnotized. For that matter, I could do more harm than good. While the police might listen to Dr. Moreau, a respected physician, on my own I didn't think they would.

But I could speak to my own attempted drowning. And I thought, *Who knows where that might lead?*

I set out once more, found a taxi, and was eventually put down in front of the police station where I'd been taken, my hair dripping down my back.

I had to wait nearly an hour for the magistrate, Bissett was his name, who had heard my case at the time. He came in, smiled at me, and said, "Sister. May I say you are a much happier sight today. Are you well?"

"I've recovered, but I'm still rather shaken by what happened to me. Have you made any progress in my case?"

"Sadly, no, I am sorry to tell you. The policeman who rescued you saw only a man running. Not enough of a description, alas. And you yourself couldn't identify him."

"I couldn't at the time, no. But when I was safe and rested, I did my best to recall every detail of what occurred. And then, not far from where I am presently living, I saw someone crossing the street who reminded me of that man. He looked up at me in a way that appeared to be recognition. Of course, I was in uniform. But during the attack, he saw my face far more clearly than I could see his. And then an omnibus came along, and when it had passed, I couldn't see him anywhere."

"You say you felt that he recognized you?"

Considering that, I replied, "When you walk down the street, and people pass you coming the other way, you may glance at them for a matter of seconds. But you aren't really noticing them. If I encountered you on the street, I would look more closely, because I remembered you. And if you remembered me, you would nod to me, or perhaps smile. There is a difference."

He'd listened carefully. Making a note, he said, "You are very observant, Sister."

"I'm a nurse. I am used to observing patients."

"And can you describe this man?"

I frowned. "There is a cinema actor, quite popular before the war. Paul something." I closed my eyes, remembering the face reflected in the glass. "I was reminded of him. Your height. Perhaps forty. Fair hair. If he was graying, one couldn't tell. Light eyes. Gray?" I opened my own.

He was watching me closely now. "I am fond of the cinema. You have just described Jean-Paul Reynaud. He is currently appearing in the Theatre Aurore."

Ah!

I looked down at my hands, clasped in my lap. So that he couldn't see the triumph I was feeling. "I remember those eyes. Very well."

"Surely you can't be suggesting that this actor was your assailant? Do you know him?"

"No." But I knew someone who might. And the facts matched too well to be a coincidence. "An actor would be good at disguising himself. He would know how to appear as a different person."

"Sister, I appreciate what a terrible experience this must have been for you. But I must ask you, why should a well-known cinema actor attack a British Sister? Why indeed would he be lying on the quay, waiting for you to approach from the bridge you were crossing?"

I wanted to say to him, *Because I knew Lawrence Minton, and he wanted me dead before I upset his plans—he'd found Lawrence and was planning to kill him. If I were dead, and Lawrence was dead, what had happened on the Mons road would be lost forever.*

Even as I was thinking that, the truth struck me. The killer must have believed Lawrence had confided in me—! *That* was why I had been a target.

But the magistrate wouldn't believe that either. An actor neither of us knew or had ever actually met, attacking both of us with intent to murder us.

I had to find my way out of this tangle. While the magistrate still accepted my account of the attack.

"You must understand. I can only tell you what I have experienced. The attack. The man I saw on the street. I can only be honest about both. How you investigate is a matter for the police to decide."

Partly mollified, he said, "Then I will take your evidence under consideration. Thank you."

I rose, preparing to leave. "Thank you for listening."

Out in the street once more, it occurred to me that whoever this man was, Jean-Paul or a stranger, he had been hunting for a very long time. Would he believe that Marina also knew what had happened?

Concerned for her, I found a taxi and ordered the driver to take me to Marina's school.

It was a small school for young women, the daughters of merchants and shopkeepers who could afford to send them there for their education. I walked into Reception and asked if I might speak to Marina Lascelles, a teacher there.

"She is occupied, preparing for the dinner we are holding for parents and guests."

I remembered: Dr. Moreau and his wife had received an invitation.

"I only need to speak to her for a moment," I replied. "Would it be possible for me to go to her, if she can't come to me?"

But I was unknown to Reception, I had no daughter here, and I was a foreigner.

"I'm very sorry, Sister. However, I could take a message if you wish to leave one."

What could I say? *You are in danger? Be careful, don't trust someone you don't know?* However well intended, such a message would frighten her. And if Reception wouldn't allow a British Sister beyond their front door—

She offered me a sheet of paper. I stared at it, trying to decide what to say. And in the end, I simply wrote:

I came to call, but you were busy. I have some news to give you about Lawrence. Could you come by Dr. Moreau's house, when you have a free morning or afternoon?

Signing it, I folded the sheet neatly and passed it back to the woman.

Mention of Lawrence would bring her sooner than later, but there was nothing in the message to alarm the dragon at this gate or the Head, if it had to pass through several hands before it could be given to her.

Thanking Reception, I walked back out to the street.

It was growing late, and the streets around the school were dark—the houses in this neighborhood were fairly large, prosperous middle-class homes, and most of the people who lived in them would either be preparing dinner or sitting down to it.

Listening to my footsteps echoing in the silence, I suddenly realized that if I were being followed, I had just led whoever it was to Marina. Information he might not have had before. And I'd just come from a police station.

Swallowing a lump in my throat, I hurried around the next corner and then waited, standing close to the stone front of the house behind me, to see if someone came after me. My hand was in my pocket, gripping the little revolver Simon had given me, but I couldn't use it until I was sure just who I might be shooting at. The worry was that I might find out too late.

But no one came down the street by the school, and feeling a little better, I kept up a brisk pace until I was on a main thoroughfare again and could find a taxi.

Dr. Moreau was still attending to his emergency, according to the maid who took my umbrella. I went up to my room and lit the fire in the hearth, feeling the chill of the evening.

I wanted to talk to Lawrence, but his mother would be there in the room, and it would be impossible to say anything.

Instead I went to the small Empire-style desk between the windows and drew out a few sheets of the notepaper in the single drawer. Sitting down, I took up the pen in the holder and began to write.

It would be as well to have a record of everything that had transpired since I first set foot in Paris. I was the only one who knew all the details, and all the people involved. And that was not wise. If anything should happen to me, who could put the pieces together and know what this Jean-Paul had done? Even if I was wrong about him, the information was helpful, useful in finding out who was behind all that had happened.

I was still writing when Matron tapped at my door to tell me that supper had been served.

Thanking her, I took the time to shove the pages back into the drawer.

Then I followed her down to the dining room.

Dr. Moreau came in very late, depressed by the death of a patient, who had also been a dear friend, and shut himself in his surgery with a bottle of brandy.

"He fought so hard," his wife told me when I asked if he had returned. "But the infection had spread too quickly."

How many times had I had to stand by helplessly, unable to stop the onslaught? In wounds it had often been caused by a tiny bit of the man's uniform buried deep by the bullet or the shrapnel, a grain or two of the filthy soil of No Man's Land we couldn't even see, caught in the torn flesh as he pulled himself into the trench and safety, or too much damage for the body to heal quickly, sealing the injury.

I thanked her, and went upstairs again, sitting in the dark by the window, staring out into the night.

This was the part of nursing that had been hardest for all of us. I was tired, it had been a long day, and I didn't feel like writing more about what had happened since I'd landed in Calais. My mood was gloomy.

There was a large clump of daffodils on either side of the iron seat in the garden below my window, and without the sun to give them color, they were a ghostly white, moving a little in the light wind that had come up. I had noticed them as they began to bloom, but I hadn't really paid much attention to them, there had been too much going on. The chestnut trees would come into bud soon. I'd been in Paris once years ago with my cousin Melinda when they were in full bloom, like candles on a tree. And violets in the market, great bunches of them for sale. I'd wanted to buy some and carry them home to my mother, but Melinda had explained that they would be wilted long before we reached Somerset. "We'll find them in Covent Garden when we reach London," she had promised. And so we had done.

Dear Melinda! She had been talking about going back to India one last time. Her husband was buried there in Simla, where he'd died. My parents had not cared for the idea of her traveling so far alone, but

Melinda hadn't asked me to accompany her, she knew I hadn't made up my mind about what to do, now that the war had ended, and might well decide to stay with the Queen Alexandra's or perhaps another nursing service—

My thoughts broke off as I realized that something was moving in the garden below.

The neighbors' little dog? She sometimes wriggled under the gate between houses and came over to visit. I suspected that the cook saved scraps for her. A pretty toy poodle, as white as the daffodils were yellow and both indistinguishable in the dark as anything but white.

I watched, thinking that the cook hadn't had much left to give her this night. The house was full of people just now, five of us and the staff. As I looked more closely, I saw boots pass the bright rectangle of the sitting room window. The curtains hadn't been drawn.

Who was walking in the garden at this hour of the night? When the grass was wet?

Suddenly I was galvanized. *No one up to any good!*

Captain Jackson had been right. We were *in danger.*

There was no time to take the Captain's revolver out of its hiding place. I caught up my coat, patted my pocket to see if my own weapon was still there, and ran out my door, taking the back stairs as quickly as I dared.

The door to the kitchen garden was unlocked, and I slowed, trying to make as little noise as possible. Slipping out into the darkness, I let my eyes adjust before moving toward the corner of the house. Taking a deep breath as I reached it, I turned quickly around it—and collided with someone coming the other way, who smothered a scream.

I stepped back and saw that it was Matron.

"You frightened me to death!" she exclaimed. "Bess, what on earth are you doing, out here in the garden at this hour?"

It was the first time she had used my given name.

But I could ask her the same thing. And then I saw in the hand pressed against her chest that she had a bunch of those daffodils.

Recovering quickly, I managed not to stammer as I said, "We must have had the same idea. I saw them from my window, and I thought they might brighten our patient's room a little."

"I saw them as I was drawing the curtains. I was going to wait until tomorrow, but then I thought I might just run down and pick a few. They would be there when he woke in the morning."

We'd been speaking quietly after the first shock of recognition, and now we turned back toward the kitchen door. It had been unlocked—I should have thought it was someone from the house, but I had just tried to warn Marina to be on guard, and never said a word to the family.

We stepped into the passage, closing and locking the door behind us.

"I'll just ask Cook if she knows of a vase I might use." She was smiling in that dimly lit little passage, but she added, "You gave me the most awful fright."

My own heart was only just beginning to slow. I asked, "How is our patient?"

She shook her head. "He sleeps more than I feel is good for him. And he doesn't seem to want to talk when he is awake. I wish I knew why. He's changed, I haven't seen him like this since the Army sent him home from France back in the autumn of 1914. He was so quiet then, but of course he was struggling to recover from that concussion and all he'd been through."

"He was concussed again," I said, making excuses.

"Who attacked him like that? Do you know? I've asked Michel and Aimée, but neither of them seems to know of any reason at all."

"When he's more himself, we ought to ask him what

he remembers." We hadn't done that since he was hypnotized.

"I suppose," she said doubtfully. "It all seems so very strange. But Paris is full of all kinds of people from everywhere you could think of. Well. Good night. Sleep well."

And she opened the door into the kitchen. I continued up the back stairs and quickly looked in on Lawrence. But I thought he might well be sleeping. If he wasn't, there wouldn't be time to talk to him . . .

I went on to my room, taking off my coat and just standing there in the middle of the floor.

What had just happened was a vivid reminder of our vulnerability. It was time to stop searching for answers and go to my father, time to tell him everything. He would know how much to tell the Regiment. Lawrence was stable enough now, we could move him by ambulance to a place of safety, have a watch put on him and his mother, and arrange eventual transportation out of France.

Marina and Dr. and Madame Moreau and the staff here would be all right, once that was done. And I could go back to nursing.

Jean-Paul or not, whoever was behind this whole horrid deception was set on murder.

In the event, I left the house before breakfast, hoping to catch my father before he left for the morning talks. When I approached the busy clerk behind the desk at Reception, I was told that the Colonel had been summoned to London, but that he was expected to arrive in Paris late this evening.

Disappointed, I left a message for him to come to the doctor's house as soon as he possibly could. And I left it with the desk clerk who had helped me before.

This time, I couldn't elude Major Webb.

He had just come through the hotel doors, removing his cap as he stepped into the brightly lit lobby. There was relief in his face as he recognized me, and there was nowhere for me to go.

I stopped, smiled, and said, "Hallo."

"Looking for your father?" he asked. "Will I do? May I offer you breakfast in his place?"

I hadn't told Madame Moreau that I wouldn't be in for breakfast, and I hesitated.

"Please," he said. "I've just received a package from my brother. He found a packet of real tea in the very back of the pantry at my parents' house. He's sent me a quarter of it. I'll be happy to share."

We were standing in the middle of the lobby, people

having to walk around us as they came and went through the handsome doors to the street.

The last thing I wished to do was make a scene. "Thank you."

He smiled and led me to the elegant dining room, where the chandeliers brightened the day. It was not quite half past eight, but most tables were filled with residents of the hotel. The waiter who came forward recognized the Major straightaway, and led him to a table for two, pulling out my seat for me, and then handing my escort the menu.

He grinned, and turned it so that I could read it as well. "You know what you prefer for breakfast."

I made my selections, and when the waiter returned, the Major gave him our order, then held up a small packet of tea.

"This is a national treasure of the British Isles. Can you make a pot properly?"

"Indeed, sir," the waiter said, trying to keep a straight face. "You are to be congratulated, sir, on the possession of this." He took the packet as if he'd just been handed the Orb or Scepter at a coronation, and with a little bow, disappeared.

"You shouldn't be using up your supply of tea on a stranger!" I chided him, smiling.

"Alas, I have no one else to share it with, and the Colonel is presently in London. As you may know."

"Yes, the desk clerk informed me of that."

"I must confess to something I should have told you in the beginning. Captain Barkley is in Versailles, keeping an eye on the conference participants, or your father would have asked him to keep an eye on the Colonel's daughter instead. That has fallen to my lot, and you've made it quite difficult."

I could feel my eyebrows shooting up in surprise.

"I know. Barkley has told me that you aren't always pleased about that."

"You've discussed me with the Captain?"

"Not at all!" he replied at once, flushing. "I did ask his advice when you shunned me whenever you saw me." He added hastily, "I have sisters—I assure you I understand. *My* father expected me to keep an eye on them, and they didn't care for it one whit. When I mentioned my difficulties to your father, he laughed, asked me if I thought you were in any trouble, and when I told him you were in Paris looking for Lawrence, he explained that he was Matron's son, and it was all right."

He had the grace to look more than a little embarrassed. "I wanted to apologize. I don't know what I've done to set you against me, but I had no intention of making you uncomfortable."

I shook my head. "My father is nearly as bad as Simon."

"Who is Simon? *Your* brother? I must say, I have fellow feelings for him."

I didn't explain that my father looked upon him as the son he'd never had.

"What did I do wrong?" he asked. "What put you off?"

"I don't know—you were a little too helpful for a stranger. And you came to Dr. Moreau's house on a pretense."

"It wasn't the cleverest tactic, was it?" he responded ruefully. "But I felt I ought to be sure it was a respectable address."

Why did men feel I was to be protected and guarded? I'd been on my own since 1914, and I'd taken very good care of both my reputation and my character. I owed that to my parents. As a nurse I'd often had to make life and death decisions on my own, and that was steadying. I'd held the hands of men who were dying, offering what comfort I could. That was sobering. My parents had brought me up to think for myself, and I had valued that. I wasn't beautiful like my flatmate Diana, who turned heads wherever she went, with men falling over themselves to do her bidding. It must be something else about me, and I didn't know what.

But I said, putting him at his ease, "Never mind. You've been honest with me, and I am grateful. And I forgive you."

"Thank you. Somehow I felt I ought to set the matter straight." He hesitated. "Your father will ask me to report, as soon as he arrives. What shall I tell him?"

Dear God. I'd come to tell him I needed his help, that matters were rapidly getting out of hand. If I said any of this to the Major, it would only reinforce his belief that I needed to be protected. He'd call out the troops. I could tell, listening to him, that he must have admired my father to have been willing to take on this duty, and my father must think highly of him to have asked it.

"Tell him that I'm well, but that I need to speak to him about Lawrence. As soon as possible."

"Where *is* he?"

"He's staying with his mother at the moment. Here in Paris." It was evasive, but I couldn't drag the Major into Lawrence's affairs. I wasn't even sure the Colonel Sahib could deal with them, complex as they were. But at least he would know just where to turn.

"That's good news. I liked him, and I've been worried about him."

And then our breakfast arrived, along with that precious tea in a porcelain pot under a dark blue cozy patterned with gold fleur-de-lis and the hotel's crest. A very proper treatment for a National Treasure.

By the end of the meal, I think we were friends, the Major and I. I allowed him to see me to a taxi and give the driver the Moreau address.

I had to admit the tea was heavenly. Made just right. For that I could forgive Major Webb almost anything.

The hours dragged. I debated telling the Lieutenant that I intended to confide in my father but thought better of it. It could easily upset him to think I'd gone to the Regiment's former Colonel. He was still as fragile emotionally as he was physically.

I considered speaking to Dr. Moreau as well. I also wanted to ask him if he still intended to call on the police, but he'd gone out when I arrived.

Worried that he'd gone to the police alone after all, I went in search of Madame.

"The death of his old friend has upset him rather badly," she told me. "They have known each other longer than I have known Michel. They were in school together, medical school as well, and they have always been the closest of friends. Michel is helping the family plan the funeral. I don't know that he will be in the mood for Marina's dinner tonight. I don't like to disappoint her, but we may have to send word that we can't

come. Would you care to go in our place? I think someone should."

I was expecting my father later in the evening. "Perhaps," I said. And left it at that.

I looked in on Lawrence when his mother stepped
out of the room for a bit, and immediately saw the daffodils there on the table by his bed. They were in a tall
cut-glass vase that showed them off beautifully.

"How lovely," I said at once. "A breath of spring."

He looked up at them. "We never had many flowers in India. I think that's why my mother loves them
so much." Then looking back at me he asked, "What's
wrong?"

"I came to ask you. Have you recalled anything
about the person who attacked you in that alley?"

He shook his head. "The *pension* was only a short
distance away, I'd got over my anger after my encounter with Bedford, and it occurred to me that I should
see if I could buy a little bread to take back with me. I
don't remember anything after that."

"He must have accosted you—given you a reason for
going with him into that alley."

"If he did, I have no memory of it." He plucked at
the coverlet. "I know, the concussion, everyone tells me
that's why I can't recall anything useful. Dr. Moreau
has asked me. You, Mother, even the policeman who

was there in that hospital. But it's a blank. I don't really remember being brought here. It's as if it happened to someone else, and I was floating above it all, being told about it."

I understood. "Never mind," I said cheerfully, "we'll find him. I promise you."

He turned away. "Bess. I have to lie here day after day, helpless, unable even to feed myself without dropping food all down my front—like an infant. I tried shaving myself yesterday morning, and my mother had to finish for me. Everyone tells me that my task is to heal. But I want to find him. After what he's done to me, I want to get my hands on him." That last was said with clenched teeth.

That, I thought, was an improvement on wanting to harm himself.

"It takes time. But it will happen. Your leg will heal, you'll walk soon enough. It was a bad fracture—it will be weak for quite a while."

"I know—everyone tells me that as well. And I lie here, and the minutes crawl by while the rest of the world goes on without me. I can't say anything to my mother—she's worried enough as it is. I can't even concentrate on what she's reading to me. But the headaches are gone. A little of the dizziness is still there if I turn my head too quickly."

"That's wonderful. It's also a good sign that your head is healing."

"Thank God, even the nightmares are gone."

"I've heard other patients say that the nightmares are often appalling, after a serious blow on the head." Then, thinking they might give me some insight into what he was going through, I asked, "Were they too dreadful?"

He frowned. "I can't recall most of them now. Just as well, I tell you. The man with no face was the worst."

"No face?"

"Well, he had a face, but I couldn't see it. Instead of eyes, there was light coming out of the eye sockets. A gray, terrifying light."

"How awful," I managed to say, looking down at his face, contorted with distaste.

And all the while I was thinking about the eyes I'd seen. Such a light gray they might not have been there at all.

"It's over now," I added soothingly, shutting out my own images. "I'm glad they are gone."

But he must have picked up on something in my voice or manner.

"What is it? What matters about the dreams?"

I told him the truth. "I was just thinking. There's a

cinema actor with very pale gray eyes. Like—like clear water on a cloudy day."

"Then he probably plays villains."

"I only know by hearsay." I sat there and talked about other things, the news about the conference—it was still bogged down in argument, or so the local newspapers claimed. I saw them everywhere, large black headlines. "You'll be walking before any treaty is signed. And you will be there to witness it."

I had tried to lift his spirits. But in the end, although he pretended for my sake, I could tell that lying there brooding was not helping him heal emotionally, however much it was helping physically.

Dr. Moreau was a man who took his obligations seriously. He spent four hours with his dead friend's family, offering comfort, advice, helping with the arrangements for the funeral. He looked very tired when he came in at four.

I was there when his wife reminded him of the dinner at Marina's school, adding, "We can always send Bess in our place, and ask her to explain why we couldn't come."

"No," he said resolutely. "We must go. She is from a good family, and she sees an obligation. She can't take us to a restaurant, or have us come to her rooms. It would not be proper to refuse. There may not be another such dinner for weeks."

She accepted his decision like the devoted wife she was, and said, "Very well. I must see that the lace on my gown is pressed properly."

"Helena hasn't left Lawrence's side since she came," Dr. Moreau said. "It might do her good to have an evening out. Bess can sit with Lawrence."

My heart sank. If I was upstairs with our patient, I might not hear the door when my father arrived.

But Madame said, "It would be good for her. But she won't leave him. I have to persuade her to come down for meals or let me draw bathwater for her."

"Ask her, all the same. She's our guest. We shouldn't leave her behind."

I was on tenterhooks the entire time she was away, and was relieved when she came back into the sitting room.

"As I thought, my dear, she is grateful but must decline. She doesn't know Marina, of course."

"Yes, yes. Well, I will arrange for the taxi." He took out his watch. "Seven o'clock? The dinner is at half past."

"Very well." Turning to me, she said, "Bess, Cook will prepare dinner for you and Helena and Lawrence before she leaves this evening."

"Thank you, that's very kind."

She smiled and disappeared up the stairs to her room to bathe and dress.

I sat in the sitting room until it was time for them to leave. Dr. Moreau was striking in his evening clothes, and Madame wore a very becoming blue silk gown with a silk-lined cloak.

I wished them a happy evening, and after my own dinner alone in the elegant dining room, I went back to the sitting room again, where I could hear my father's knock.

Cook and the maid bade me good night before they left, asking if there was anything more I required, and I thanked them, sending them on their way.

Matron came down to tell me she was going to have her bath, and asked if I could sit with Lawrence for half an hour while she did. He really didn't need to be watched every minute now, but it was as if she feared he might disappear if no one was there.

We talked about the war, about the peace conference, about Marina's school. And then he asked, "Do you believe in the Angel? At Mons?"

"I do," I told him. "It's always possible that all those tired men, struggling to keep the Germans at bay, needed a miracle, and they conjured up one. On the other hand, it was just as possible that a miracle happened."

"Why did he turn his back on me?"

Oh, dear. This was important, and I had to get it right.

I said, "I rather think it might depend on where you're standing and what you could see. Like a rainbow, perhaps. I remember a summer storm when I was a child, and the rainbow after the worst had passed looked as if I had only to go to the smithy on the far side of the village to find the end of it. But there really was no beginning or end. That was only how it appeared from where I lived. My father, coming back from London, saw it from a different vantage point, and he thought the end might be in our back garden. It was altogether gone when he arrived, but he came striding in the door, asking if I knew I lived in a rainbow. And he had to explain that, because I was sure it ended just beyond the village. I told him roundly that it had never been in the back garden."

He considered me. "You were stubborn, even when you were a child."

"Not stubborn, no. I was so certain about the rainbow. I'd seen it with my own eyes."

"And I saw the Angel with my own eyes," he said slowly. "But I was very likely between our lines and the Germans. His back would naturally be toward me."

"The Angel had more important matters to attend to than turn and look for you," I told him lightly.

He smiled wryly. "I expect he did. It was a very long time before I mentioned seeing the Angel, you know. I thought at the time that it was all in my head."

"I expect you weren't the only one who was afraid to say anything."

He was silent for a time. "Why did it appear on the Mons road, and not at the Somme? We needed an Angel badly there. Or Verdun, the French equivalent."

"I don't know how Angels make decisions."

He laughed, as I'd intended him to. Then he said, "You're right, we were badly outnumbered and being pushed back faster than we could hold on. If ever we needed divine intervention, it was during that retreat."

Matron came in just then, smiling and saying, "I heard the sound of laughter."

Before I could reply, Lawrence answered her. "Bess was telling me about the problems with the peace talks."

She turned to me. "Is your father in France, with the talks?"

"He has been, yes."

"Please tell him hello for me. It would be lovely to see him again. How is your mother? Is she here with him?"

"She's well, in Somerset at the moment."

I wished them a good night, then hurried back to the sitting room.

It was eight-thirty by my little clock, pinned to my apron. The clerk had said *late,* and I gathered from that it might be any time after nine o'clock. I should have thought to ask Major Webb when the night train from Calais came in.

On the footstool by Madame's chair, there was a catalog of an exhibit of paintings at the Louvre. It was dated May of 1914, but I sat there turning pages with half an ear to the door. The fire on the hearth was comfortably warm, I had chosen Madame's comfortable chair, and I could feel myself growing drowsy. If he wasn't here soon, he would encounter Dr. and Madame Moreau returning from their dinner.

At a quarter to ten, neither the Moreaus had come in, nor had my father appeared.

Then the case clock was striking eleven.

I was suddenly wide awake.

Dr. and Madame Moreau should have been home by now. Remembering the dark street that ran past the school, and how far I'd had to walk to find a taxi, I realized how vulnerable they might be.

But the dinner could have run long—they could be touring the school with Marina afterward. I knew how much Madame liked her. And Dr. Moreau might enjoy that as well.

I went to the window overlooking the street. No sign of a taxi.

Should I find one, and go to look for them? I wouldn't be here when my father came, but I could leave a note at the door. What if I missed them as they took another route back to the house? But that would leave Lawrence unprotected, and Matron.

It was a dilemma, and I was trying to convince myself that the doctor and his wife were perfectly safe, when Matron came up from the kitchen quarters with a pretty bouquet of tulips held in both hands.

"I nearly forgot to pick these. I meant to before my bath and it completely slipped my mind. Michel had mentioned they were blooming. Aren't they lovely? Do you know where I can find another vase?"

"I have no idea. The kitchen? Didn't you find one there for the daffodils?"

"I didn't see where Cook got it. She just handed it to me. And these need water to keep them fresh. Michel tells me it won't be much longer before their lilacs bloom. We've always had lilacs at home."

We were walking back to the kitchen together. "Yes, we do as well. When the wind blows, I can smell them from my bedroom windows." We set about searching, finally locating a clear glass vase in the back of a cupboard. But it was too tall for the tulips, and we started again. Over my head, the bell for the front door rang as it opened and closed, and I felt a surge of gratitude that Dr. Moreau and his wife were safely home.

Matron was on her hands and knees in front of the dresser, looking on a lower shelf. "Aha!" she exclaimed, and held up a shorter but very pretty china vase that was the perfect match for the tulips.

I left her to fill the bowl with water and arrange the flowers, hurrying out to the sitting room to ask how the evening had gone.

It was empty, and I went out to the hall.

No sign of Dr. Moreau's hat or his coat. Madame had very likely taken her cloak upstairs to put it away. But where was his?

I started through to the surgery to see if he'd gone in there for a moment, and as I opened the door, I heard a crash. Glass breaking somewhere back in the house—

I ran toward the kitchen, but Matron was still arranging the tulips. Nothing had fallen—nothing was broken.

Lawrence could have dropped his glass—

She looked up in dismay at me as I came to a breathless halt. "What is it? What do you need?"

"Did you hear something fall—or break?"

"No—I—"

I interrupted, saying in a low voice, "I could be wrong, but please, listen to me. Go out into the garden, quietly make your way around the house and look for a policeman. Bring him back here as soon as you can."

"Bess? What is it?"

"I don't know. But I think someone else is in the house."

"Michel and Aimée just came in—we heard the bell."

"It wasn't them. I've just looked."

"Lawrence!" she exclaimed, realizing he was alone upstairs.

"Shhhh. Please, go out through the garden and find a policeman. Quickly!"

"No, I must go to him. You find the police."

"Matron. We're wasting time. You have no idea what is up those stairs, and I do. I've a very good idea. You must go and bring us help."

She shook her head. "He's my son."

"And while we argue, he may be dying. If you love him, *go!*"

I turned and opened the door to the back stairs as quietly as I could. He must have been watching the house. He must know there are only two women and a wounded man here.

I was already fishing my little revolver out of my pocket as I ran lightly up the stairs. The door at the top was closed, as it should be. I paused there only long enough to catch my breath, then opened the door.

Raised voices were coming from Lawrence's room. I recognized only one of them. I walked carefully down the passage to the partly opened door, and slowly looked around it.

Lawrence was braced on his good arm, and on the floor by the bed I saw the vase of daffodils, glass shards and bruised flowers everywhere in little pools of water. But I couldn't quite see who else was in there with him.

A rich baritone voice, stage trained, spoke. "Never mind, I'll find them. If that vase doesn't bring them running, your falling down the stairs will. I counted. There are fourteen of them, narrow treads. It's a very long way for you to bounce."

"Don't try it," Lawrence said angrily. "You don't have a weapon now. I can still knock you down. I did by the river. That's why you carried a rolling pin the next time."

"Of course I did," the voice replied, taunting. "But I don't need a weapon now." He must have surged toward the bed, because suddenly he was there, in my line of sight now, and he raised both fists together, over his head, to bring them down on Lawrence's half-healed broken leg.

"*No!*" he cried, desperately trying to swing it off the bed and out of reach.

The face between the raised arms was twisted by something that was more hate than anger, and I didn't wait.

I fired.

The shot struck him in the right shoulder, and Jean-Paul cried out in pain and shock, turning toward me. Those pale gray eyes were darkened with fury.

With a roar, he came toward me, arms outstretched, intent on what he would do when he caught me. Ignoring the pain, his mind was on nothing but me, in the doorway.

I moved back, fired again, this time at his knee.

He dropped like a stone, and then rising up on his elbows, he tried to crawl toward me.

I didn't want to kill him. Backing away, I quickly found my body up against the passage wall. There was nowhere else to go. If I fled down the stairs, I left Lawrence at his mercy. And he was still pulling himself across the floor toward me, still roaring, even with the weapon pointed directly at him.

Lawrence was shouting something, but I couldn't hear him. I watched in fascination as the wounded actor struggled toward me.

"I will kill you," I said as coldly as I could. "If you don't stop."

But he was out of the room now, a matter of feet away, and I had to make a decision.

One more foot agonizingly gained. And then another.

I fired a last time, and this time he crumpled to the floor, his left arm broken. Screaming obscenities in such a fury that he still felt nothing.

I heard the front door open. "Up here," I shouted, thinking it was Dr. Moreau. I had the ridiculous thought that he was going to ruin his evening clothes, attending to Jean-Paul.

But it wasn't the doctor, it was the Colonel Sahib, taking the stairs two at a time, his long legs bringing him up them at great speed.

"Bess? For the love of God—"

I handed him the little revolver. "There's one shot left. I tried not to kill him."

He put his arm around my shoulders as Lawrence shouted, "Bess! Are you all right? What's happening? Damn it, *someone tell me what's happening.*" He couldn't see me from where he lay.

"It's all right," I called. "It's over."

"Er, who is the wounded man?" the Colonel Sahib asked me.

"He's a French actor. He tried to kill Lawrence Minton—he's there in the bedroom—and he tried to kill me. He *did* kill a young girl."

Beyond the buttons of the Colonel Sahib's coat, I saw Matron, her hand covering her mouth as she looked up the stairs in horror.

"Lawrence is safe," I said to her. "He isn't hurt." Glancing up at my father, I said, "I expect I ought to do something to stop the bleeding."

And my calm, collected father, looking at the dark red smear from Lawrence's bedside to a foot from where I'd been standing, said harshly, "Let him bleed."

In the event we did no such thing.

Once she had assured herself that Lawrence was upset but truly unharmed, Matron knelt by me in the passage and worked with quiet efficiency on Jean-Paul's knee as I dealt with his shoulder and arm wounds. His single-minded determination had kept the pain at bay as he came after me, but it had finally overwhelmed him, and he lay there now, his eyes tightly shut and his jaw clenched against it.

I thought in other circumstances, he'd rather die than allow us to attend to him, but his suffering was mounting with every passing minute and even his stoicism was wearing thin. The Colonel Sahib stood guard until the ambulance and the police arrived, but there was no possibility of escape. Jean-Paul could hardly move.

I found it difficult to be sympathetic, all the same. He would have killed me if he could, and then Lawrence. Matron as well, if she'd rushed back inside. I'd seen that in his pale eyes as he crawled toward me, his will stronger than his body, and for seconds that seemed to go on forever as I stood there watching him, I'd feared I'd have to kill him to stop him.

Still, it was easy to understand how grief might turn a man's mind, even how it might turn him into a killer. His daughter, as I learned much later from the magistrate who took our statements, was with the nuns in Rouen. She had never fully recovered from the nightmare she had endured. Her father had found her wandering the road out of the village, bloody and wounded, having been left in that house for dead. A constant reminder of all he had lost.

By the time Dr. Moreau arrived ten minutes later, he had only to supervise the rest of our work. The knee was shattered, but the arm was a clean break, and the shoulder wound was in the muscle. He brought more dressings from his surgery, and something for the patient's pain. I don't think Jean-Paul was grateful for the relief, but he didn't refuse to swallow the medication. By the time the police and the ambulance finally arrived, he was groggy, unable to answer questions. The police turned first to Dr. Moreau, who deferred to my father to clarify the situation.

Later, I asked, "How was Marina? And the dinner?" as we watched the attendants slide the stretcher into the ambulance. A policeman climbed in beside it and was ordered not to let the prisoner out of his sight.

"It was odd," Dr. Moreau said, shrugging. "She hadn't sent the invitation."

"She hadn't? But it appeared—it appeared to be *real*. And she was preparing for the dinner when I was there only yesterday."

"Apparently it's tomorrow night. No invitations had been sent out, anyway. There was no need. The students were to ask their parents to attend. But after she'd finished her duties, we took her out to dine. We could do no less. And it was a very pleasant evening. What has happened *here*? And who was this man lying in the upstairs passage? I've never seen him before."

"He's the man who nearly killed Lawrence."

"But what is he doing *here*?"

"He came to finish his handiwork."

"*Mon Dieu*! Who shot him? Your father?"

"No. I had to. He was going to kill us."

He turned to look at me. After a moment, he said quietly, "That was very brave of you."

For the first time, some of the tightness in my chest went away.

Madame and Matron were in the sitting room. My father was still speaking to a senior policeman.

Matron had almost literally run into the Colonel Sahib arriving to speak to me—he was just stepping out of a taxi as she was frantically searching for help. He didn't wait to listen to what she was trying to tell him. He could hear the gunshots and came through the door that Jean-Paul had left unlocked for his own escape, and up the stairs, leaving Matron to follow. She had had the good sense to send the astonished driver to find the nearest policeman.

When the ambulance had taken Jean-Paul away, under guard, we sat in the parlor as I gave a policeman the simplest account of the evening, knowing I'd have to repeat it again when we were interviewed in the morning by the magistrate in charge. The policeman hadn't recognized Jean-Paul, but someone at the hospital or police station would do so during the night, I was sure. I was glad I had witnesses. The police had ignored me until they learned who had done the shooting. It was assumed that Matron and I had been summoned by Dr. Moreau to help him deal with the wounds.

It was well after two in the morning when we crawled into our beds. My father had insisted on staying the night, and a cot from the surgery was made up for him in the sitting room.

I had a few minutes to speak to him after the others had gone up the stairs.

"If you'd taken Major Webb into your confidence, he might have been able to help you a little," my father chided me. "We'll have to keep this from your mother, you know."

"Even if I had trusted him, he wouldn't have been here tonight. But yes, for Mother's sake." Still, she would find out in time. She always did. *Sparing her* never worked for very long.

"What's this about that man trying to drown you?"

He had been present when I spoke to the police tonight.

And so I told him everything I knew. He listened without comment, but I watched the line of his mouth tighten as I talked. "And there you have it," I said, when it was finished.

"Good God, Bess. I had no idea you were in this much danger."

I said thoughtfully, "I don't know what Jean-Paul believed at the time. What his daughter, if he ever found her, knew or understood about the murders. I expect he has been looking for a scapegoat for a very long time."

As I finished, I caught a fleeting expression on my father's face. There and gone so quickly I wasn't sure I'd read it correctly: he was seeing himself in Jean-Paul's shoes, if anything had happened to us, my mother and me. He wouldn't have stopped until he had found whoever was responsible.

A little silence followed, uncomfortable on my part.

Then he said in his normal tone of voice, "The Sergeant's body was still there at the house, you said?"

"Yes, Lawrence hadn't been able to carry it back to his own lines." I realized where he was going. "You're right. Jean-Paul would have seen the man's insignia. What regiment had been there. And he could most certainly see that the Sergeant had been dead well before that family had been shot. There were no German bodies in the house. He'd *assumed* that the English were to blame. A starting point."

What's more, he'd befriended Lieutenant Bedford— who was also in that regiment. How many others, until he'd found Lawrence Minton?

"If Minton hadn't been seconded to these talks, the man might never have found him."

Happenstance . . . But theater companies traveled, didn't they? He might have found his way to England eventually. He'd waited this long, after all.

Changing the subject, the Colonel Sahib said, "Go to bed. Before you fall asleep on your feet." He rose from his chair, and as I stood up, he bent forward and kissed me on the cheek. "Good night, love."

I went upstairs, uncertain whether I would sleep or not. Someone—Matron perhaps—had taken a mop and water to the bloodstains where I'd shot Jean-Paul, and the wood was still damp in places. I was grateful to her.

I had had to give my little revolver to the police for the time being. It would be returned, I was told. But I didn't think it would be.

The house was quiet. I undressed, got into bed, and then sat bolt upright again.

When the ambulance and the police had arrived, neighbors had come out into the street to see what was happening. They'd heard the shots, of course. They were worried.

I had had other things on my mind just then, but now I remembered something.

Standing back on the far side of the street, in the shadows, was Captain Jackson. As soon as he saw me, the worried expression on his face changed to relief. There hadn't been time to think about him, and I didn't see him after that. Whether he'd gone or stayed.

The police were back in the morning, and afterward we went to the station to give our written statements. It was unnecessary to mention Lawrence's dependency on laudanum or his suicidal feelings. I simply wrote down the facts in the case, from Jean-Paul's belief that a British officer had killed his family, to his search for that man, and his obsession with revenge. Whatever anyone else chose to write was his or her affair. I told the absolute truth. Just not all of the truth. Jean-Paul had been found in Lawrence Minton's sickroom, he himself could attest to that, and while the police were not happy that I'd shot him, they decided that my lack of skill with a revolver and my terror had resulted in three wounds, none of which was fatal.

I didn't tell them that my aim was true.

They didn't search my room, and so they never discovered Captain Jackson's revolver. I was glad I hadn't had to explain having *two* weapons in my possession.

It helped that the respected Dr. Moreau could tell them that he and his wife had been lured away from the house. And Jean-Paul hadn't come to the house until he was certain that the doctor had taken the two women to a restaurant and had ordered their meal. Witnesses later placed him on the street outside the windows.

I returned from the police station to find Captain Jackson waiting for me across the street from the house.

"Are you all right?" he asked at once, when I stopped to speak to him. "What happened?"

I gave him a brief account.

He swore under his breath. "I followed the doctor and his wife. I thought they were the intended target. And nothing happened. I came back here, to find police and an ambulance at the door."

"Why should they be a target?"

"I wasn't the only one following them."

"Do you still have that rolling pin?"

"Yes. Shall I take it to the police?"

"Would you mind, terribly? They will not be pleased that you didn't turn it in straightaway."

His drawl came back. "Well, as to that, I just knew it had blood on it. I couldn't say whose blood it was."

"Come in and meet my father. He'll be returning to the house as soon as he's finished his own statement and his interview. And I must return your revolver."

Surprised, he said, "Didn't the police take it as evidence?"

"No," I said, smiling. "I couldn't get to yours. I had to use my own."

He stared at me. "I didn't know you had one." Then, considering the matter, "Did you miss, trying to kill him?"

"I didn't want to kill him. Just to stop him. And I succeeded."

Captain Jackson howled with laughter then, bent over with it.

More than a little put out, I said, "I don't see anything funny about that."

"No, ma'am, I expect you don't," he answered when he'd caught his breath. "My mother would like you. I have never seen her miss anything she aims to shoot. With revolver or rifle. New Mexico wasn't always civilized, you know. My father taught her well."

In India, I'd been taught by my own father, and Simon had seen to it that I practiced regularly. He would take me out riding and find a quiet place to put up targets, a place that wouldn't bring the regiment or anyone else charging down on us if they heard the shots.

I realized that I hadn't had time to ask my father if he'd seen Simon in London, or if he'd even returned from Scotland.

Madame Moreau was in her sitting room with Matron, and so I took the Captain into the parlor. But when I started upstairs to fetch the revolver, he asked if he might meet Lawrence Minton. And so I took him with me.

Lawrence was tired from his own session with the police, and I thought for a moment he wasn't happy to have to deal with another stranger. But I shouldn't have worried. The Captain was affable and soon had Lawrence smiling. I left them together and went to take off my coat. When I came back, they were exchanging war stories, and I left them to that as well. It was, I thought, an antidote to his own boredom and his mother's constant presence.

Captain Jackson, I told myself, starting down the stairs to wait for my father, could cajole a post into talking to him.

Later he met my father and Dr. Moreau, but I found a moment to return his revolver. And before the Colonel Sahib left, I asked him for news of Simon.

He shook his head. "Your mother told me that he hadn't returned to the cottage."

I had to leave it at that. Matron had come up behind me to tell him good-bye.

When the police had everything they needed, I was allowed to return to England. They kept my little revolver, evidence for the trial. But I could always ask Simon to find another one.

Matron was staying a little longer, until Lawrence could travel.

I went to see the magistrate before I traveled to Calais. I asked him what would become of Jean-Paul.

He studied me for a moment. "It's a very sad case. But there are other circumstances to be considered. Still. The court will decide his fate. He pleaded guilty, you know."

I hadn't known that. But somehow I wasn't surprised. He was clever enough to save himself from the death penalty. I was glad that Lawrence would be leaving for England in another few weeks. I didn't think that Jean-Paul felt either remorse or guilt. He couldn't let go of the past. And if he ever got the chance, he would still take his revenge if he could. He would find *someone* to blame.

I said, "Just as well. It will be easier on Lieutenant Minton and his mother, if they don't have to face him in a trial."

"And you, Mademoiselle?" He waited for my answer.

"I must go back to my patients in England. It's where I belong."

He nodded. "That's for the best." He glanced at a file on his desk, but didn't open it. "You were involved in another matter in Paris. Before the war ended."

"Yes. Again, not by choice."

"Have a safe journey, Mademoiselle."

I took that to mean I was to stay out of trouble for the remainder of my visit.

I intended to do just that.

With nothing to keep me in Paris, I arranged to leave the next day. My father was unable to accompany me after all. He was needed at the negotiations. I said my farewells to Dr. and Madame Moreau and to the cook and maid, before going up to tell Lawrence and his mother good-bye.

He was rather gruff. "I have some regrets," he said, giving me his good hand. I knew he was talking about what had happened in St. Ives. "I lost my way, and I couldn't find it again."

"Well," I said, smiling. "It's behind us, now, isn't it?"

"Yes. Thank you."

Matron said good-bye as well. "There are orders waiting for you in London."

I didn't ask what they were. It could wait until I was in London. I still had decisions to make. In case.

As Dr. Moreau carried my valise out to the taxi, I saw that Captain Jackson was waiting by the door.

"It's just as well for you to be escorted to the coast," he told me. "Look what happens, ma'am, when I let you out of my sight."

"You're going to England?" I asked, not expecting that.

"No, ma'am, I'm planning on staying in France a little longer. But I'd feel better seeing you step on that ferry bound for Dover."

Exasperated and amused, I said, "Oh, very well. I might as well have someone to talk to."

He grinned. "You know I'd just sit there in the next compartment, if you didn't care to speak to me. Oh, and Captain Barkley asked me to tell you good-bye, and that he was sorry he never got an opportunity to come to Paris."

As it happened, the Captain made the journey a pleasant one, and he kept his word, carrying my valise down to the salon before leaving the ferry.

We were saying good-bye, they were waiting to cast off, and he said, "I don't know that I'm supposed to tell you this, Bess. But if you see Simon, please give him my regards."

He turned, was down the gangway in those long

strides of his, out of reach on the dock below. And the crew were just waiting to swing it aboard.

I shouted over the cries of the gulls, "How do you know Simon?"

"Oh, we ran into each other a time or two during the war. I rescued him once when he was trapped behind the lines. A quick in and out," he shouted back.

"Did he ask you to keep an eye on me? Is that why you were in Calais when I arrived? Where is he?"

But the ship was pulling away from the dock, the engines making their own racket.

And Captain Jackson stood there, grinning up at me as he answered. But I couldn't hear what he was saying.

About the Author

CHARLES TODD is the author of the Bess Crawford mysteries, the Inspector Ian Rutledge mysteries, and two stand-alone novels. A mother-and-son writing team, they live on the East Coast.

HARPER LUXE

THE NEW LUXURY IN READING

We hope you enjoyed reading
our new, comfortable print size and found it
an experience you would like to repeat.

Well — you're in luck!

HarperLuxe offers the finest in fiction and
nonfiction books in this same larger print size and
paperback format. Light and easy to read, HarperLuxe
paperbacks are for book lovers who want to see
what they are reading without the strain.

For a full listing of titles and
new releases to come, please visit our website:

www.HarperLuxe.com

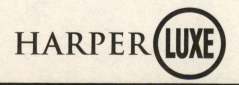

SEEING IS BELIEVING!